"I can categorically state 1 of book I would pick up. extremely gifted and excitii and growing and changing manages to leap beyond the cliches of the genre and stand as an original work. I look forward to more from her in the coming years."
—Cliff Graham, Author of *Day of War*

"*Until Forever*, by Darlene Shortridge, is an incredible journey that pulls the reader into a world of emotions that can only be described as absolutely powerful. Often, beauty comes from tragedy, as well as the compelling truth about the power of prayer, the freedom of forgiveness, and the love of God. I urge everyone to read this book because it gives the reader an opportunity to experience the love of God through the heart and soul of a parent, the kind of love that will last *Until Forever*."
—S.B. Newman, Author of *The Night Eagles Soared*

"*Until Forever* delves into the difficult realms of reconciliation, redemption, and forgiveness. Shortridge illustrates a story that is at times poignant and compelling. I found myself vicariously experiencing Jessi and Mark's tragic loss and desperately wanted them to be fully healed and restored. If you battle with the perception that you are unconditionally loved and forgiven by God, this novel is for you."
—Jeral Davis, Author of *Tomorrow*

"*Until Forever* has made me stop and realize that God's timing is perfect, unlike ours. What happens in our life today defines Gods greatness.
 The things good and bad are used to bring you closer to him. Great story, very deep!"
—Kathy Kelly, Assistant Worship Leader

"Darlene Shortridge is a talented new writer who brings a lot of creativity to the craft. Her compelling cadence drew me from one page to another, and I found it hard to put her book down. *Until Forever* is one of those captivating books that will inspire you as well as entertain."

—Marilyn Jackson, Former Editor, Women's Speaker, Pastor's Wife

"*Until Forever* is a beautifully written novel about the restoration power of God working in the most tragic situations. This book will remind you of the love God has for His people and of His ability to work good in every situation."

—Pastor Charles L. Butler, Jr. Covenant Church Fox Valley

"Darlene Shortridge has written a wonderful book. *Until Forever* is the kind of book that the reader can invest himself into. I found myself wondering how I would react in the same circumstances. Would I hold onto grief in the same way, or would I be able to move on with my life? How would I handle forgiveness? I think it is the mark of a good book when the reader is able to move past the story and make life decisions for himself. *Until Forever* is a thoughtful book with a great message. The storyline is compelling, and I found the book hard to put down. I recommend that you add *Until Forever* to your reading list."

—Elaine Littau, Author of *Nan's Journey*

Until Forever

WOMEN *of* PRAYER SERIES

darlene shortridge

Until Forever

Darlene Shortridge
Matthew 19:26

TATE PUBLISHING & *Enterprises*

Until Forever
Copyright © 2010 by Darlene Shortridge. All rights reserved.

No part of this publication may be reproduced, stored in a retrieval system or transmitted in any way by any means, electronic, mechanical, photocopy, recording or otherwise without the prior permission of the author except as provided by USA copyright law.

This novel is a work of fiction. Names, descriptions, entities, and incidents included in the story are products of the author's imagination. Any resemblance to actual persons, events, and entities is entirely coincidental.

The opinions expressed by the author are not necessarily those of Tate Publishing, LLC.

Published by Tate Publishing & Enterprises, LLC
127 E. Trade Center Terrace | Mustang, Oklahoma 73064 USA
1.888.361.9473 | www.tatepublishing.com

Tate Publishing is committed to excellence in the publishing industry. The company reflects the philosophy established by the founders, based on Psalm 68:11,
"The Lord gave the word and great was the company of those who published it."

Book design copyright © 2010 by Tate Publishing, LLC. All rights reserved.
Cover design by Amber Gulillat
Interior design by Lynly D. Grider
Author photo by Photography by Jonna

Published in the United States of America
ISBN: 978-1-61739-244-3
1. Fiction, Christian, Romance   2. Fiction, General
10.10.19

For my husband, Danny, and my children, Jonna and Jeremiah.

Acknowledgments

I would like to thank everyone at Covenant Church Fox Valley for your support, prayers, and encouragement, with special thanks going to Pastor Charles Butler. The time spent on your knees for this project would have been enough. You chose to go above and beyond by encouraging, reading, and telling everyone, whether they wanted to hear it or not, about this project. The love and dedication you show to each member of your flock is a testimony to the great call God has raised you to. Thank you.

Thank you to Bonnie at Bonnie's Hair Design in Kimberly, Wisconsin. You did a fabulous job!

Ed and Kathy Kelly, Wayne and Marlene Cornwell, John Shortridge, thank you for your belief in this project, your prayers, support, and encouragement.

Thank you, Jonna and Jeremiah, for sharing your mother with the world for a little while. When I am not writing, surely I make up for the quality of meals you ate while I was. Jonna, you are the best assistant a writer could ask for! I love you both so much.

I would like to thank my husband, Danny. You have been supportive of this novel since the day I began writing it. When I would skip a day of writing, you would gently remind me to write every day. When hot meals were not on the table and clean clothes in the closet, you would burn some grilled cheese and stuff the washer full. Everything I do, I do better because of you. I love you…until forever!

Much thanks to everyone at Tate Publishing working to make this project a success. I appreciate all the hard work and commitment that each of you have contributed. Collaboration is not always easy, but always worth it.

Without God, the story in me would never have seen paper. I am so thankful for every gift he has given me, especially his Son, Jesus, who gave his life for mine. To God be the glory!

Foreword

My husband and I served as pastors for approximately thirty years. Of all the people we worked with, met, and led during those years, some people seem to stand out. Darlene is one of those people.

She was and is created by God to be a communicator. She comes from at least three generations of anointed professional quality communicators, both in music and the Word of God. We have had the privilege, and sometimes great challenge, of walking with her family members.

Even though *Until Forever* is a work of fiction, the characters could easily be real people, in real circumstances, experiencing real tragedy. Just like real life, they have the opportunity to find answers to their questions and obtain victory. Many of the experiences the characters go through parallel Darlene's walk through life—times she has had to endure, walk through, cry through, fight through, and come out the other side of much wiser with a deeper faith, restored joy, and a fresh love of people and the Lord.

You are going to see yourself in this writing, as I did, and who knows what new insight you will gain or what the Lord might whisper to you as you walk with the characters through this journey entitled *Until Forever*.

—Linda K. Johnson, retired pastor's wife

1

Jessi Jensen watched as her husband rubbed her son's hair, and grinned. "We'll be fine. Don't worry so much. Go on. I'll even have supper ready for you when you get home."

Jessi couldn't help but show apprehension. After all, Mark had just spent six months in rehab. He hadn't taken a drink in over six months, and he was Ethan's dad, but could she trust him? She had learned the hard way a long time ago that trust was a word she could not use in the same sentence with her husband's name.

Mark walked over and smiled at his wife. "Honey, I'm done with all that stuff. I love you. I love Ethan. There's nothing I would do to risk your love or jeopardize our lives together. Please believe me. We'll be okay. I promise."

Jessi bent down to give her son a hug and kiss. They rubbed noses, and Ethan giggled. "Mommy, you always do that."

"What does it mean, Ethan?" Jessi asked, her eyes shining with the threat of tears. Her love for her child overwhelmed her. She'd never had anything in her life that meant so much to her. Not Blackie, the lab her parents had finally permitted her to have when she was six, nor Miranda, her favorite doll that she took to bed with her each night as a child. Nothing she could have ever imagined or experienced could have prepared her for the love she would pour out for this child.

Ethan looked up with an expression you wouldn't expect from a four-year-old. "It means that I love you and you love me until forever, Mama. Just like Jesus. Right, Mama?"

"Yes, sweetheart. Until forever I will love you. Always remember that, Ethan—until forever." Jessi rose from her place next to her son and managed a half smile for her husband. "Take care of him, Mark. I'll see you around four thirty."

She grabbed her school bag and headed out to a cold car with a feeling of dread. If only she had faith like Aunt Merry and her little Ethan, then maybe this wouldn't be so difficult. She closed her eyes for a brief second and tried to pray. Nothing. It would never change. God didn't help losers like her, and he certainly didn't have time to listen to her whining.

She could see why God loved Aunt Merry and Ethan. Of all the people in the world, these were the two she loved the most. Who wouldn't love them? They were the kind of people who inspired others just by watching them. They didn't have to speak a word. The love within them said it all. One look into their eyes, and a person experienced a sense of peace. Aunt Merry had her wisdom and unconditional love, and Ethan with his wide-eyed wonder and innocence. The sound of pelting ice pulled her out of her reverie.

Great! Freezing rain again, she thought. *I'll have to call Mark and tell him if he's going out to be careful. I am so sick of these Oklahoma winters.*

She slowly pulled out of the driveway and headed to Roosevelt Elementary School, where she taught a classroom full of third graders. Her mind quickly shifted to the task at hand: making it to school in one piece. Why school hadn't already been called off, she couldn't fathom. "Nothing to do now but keep on going," she muttered to herself. "Tomorrow the sun will be out, and it'll be sixty. Crazy January weather. A couple more miles and I am home free, at least until school is out."

Driving slow did have its advantages, Jessi reminded herself. Lately she was in too much of a hurry to take the time to look at the stately old homes that surrounded her school. Someday she would love to live in a house like one of these—two-story, brick homes with white shutters and brick sidewalks leading up to big front doors with brass knockers; front porches with porch swings that spanned the entire front of the house. Some of the homes still had Christmas decorations up. Big, fresh green wreaths with red bows hanging from second-story balconies and candles lit in every window. Even brightly colored lanterns with little tea lights graced the steps to a few of the homes.

One night she had taken Ethan on a Christmas-light drive, and she purposely drove through this neighborhood. She had fallen in love with the lanterns and the candles, all the decorations, really. Something about a candle in a window made a place feel inviting, like you could go in and sit by a fire with a mug of hot chocolate and a good book. The tree would be brightly lit with gifts underneath and a train track running completely around it. Antique glass ornaments of all shapes and sizes would hang from each limb, and an angel would grace the top, watching over her keep. She could still picture the look on Ethan's face as he took it all in. He was in awe over everything. Ethan had his favorites too: the snowmen with eyes of coal and carrot noses, Santas and reindeer on rooftops, and oh, the lights—bright white lights, blue ones, or all the multi-colored sets. He couldn't get enough of them. Some flickered, and some raced along. Faster and faster, just like his race cars at home. He even rounded out the scene with his own sound effects—*zoom, zoom*. What surprised her most was when he wanted to stop the car and get out for a nativity scene. "Mom, please," he'd pleaded, and she'd never been able to deny those eyes when he really put his all into it. They stopped for a little while, and she watched as he went from life-sized camel to cow to lamb. He would stand at each piece for a minute or two. Finally, he ended up at the manger. When he knelt down on his knees and bowed his head, tears formed in her eyes. Normally, she took his faith with a grain of salt, knowing he was a four-year-old boy who was greatly influenced by his great-aunt Merry, who watched him while Jessi was working. This time she did not know why she let this simple act of obedience to a God she refused to serve bother her.

On occasion when Jessi would let herself drift, she liked to think about what others had and what she was lacking. On occasion she became quite maudlin, and she forgot exactly what she had to be thankful for. It usually happened when something in her life was considerably stressful. She would find herself wandering, daydreaming about living in someone else's life or the "once upon a time" dreams she had had and how far away she was from seeing them become a reality.

Maybe this time Mark would be able to stay dry and hold down a job. Her own salary was steady, but it wouldn't allow her to live in a neighborhood like this one or eventually get that great play set Ethan had wanted for Christmas. Money was always just a little too tight. Expectations were always a little too high, and too many times reality was a bit too much of a letdown. She'd done her best for Ethan with Christmas this year. She found him a great refurbished two-wheeler in the perfect colors: blue and red. It had tassels hanging from the handlebars and a horn that he just loved honking. But she wanted to do more. She'd loved their little house when they first bought it. She knew it would be a first home, and she was okay with that. They would fix it up little by little, and as their family grew, they would move into something bigger and start the process again and again until they were in their dream house. Where did all those dreams go?

I guess the ice is giving everyone a hard time this morning, she thought as she pulled into an empty parking lot. The only other car was Principal Davies'. She half skated across the parking lot as she made her way to the school building. The sound of silence that greeted her as she walked in the door was altogether unnatural for a school. At the very least she should have heard teachers chatting among themselves, chalk clicking upon chalkboards in preparation for a day of learning, and the sound of a typewriter emanating from the office as Julie, the school secretary, typed memos from her perch behind the counter. Nothing but silence.

"Hello, is anyone here?" Jessi yelled out, knowing full well that Dr. Davies was somewhere in the building.

Not only was his car in the parking lot, but the doors were unlocked. At least the teachers' entrance was.

"Jessi? Is that you?" Dr. Davies rounded the corner, probably coming from the copy room. "Didn't you receive my message? I left a message on your voicemail that school had been cancelled for today. This ice storm is going to be a killer."

Jessi groaned and glanced outside. She had forgotten to charge her cell phone. Her windshield looked like one of those glass block showers. Everything was out of focus. Heading straight home now would definitely be a problem. At the very least, the roads wouldn't be drivable until the rain stopped. She wasn't sure if the city even owned salt or sand spreaders, let alone was able to pay someone enough to risk their lives trying to save someone else's. Probably not.

The words "Looks like I'll be getting caught up on some of my grading today," managed to escape from her lips, when all she really wanted to do was get back in her car and head home. She resigned herself to her day, even though her heart screamed for a second chance. If only she had checked the messages before she and Mark had their semi-argument she would be at home right now having breakfast with her son. If only. Her life thus far had been a series of "if onlys." If only Mom and Dad had loved each other enough to stay together. If only I had listened to the voices in my past telling me that Mark was nothing but trouble. No, that's not right. Then I wouldn't have Ethan, and I would do anything for Ethan ... even marry Mark again.

As she entered her classroom, her mental to-do list caught up with her. She made her way to her desk and began to check items off her list. It felt good to be getting something done. With everything else happening in her life, she hadn't been able to keep up with her schoolwork. As she immersed herself in her work, she completely forgot about calling Mark.

. . .

By eleven, things seemed to be getting a bit better. The freezing rain had changed to rain as the air warmed up a bit. Mark figured this was as good a time as any to head out and grab the ingredients he needed for dinner. "Come on, buddy. We have to run to the store. Where's your coat?"

Ethan went to his hook in the hallway where Mom put his coat and his backpack. He grabbed his coat, which was bright orange (Mom said it was easier to find him in a crowd that way), and walked back to his dad, who helped him put it on. "It shouldn't take us too long. Your mom still likes spaghetti, right?"

"She loves it, especially the cheese bread," Ethan said, speaking more for himself than his mother.

Together they headed out to the garage, where Mark's car had been sitting for the last six months. He still had his license, as his rehab stint hadn't been the result of an accident. He'd willingly checked himself in to prove to Jessi that he didn't have a problem. He figured if he went willingly, she would know he really wasn't an alcoholic, as she so loved to call him. And he'd proved himself. He didn't have a problem. A guy with a problem wouldn't be able to go six months without a beer, right? He couldn't figure out what the big deal was. What was so wrong with a beer now and then? And what was with her attitude this morning. It was like she didn't trust him with his own son. Well, Ethan was his son too, and he had just as much of a right to be with him as Jessi did. As far as he was concerned, she sheltered the kid a bit too much for his own good. If he was going to learn to get along in the real world, he was going to have to be in it once in a while. And besides that, she was going to turn him into a mama's boy. That was out of the question. No son of his was going to be some whining wimp tied to his mama by the apron strings. It was time to take over the education of young Ethan and teach him to be a man.

Mark opened the car door and helped Ethan get buckled in his booster seat. That was one thing he would not challenge Jessi on. She'd blow up if she ever found out Ethan wasn't in his safety seat. Their man-to-man talks would have to be from the front seat to the backseat, not like Mark and his dad's—sitting next to each other in his dad's old Buick, his dad with a beer in his hand, and him with a root beer, just like Dad. *Someday I'll be just like him*, he had thought to himself. He would picture himself sitting in the front seat of a car like this one on a hot summer day with a nice cold beer. Nowadays you couldn't even have a beer outside of the car and then drive, let alone tool along with one. Course, he didn't let laws keep him from having fun when he was younger. He and his buddies would pick up a case and cruise down country roads like there was no tomorrow.

Yep, the fun stopped about six years ago, when he met Jessi. Granted she wasn't a religious freak like her aunt Merry, but she was pretty straitlaced—no partying, no swearing, and certainly no fooling around before they were married. She was up front with him about that. He figured she was lying to him about the religion stuff. It turned out she wasn't. She didn't have time for a God who would allow so much pain and suffering in her life. Then she figured she wasn't worthy of his love anyway. He could never figure that one out. If ever there was someone worthy of God's love, it was a goody-two-shoe like his wife. He had never been attracted to teachers' pets or Ms. Perfects before. She definitely fit into those categories. For the life of him, he could not remember what it was that had attracted him to her in the first place. She was pretty, that was for sure, with her blond hair and dark eyes. Dark brown. He'd never seen such dark eyes before. Indian eyes, she had told him later. He first noticed her at one of the college hangouts near Oklahoma State University. She'd been sitting with her friends at a table, and they were laughing and carrying on, and he couldn't take his eyes off her. He'd asked her to dance, and they danced a couple of numbers before he offered to buy her a beer. She politely declined the beer and asked for a Sprite. He should have figured something was up with that but then dismissed it with the thought she was probably letting up because she was driving. Talk about wrong first impressions. Later he'd learned the only reason she was even there was because it was one of her roommates' birthdays and she was in the minority when it came to choosing the place to celebrate. He'd gotten her number and promised to give her a call. After putting it off for a week, he was unable to get her off his mind, so he called her. They decided to get together the following Saturday for the OSU vs. OU football game. Being big rivals, the game promised to be packed to the hilt and a great showdown between two good football teams. About a half hour before kickoff, Jessi met him outside the stadium, as planned. He was duly impressed by her knowledge of football and didn't mind letting her know. She had played flute in the marching band all throughout high school and had never missed a game in four years. Sometimes she lost her voice from yelling so much but never missed a game. Therefore, she developed an understanding of football, if not a love of the game.

The next thing he knew it was a year later and they were standing at an altar saying "I do." A year after that, Ethan was born. Everything had been a series of up and downs since then. She had her teaching degree and had no problem securing a job in Oklahoma City, teaching inner-city third graders, while he drifted from construction crew to construction crew. It seemed as though he would just get in a rhythm at one job and then they'd let him go. So he'd been late a few times and had a couple at the local bar with his burger at lunch. Everyone else was doing the same thing. Shoot, a couple of times his crew chief drank one down with him. He still couldn't figure out what the big deal was. Mark jumped when the car behind him laid on the horn. Green light.

Mark pulled into the parking lot of the grocery store, looked back at Ethan, and started to say something when he noticed Ethan was sound asleep in his car seat. *Well, I suppose if I lock the doors he'll be just fine. I just need a couple of things, and I'll only be a minute*, he thought to himself. Mark hurried into the nearly empty store and found the pasta, sauce, and French bread. He bought some cheese and the makings for a salad and then hurried out to where he left Ethan. He found him right where he left him, sound asleep. He wasn't sure if Ethan still took naps, but today he did.

Mark took a different route home, thinking the roads might be a little better than they were on route to the store. He saw the sign before he could really even read it: Pappy's Bar and Grill. And it beckoned him like a lighthouse guiding a lost ship. *I'll just go in and say hi to everyone*, he reasoned with himself. He looked back at Ethan, who was still sleeping soundly, and figured if he was okay in the grocery parking lot he would be fine for a few minutes while he went in to see his friends. He wouldn't drink anything; he'd promised Jessi. He'd just say hi. He got out, locked the doors, and headed straight for the door.

Ethan woke up and looked around. He was cold. He let himself out of his car seat and curled up on the backseat of the car with the blanket his mother kept handy for emergencies. He recognized it for its warmth, curled up, and went straight back to sleep on the backseat of the old Buick.

It wasn't until lunchtime that Jessi remembered to call home. No answer. She tried calling several times while she ate lunch. Still no answer. She closed her eyes and rested her arms and head on her desk. She breathed deeply, wishing she had remembered to call earlier.

It was something she would never forgive herself for.

2

Mark's friends finally talked him in to having a couple of beers with them. They sure tasted good, too. One followed another and then another. He lost track of time but knew he should be doing something else, so he finally said his good-byes and left. He almost fell on the ice trying to get back to his car. He slid in the front seat and started the car without a backward glance at his son sleeping on the backseat. Truth be told, he didn't even remember Ethan was in the car. He shook his head, trying to clear up his vision. He pulled out of the parking lot rather cautiously, the way a drunk usually does.

If it hadn't been icy, he probably would have been pulled over for weaving back and forth across the middle line. Unfortunately, most of the police were dealing with traffic accidents and helping the power company guard downed lines. One drunken dad, with his four-year-old son sleeping in the backseat, left the parking lot going the wrong direction on a road heading out of town.

Mark couldn't remember where he was going, let alone how to get there. It seemed as though there were voices in his head playing tricks on him and they were all talking at once. Nothing was making sense, so he just drove—back and forth, weaving to and fro. Before long Mark was nodding off and then jerking his head back up. Finally, he nodded off and didn't wake up until it was too late. He slept through tires hitting the gravel on the side of the road and the front of his car hitting a tree head-on. He slept through both Ethan and himself being thrown from the vehicle. One major difference was Mark weighed a lot more than Ethan did. When he did wake up, he found himself lying in a ditch. He tried to stand up but couldn't make it to his knees. From a distance he could hear a very small voice saying, "Daddy, please help me; please, Daddy." Mark belly crawled out of the ditch toward the small voice that he now knew was his son. He dragged one of his legs, which was twisted and lay at an odd angle behind him. He saw the car with the front end smashed up against a tree. On the street about twenty feet from the car, he saw Ethan. Ethan was laying very still for a boy of four. Mark instinctively knew that something was very wrong with his son, who was still quietly calling for his daddy, "Please, Daddy, please. Help me."

Mark crawled to where his son lay and started sobbing. He couldn't get help for his own son. He lay there next to Ethan, trying to give him what warmth he could, and waited until a passing car stopped to help. He would always remember the desperate cries of his son pleading with him for help. More importantly, he would always remember not being able to help his own son.

The police arrived on the scene just three minutes after the first passerby called in the accident. By the time they arrived, both father and son were covered with blankets in an effort to keep them warm. There was glass everywhere, and Ethan had bits and pieces embedded in his face and forehead. No one dared move the boy. The ambulance arrived right after the police and quickly transported both father and son to the nearest hospital. Mark's wallet was checked for identification and residence. His blood was drawn, and tests confirmed what was already suspected. He was legally intoxicated, and his alcohol blood level was a .14, well above the legal limit. He suffered from multiple breaks in the right leg and two broken ribs. Ethan didn't fare so well.

Jessi was beside herself trying to reach Mark at home. She decided to brave the elements and head home. She'd already done the distance once today. As long as she was extremely cautious, she should make it back again. As soon as her car left the parking lot, the school phone started ringing. After listening to the messenger on the end of the phone line, Dr. Davies ran out of the building just in time to see Jessi's taillights grow dim and then disappear in the distance.

Jessi let herself in to the front door and looked around for a note. She did not find one. Next she checked phone messages. The first one was indeed from Dr. Davies. "Jessi. Hi, this is Dr. Davies. School has been cancelled for today because of the ice storm. I'll see you tomorrow."

There were two other messages, one from Aunt Merry inviting Jessi and Mark to attend church with her and Ethan and to have lunch at her house afterward. This was no surprise, as she extended this invitation at least once a month.

Jessi shook her head and had a wry smile for her aunt. "She sure doesn't give up easy, I'll give her that."

She made a mental note to talk to Mark. If they were going to make a go of this marriage and be a good example for Ethan, maybe they should start attending church together. No one would have to know it was for appearances only. It was only an hour once a week, and it would make Ethan happy, not to mention Aunt Merry.

The next message caused her to catch her breath. "Hi, Mrs. Jensen, this is officer Burtell with the Oklahoma City Police Department. Your husband and son were involved in a car accident today. We tried to reach you in person at home as well as by phone at your place of work. They have been taken to Baptist Medical Center on NW Expressway. Please enter at the emergency room, and the nurse at the registration desk will direct you to where your family members are."

That was it. No reassuring words, no explanations, nothing.

All the way to the hospital, Jessi pleaded with God. "God, if you would just let Ethan be okay, I'll do whatever you want. I'll go to church. I'll give money. I'll move to Africa—anything, God. Please just let him be okay." She tried cutting every deal she could think of. She promised him everything she had—all her worldly possessions and her health—not stopping to think that the only thing he might want was the one thing she did not offer: her heart.

Jessi pulled into Baptist Medical Center at the emergency entrance at 1:23 in the afternoon and ran into the hospital. She grabbed the first person she saw that looked like they worked there. "Where is my son? I'm Jessi Jensen. My husband and son were brought in here a little while ago. Where is my son? Please take me to him."

The nurse smiled at Jessi and led her to the reception area. Giving the receptionist a look that Jessi did not at all know how to interpret, she introduced her. "Sandy, this Mrs. Jensen. She is looking for her husband and her son. Could you please see that she is taken care of?" With that, she turned and continued walking in the direction she had been pulled from.

Sandy smiled at Jessi. "I will phone the doctor and let him know you are here."

With her patience wearing very thin, Jessi stood by the receptionist's desk and waited. A few minutes later, who she assumed to be a doctor appeared by her side.

"Mrs. Jensen, I am Dr. Peters. Why don't we go over to my office so we are a bit more comfortable?"

Jessi wordlessly followed the doctor.

She sat across from him and calmly asked, "Where is my son?"

"Mrs. Jensen, I'm not sure of how much you know or if you know anything at all, so I am going to assume I am the first person to actually speak to you since the accident. I will start with your husband's condition. Mark was brought to the emergency room via ambulance. He has multiple contusions and several fractures in his right leg. He will need surgery to be able to walk properly, as he also fractured his right ankle. He has two broken ribs and a punctured lung. He's in pretty good condition, all things considering. The police will want to speak with you as soon as you are able to, to discuss the details of the accident. Mrs.

Jensen, medically speaking, I must tell you that Mark's blood alcohol level was .14. Your husband had been drinking before the accident."

Jessi closed her eyes, and a tear escaped and ran down her cheek. "Please tell me that Ethan is okay. Please tell me he wasn't hurt."

Dr. Peters took a deep breath and began. "Unfortunately, Ethan wasn't as lucky. He was thrown from the vehicle on impact and has suffered an acute subdural hematoma from a traumatic injury to the head, which means he developed a blood clot, and he is bleeding internally from the tissue that protects and cushions the brain from the skull as a result of his head hitting the icy road. He is in surgery now, and surgeons are working to drain the fluid from the brain. He was conscious at the scene of the accident but slipped into a comatose state before he reached the hospital. Studies have been done showing that patients with severe head trauma often have a better chance of recovery when their body temperatures were lowered into a semi-hypothermia state. These studies were not performed on four-year-old children, Mrs. Jensen, but we are hopeful that in this case the elements have made a positive contribution to your child's recovery.

If Ethan makes it through the surgery, as we are hopeful he will, and if there are no further complications, then the best-case scenario would be for Ethan to come through the injury completely unscathed. The more likely scenario would be Ethan coming out of his coma with a combination of various types of side effects that range from vision problems to seizures. But that would be okay. As a matter of fact, better than okay. We can deal with the various symptoms that are caused from a trauma to the head. Worst-case scenario would be for Ethan to not recover from surgery and/or return to consciousness from his comatose state. We will cross that bridge when and if we have to. There are other relatively minor injuries compared with the brain trauma. He also has a fractured pelvis, a broken left arm, various contusions, and..."

Jessi couldn't take anymore. She wasn't even sure she heard everything the doctor had told her. At first, she started to shake. Then she began sobbing, with her sobs turning into screams.

Anticipating Ethan's mother's reaction, Dr. Peters instructed his assistant to be ready to lend a hand in the event that she would become hysterical, an occurrence that happened with mothers on a regular basis when their children were seriously injured. He was actually surprised she made it through as much information as she did.

Nurse Jacobson entered the room as soon as her pager went off. She held Jessi's hand and spoke to her in low tones, trying to calm her down, "Jessi, I am going to give you a sedative to help you calm down. You are beginning to hyperventilate, and we need you to be coherent enough to listen and make informed decisions regarding Ethan's, as well as your husband's, care. Please, for Ethan's sake, you need to be calm."

Jessi managed to shake her head between sobs, and the nurse rolled up her sleeve and administered the sedative. It was a couple of minutes before Jessi's breathing became noticeably slower. Even with the medication she was unable to control the tears, which were flowing at a slower yet constant rate.

Nurse Jacobson, concerned for Jessi's well being, asked, "Is there someone we can call who can sit with you while you are waiting for Ethan to come out of surgery?"

Jessi covered her face with her hands and breathed deeply. "Aunt Merry. Yes, Aunt Merry. She'll know what to do."

Jessi gave the nurse the phone number and waited in the private waiting room she had been shown to. She couldn't sit, so she paced back and forth from one end of the room to the other, not thinking, not praying, not anything. She was barely managing to breathe. When Aunt Merry walked into the room she wrapped Jessi in her arms and closed her eyes while her own tears slipped down her face. When every tear possible was spent, Jessi explained what the doctor had told her. She wasn't sure of the technical terms, nor did she remember his "relatively minor" injuries. She did remember his head injury, the blood clot, and the surgery that was now being performed to drain the fluid off the brain. She also remembered him being in a coma and possibly never waking up.

Everything else she had been told, including the hope the doctor had tried to convey, was a blur. "Oh God, what am I going to do?"

Sometime later, after Jessi slipped back into a habit of pacing, stopping, staring at walls, and then pacing again, the surgeon entered the room.

"Mrs. Jensen, I'm Doctor Phillips, Ethan's surgeon. The surgery went as we had hoped. We drained the fluid that was accumulating, repaired the damaged tissue, and inserted a drain for any fluid left as a result of the surgery. Ethan is in the recovery room now, and you may go in and see him for a few minutes. He is still under anesthesia and still in a coma, so he will not be responsive. We still encourage you quietly talk with and touch Ethan, maybe hold his hand or rub his cheek. Reassure him; let him know you are here and waiting for him to wake up."

Jessi followed Dr. Phillips to the recovery room where Ethan had been placed. She had been given five minutes to see her son. Five precious minutes. It wasn't enough. Her eyes welled up when she saw the tubes coming from everywhere. Bandages were wrapped around his head. His left arm was in a cast, and there were bruises and scratches on his face. He was the most beautiful child she'd ever laid eyes on. She tried to maintain control; Ethan needed to hear her being calm. "Hi, Ethan, it's Mommy. I'm right here beside you, baby. How are you feeling?"

She lightly rubbed his cheek with the backside of her hand, being careful so she wouldn't cause him any more pain than he had already endured. Her darling baby boy. How could she have let this happen to him? This was not where he belonged. He should be outside kicking his soccer ball or riding his bike. He was always so full of life and energy. She could barely keep up with him, and then not for long. Looking at him now, she had to wonder where that little boy was—the little boy who loved Spider-Man and anything with wheels; the little boy who could eat pizza for every meal. Her little boy. The one she loved more than life itself and would gladly trade places with were it possible.

"You and Daddy had an accident, sweetheart, and you are in the hospital," she explained, hopefully calming any fears he might have. She didn't want him being afraid and not understanding where he was. "The doctors are doing a good job fixing you up so you can come home with Mommy. As soon as you are all better, Mommy will go to church with you and Aunt Merry, just like you wanted me to. But first you have to wake up and get better so we can all go together, okay? I love you, Ethan. I will be here waiting for you to wake up."

An ICU nurse stopped and motioned to Jessi that time was up. She wasn't ready to leave him.

"Sweetheart, I have to go out for a little while, so you can rest and get better. The nurses are taking good care of you while you sleep, and Mommy will be right outside your room waiting for you." She bent down and softly kissed his cheek and rubbed his nose with hers and whispered, "Until forever, Ethan. I will love you until forever."

Jessi returned to the waiting room, where Aunt Merry was waiting for her. Aunt Merry didn't ask any questions, for which Jessi was extremely grateful, although she did offer a vending machine cup of coffee. For this too Jessi was grateful. She couldn't think of stomaching food, but coffee was a welcome sight.

She was told she could visit him every hour for five minutes until he was removed from ICU recovery. When he was moved to his room, she would be able to visit with him as much as she'd like.

Aunt Merry waited until Jessi had settled down in a chair to broach the subject she was thinking about. Sitting down next to her, she looked at her favorite person in the whole world, in her world. If at all possible she would take every ounce of pain Jessi was experiencing and put it all on herself. She hated to see the child hurting. Still, she had to ask. "Jessi, have you called your mom yet? She needs to be told."

Jessi looked at Aunt Merry with an almost puzzled look. "I hadn't even thought of it. She wouldn't have time for us anyway. She never has before. Why would this be any different?"

"Jessi, you need to give her a chance. At least call her and let her know her grandson has been in an accident. If you want, I'll call her for you."

"Do what you feel is best. I don't know anything anymore."

Aunt Merry patted her knee and rose to use the telephone. A half hour later Jessi's mom, Patty, came walking through the room. Aunt Merry wasn't sure what to expect when she arrived, but it sure wasn't what happened. Jessi took one look at her mother, and she cried out and ran to her. In the half hour it took Patty to get to the hospital, she found a maternal instinct that she had beforehand lacked. "Oh, Jessi. I'm so sorry. I'm here, sweetheart."

They were the words that Jessi had needed to hear her entire life. Jessi clung to her mother, crying. "Mom, I'm so scared. I don't know what to do. I don't know how to make him better. What do I do?"

Even though Patty didn't have reassuring words that would make Ethan all better, her touch seemed to soothe Jessi nonetheless. She continued to hold her daughter close. "I don't know, baby. I just don't know. We could pray, Jessi. That's all I know." Patty had never been a godly woman and wasn't sure she wanted to risk being called a hypocrite, but at the time it seemed a good thing to say.

Jessi nodded her head in agreement, thinking of her own conversations with God, promising him anything if he would just heal her little boy. Deep inside she knew it was more bargaining or bribing than praying, but it's where her heart was at the time. Patty stayed with Jessi and became the protective mother that Jessi so needed.

Jessi felt drained, depleted, and completely void of any feeling besides desperation and utter hopelessness because she wasn't able to help her son. She had finally settled into a comfortable chair to wait for her next five minutes with Ethan when two police officers walked into the waiting room. She correctly assumed that they needed to speak with her, but she did not have the energy or the will to rouse herself from her resting place. She knew that eventually someone would notice she had not asked about her husband, nor had she gone to see him. She supposed this would be the time to disclose the whys.

"Mrs. Jensen?" the female officer asked, looking straight at Jessi.

Jessi took a deep breath and slowly started to rise from her chair when her mother spoke up and crossed the room to greet the officers. "I'm Jessi's mother. Is there something I can help you with?"

The officers looked at each other. "We'd like to talk with Mrs. Jensen about the accident."

"Well, as you can guess, my daughter is in no condition to talk with you about anything. She's had a major trauma, in case you hadn't heard, and I'm not going to let you upset her any further."

Jessi walked to where her mother stood and put an arm around her. "It's okay, Mom. I have to hear it sooner or later anyway." She looked at her mother with more love than she had thought possible. "But thanks."

Jessi looked at the officers. Patti, still by Jessi's side, reached over and gave her hand a squeeze. She stayed by her daughter's side and continued to support her through everything she was told. Eventually Jessi would need to give all her thoughts and feelings voice. For now all she was capable of dealing with were the voices in her head. Aunt Merry was wise enough to know this, and her mother was learning. Jessi greeted the police officers with no more than a nod. Not even her eyes could smile.

"Mrs. Jensen, we are sorry to be bothering you right now, but we would like to fill you in on the accident details. Your husband had a head-on collision with a tree. When he arrived at the hospital, they administered a sobriety test, and his blood alcohol level was .14. If someone's blood alcohol level in the state of Oklahoma is .08 or higher, they are considered legally intoxicated. Mrs. Jensen, your husband is going to be charged with DUI as well as vehicular assault. This will be his third DUI charge. He is looking at probable jail time as well as considerable fines. We have witnesses at Pappy's Bar that said Mark had had four beers and had a couple of shots during his one-hour visit to the bar. During that time, Ethan either crawled out of his booster seat to wrap up in the blanket found on the scene, or he had never been in his seat. Upon impact, both passengers were thrown through the windshield. Mr. Jensen landed in the ditch, and Ethan landed on the road. Mr. Jensen drug himself from the ditch to Ethan's side. They were both transported to Baptist Hospital via ambulance. We are sorry to have to give you this information at this time, Mrs. Jensen, but as soon as Mr. Jensen's medical conditions allow, he will be taken into custody. We didn't want this to come as a shock to you on top of everything else that is happening."

Even though Jessi was not surprised by anything she heard, it still breached a part of her reality that she didn't want to deal with. "It isn't a shock to me, officers. In fact, it would be a great relief knowing he's someplace my son will never be. As far as I'm concerned, when you lock him up, don't ever find him again. He should never see the light of day. Is there anything else you feel you must share with me?"

"No, ma'am. We just wanted to give you the details. If you have any questions for us or need any information at all, please don't hesitate to call."

The officer with the nametag "Officer Wells" on his shirt handed Jessi a business card with his name and phone number on it. Both police officers turned and left.

Once again the tears fell, and Jessi buried her face in her mother's shoulder. It felt good to have a mother, even if it was a little late in life.

Every fifty-five minutes of waiting gave a person a lot of time to think. Jessi had been wondering how Ethan was thrown from the vehicle when he knew he wasn't to be out of his booster seat in the car. Now it made sense. He had gotten cold, and she had put a blanket in the car just for that purpose. She remembered the day she had carried it out to the car along with other emergency items for cold weather. Ethan had watched and questioned his mom, "Mama, why are you putting all those things in the car?"

Jessi had explained that the supplies were for emergencies. If they broke down in the cold weather, they would need water, and they would need the blanket in case they got cold. They would also need candles and a flashlight. He remembered the blanket was for getting warm in the cold—something intended for good, destined to harm.

Jessi finally decided to face her husband. She knew it had to be done sooner rather than later. Later would probably be wiser, as she hadn't slept in over twenty-four hours. She was tired, hungry, impatient, and desperately praying for a miracle from a God she had refused to serve. Later might be wiser, but later wasn't happening. She stood up from her seat. "Mom, Aunt Merry, it's time I see Mark. Now that I know what happened, I have to get it over with. I'll be back in a little while."

Both women wisely stayed where they were and let her go alone.

She had to face him now, today, or not at all. Jessi walked to his room. When she walked through the door he was lying on his bed with his eyes shut. That was easy, she decided, and started to go back out into the hallway when she heard his voice.

"I'm not sleeping, Jessi. I can't sleep because my mind won't let me, and if I do fall asleep my nightmares won't allow me to remain sleeping. I'm surprised it took you this long to come and see me. What, am I not important enough for you to take a few minutes out of your busy schedule to come see me?" He opened his eyes and turned to look at her.

Jessi's mouth fell open. "What? What did you say to me? You almost kill our son, and you are wondering why I took so long to come and see you? Of all the stupid, idiotic things to question."

The pain and rejection Mark had felt all his life surfaced. "Yes, I know. You have been by Ethan's side, not moving, being the dutiful mother. You've been the dutiful mother since the day he was born. If you had been the least bit a dedicated and loving wife, then we might not be here right now. But no, I've had to sit in your backseat since the day that kid came into our lives. You could have at least checked to see if I was okay. Maybe you could have shed a few tears over me. But no, I'm just not worth it, am I?"

Jessi couldn't believe what she was hearing. She was almost too stunned to even reply. Almost. She said the first and only thing that came to mind. "Go to hell. Go straight to hell. If I never see your face again it would be too soon." She turned and left the room. Her joke of a marriage was over. She returned to the ICU recovery waiting room and waited for her next five minutes with her son.

Six months later, Jessi was sitting next to her son's bed and reading his favorite book to him when the doctor came into the room. "Jessi, we need to talk."

Knowing how she felt about discussing Ethan's health situation in front of him, Dr. Phillips motioned for her to follow him out to the hallway.

Jessi looked at Ethan and said, "Sweetheart, Mommy will be right back. I just have to talk with the doctor for a few minutes." She laid down the book and went into the hallway. "Yes, what is it, Dr. Phillips?" she questioned.

"Jessi, I know we have been over this, but there still has been no change in Ethan's situation. How long do you plan on letting him continue like this? The ventilator is all that is keeping him alive. There is no, nor has there been any, brain activity since the accident. You work all day then come here till we kick you out. You go home, go to bed, and do it all over again the next day. How long is this going to continue? You need to make a decision, Jessi."

Jessi's eyes filled with tears. She didn't say a word, just turned, walked back into Ethan's room, picked up his book, and started reading again. She closed her eyes and breathed in deeply. She wasn't ready to let go. *Why do they keep asking me to let you go?*

Another ten months went by. It was Ethan's sixth birthday, his second birthday celebration since the accident. For his fifth birthday she had brought in cake and candles and birthday hats for everyone to wear. The nurses on duty and Aunt Merry joined her in singing "Happy Birthday." They talked to Ethan as if he would wake up at any moment. On his second birthday in the home, the one they had just celebrated, Aunt Merry was the only one who celebrated with her. Christmas had come and gone. She had scrounged and scrimped and bought him that outdoor play set he had wanted for the previous Christmas. She was so excited when she told him about it. She'd even hired the store handyman to come and put it together for her. It was all ready for him to wake up and come home to play on it. It still sat in the backyard, unused.

Jessi now spent every Saturday afternoon reading to Ethan at the long-term care facility where he now lived. She loved just sitting next to him and talking to him. She would tell him about her day and how work went. It especially gave her joy to talk about all the kids in her third grade class. On this particular Saturday afternoon, Dr. Phillips had made a point of being in the hallway when Jessi came to visit.

"Hi, Jessi." They were on a first-name basis after all this time. He called her Jessi, she called him Doc.

"Hi, yourself, Doc. How's my boy today?"

"The answer's the same, Jessi. It's always the same. We need to talk, and this time I need you to answer me." Doc led Jessi to the lounge, where he poured both of them a strong cup of coffee. "I know you don't want to hear this, Jessi, but it's been over a year and things are not getting better. In fact, things are getting worse."

She understood what he was saying. She had been giving Ethan baths on Saturdays now for a few months. She had watched as his sores had gotten worse. It seemed no matter how much she and the nurses turned him, the red, open sores were always a constant in his life. He had lost a considerable amount of weight. He was a shell of what he once was. His muscles had to be stretched daily, and still problems were developing.

Jessi looked at the floor. She had known this day was coming. "Doc, Easter is in a few weeks. Let me spend it with my son, and if he hasn't made a change for the better, we'll talk."

Doc nodded his head. It was the most he'd gotten from her thus far. Her resolve had cracked seeing her son in his current condition. When the nurses had asked his permission for Jessi to start helping with some of Ethan's more basic needs, he'd agreed, hoping she would see the kind of life she was allowing her son to live. He was seeing the results of that decision. Hopefully, come Easter she would see that setting her son free would be the best all around for everyone, especially Ethan. Jessi walked back into Ethan's room and finished reading his favorite story to him. Doc picked up his file and slowly headed to his car. He had done everything that he could think of for Ethan. There just wasn't anything left to be done.

Easter passed with no changes. The hardest thing Jessi ever had to do was pull the plug. It was early in May that she sat by her son and watched him breathe his last breath. Tears coursed their way down her cheeks as she said good-bye. Aunt Merry sat by her side and held her hand. She too wept.

Ethan was buried in the Oaklawn Cemetery. His tombstone simply read:
Ethan Richard Jensen
January 27, 1994–May 6, 2000
Beloved Son

3

Meredith Duvall opened the door for the first of her guests. Well, really she called them friends, but anyone who graced her door was treated like a guest. One by one, Caroline, Betsy, Mabel, Judy, and Georgina all made their way into Meredith's dining room. First, they spent time catching up with one another and what was happening in their lives and the lives of their children. Snacks were shared, and tea was poured for a time of fellowship. Soon a quietness settled upon all of the ladies, and they made their way to the living room. Each woman retreated to her own private prayer closet, whether it was kneeling by the sofa or sitting upright in a chair because of arthritis. It didn't matter, as God knew each heart and where each woman was coming from. They had been meeting for years together to pray. A couple of their original prayer partners had gone home to be with the Lord. A few new ones were added. God brought them in, and God took them home. While it was in some ways sad, they all knew where their final destination would be and they all longed for the day when they would be told, "Well done, good and faithful servant."

In the meantime, they all had a purpose here on earth, and praying together in one accord they saw many miracles happen. Most of the time, their prayer hour was a quiet time. Sometimes one or more of the women would pray out loud, wanting the backing prayers of the whole group. Most of their petitions remained the same, for the miracles usually didn't happen overnight. They certainly happened; they just took time. When a woman entered the group, she added her unsaved loved ones' names to the prayer list. This prayer list was their main goal. They didn't pray for things that would pass away; they prayed for the things which would not pass away.

Before Ethan had gone to his heavenly home, Meredith had been sorely tempted to deviate from their normal order of things to pray for his healing, not that she didn't do this in her own prayer time (as did many of the other women). But long ago this particular time was set aside for the saving of souls. She already knew that little Ethan, should he die, would be waiting for her with the Father. That little guy had more faith than most adults she knew. She would never understand the ways of God, and what was done was done. So all of her efforts went into praying for Jessi and Mark. Her patience was beginning to wane, and she needed the strength of her fellow prayer warriors to help build her up.

Meredith loved music, and knowing the power there was in worship, she began to sing. "I love you, Lord, and I lift my voice, to worship You, oh my soul, rejoice..." All the ladies joined in. Their voices lifted as one unified voice in worship to their heavenly Father. One song led to another, then another. Each song was a powerful expression of love to their creator. Gradually, the music faded and the prayers began.

Kneeling on her favorite chair, she began to pray out loud. "Dear Father, I love you, Lord. Oh, how I love you. You know my heart's cry, even before I speak it out loud. Lord, you know it. Even so, Lord, you have made me a promise, and I am here to respectfully ask for that promise to be fulfilled. I love that girl. She was the daughter that I could never have. I practically raised her while her mama and daddy were off doing their own thing. She was my own answer to prayer. You blessed me so much when you put that little girl in my life. Father, please, she is going through so much right now, and she needs you more than she knows. Only *your* strength will be able to get her through all she has to endure. Father, surely you, Maker of the universe, know that. Please, Lord, let it be soon that the angels in heaven are rejoicing over her name being added to the Lamb's Book of Life. Father, I beg of you to protect her. I also know that you have a strong calling on her husband, Mark, Lord. Only you know what that is and what it's going to take to get him to recognize it. I am but flesh, Lord, and it pains me sometimes to see that man hurt Jessi like he does. Yet I know that he too is your creation and you love him with a love my sinful self will never understand this side of heaven. Oh, Lord, let your will be accomplished soon and let the pain come to a halt, just for a season of rest. Even you rested, Lord. How much more is rest needed for a frail sinner, Father?"

Many tears fell, and many prayers were lifted that day on behalf of Mark and Jessi. As each woman felt a release from the Holy Spirit, she would quietly leave and make her way home. Meredith lifted her eyes to see an empty room. She was the last one to be released from prayer time, and rightly so. It was her little girl they were praying for.

4

Mark turned to look at the building he had slept in, eaten in, breathed in, and lived in for the past six years. He remembered the day he was first brought here. He'd had his day in court and had been found guilty. He was sentenced to prison for his third drunk driving charge. His sentence was considerably longer because of the vehicular assault charge involving a minor, his son, Ethan. He'd walked into the Oklahoma State Reformatory in Granite, Oklahoma, with an attitude the size of Texas. It had taken a while, but eventually his attitude was chipped off his shoulders one knock at a time. He was mad at the world when he was sentenced to spending the next eight years of his life in prison. The object of most of his fury was Jessi. She was the reason he was here, and he hated her with a passion. He wasn't able to unleash his anger toward Jessi. He'd never had the opportunity to look upon her face again, so he directed it toward anyone he came in contact with—the guards, the other inmates, the cooks (though he learned to rein in his temper as he maintained a healthy appetite), as well as the chaplain.

The only person who saw the defeated, broken man he'd become was the only person who had ever visited him, his sister, Julia. His brother, David, gave up on him long ago and would have nothing to do with him, even more so when he heard why Mark was in prison. During his first and only outburst at his sister, when she visited for the first time, she stood to leave and told him if this was what she was in for by coming, she wouldn't be returning. He quickly apologized and asked her to please sit down. This was also when he started to realize just how beaten and broken he was. Later that night in the infirmary, after being beaten by a couple of inmates who were tired of his macho attitude, while sleep still alluded him and nightmares occupied what little sleep he did have, he realized that his life was not worth living. There was nothing left to live for. His wife had divorced him. She wouldn't take his phone calls, and the few letters he sent her were given back to him with "return to sender" stamped on them. He'd killed his son while he was drunk driving. He couldn't stand the skin he lived in, the smell of himself, his face in a mirror, or the haunted, lost look coming back from eyes that always stared him down in his reflection. He wanted out. He wanted to die.

The nurse on duty had thought Mark was asleep when he left him for a few minutes to get a sandwich and a cup of coffee. It was just enough time for Mark to hobble over to the nurses' supply cabinet and get a razor blade. His hands, which were swollen from the fight he'd had earlier and proof that he did get in a few good jabs, were almost too sore to handle the small razor blade. It took too long to get his bandaged hands to cut through the skin on his left wrist. He had just made the final cut when the nurse returned. His only hope was he would be too busy with his sandwich and coffee to look in on him. He heard shouts just as he passed out.

When he came to his left wrist was bandaged, he was in restraints, and a guy in a white robe was standing over him, seemingly in prayer. At first he thought he might be dead and he was being given his last rites. Then he figured out he wasn't dead and the guy was the jail chaplain. He was about to curse him and tell him to leave when he felt a strange sense of *déjà vu* came over him. He suddenly had a memory of his grandmother in prayer. He would sit and watch her, knowing that what she was doing was a sacred thing. He loved to watch his grandmother pray. She looked peaceful. His grandmother had passed away when he was six years old, so why he remembered such a thing, he did not know.

Although he questioned the motives of the chaplain, he remained silent. He had desperately desired the feeling of nothingness death would bring him, and he was sorely disappointed that once again he couldn't properly complete something once he had begun. If he had succeeded, he would be floating along on a cloud of nothing right now. No more guilt and no more nightmares. His life had become a living hell, and he wanted out. Someone, namely the chaplain, cared enough about to him to pray over him. Mark wanted to know why. He quietly watched the chaplain pray. Suddenly the chaplain lifted his eyes and met his own. What Mark saw shocked him. He saw love and understanding, not condemnation and pity. He saw compassion and forgiveness, not judgment and hatred. What he had really seen was God's love; he just didn't know it yet. He hadn't spoken a word to the chaplain that night. And the chaplain didn't say anything to him. He just finished his praying and then turned and left.

A week after being admitted to the infirmary, even though he was still a bit sore, Mark's injuries were healed enough that he could go back to normal prison life. Get up, eat breakfast, wander around the courtyard, eat lunch, read a book, watch some television, eat supper and watch some more television, and then get locked into his cell for the night, get up the next day, and do it all over again. He knew that some of the guys went to a church meeting on Tuesday nights. Normally he avoided the Tuesday meeting completely. This Tuesday was different. He wanted to attend just to check out the chaplain. He couldn't get the guy out of his head. Mark had received a gift, a picture of hope. The guard escorted him to the chapel. He slipped into the last row of chairs and waited.

Chaplain Bill was a normal guy who worked a job, had a family, mowed his lawn every Saturday afternoon, and went to church on Sundays and Wednesdays. He also happened to care a great deal for some guys who didn't have a normal life. As a matter of fact, you could say Chaplain Bill loved these guys. He considered the men at Oklahoma State Reformatory his mission field. They were the ones that God had appointed for him to reach with the gospel of Jesus Christ. He prayed for them daily. He met with anyone who asked him to, no matter what their crime. Most of the time, he didn't even know what crimes had been committed. He didn't care. Jesus loved them, every one. If it didn't matter to Jesus, he couldn't let it matter to him. That was his motto: Love them and lead them as they are. God will do the rest. He called out a few hellos and asked a few of the guys how they were. The men were making their way into the room and sitting on the metal folding chairs when he stepped to the front of the room. When his eyes rested on Mark sitting in the last row of chairs, he took a quick breath and held it a second before letting it out. He continued calling on a few men by name but still questioned God about the man in the back row. *This is the one, Lord. I don't understand it, but I trust you, and I will do as you ask.*

He had made it his mission to learn as many names of the prisoners as possible, especially the ones who regularly came to Tuesday meetings. When a new person attended the group, he would add his name to his list and pray for him daily. No matter how long it took, he prayed for each one of his little flock daily. He'd watched many men grow in their faith while under his tutelage. Some went on to teach Sunday school in their home churches. He'd even seen a few go to Bible college and then go into the mission field or youth ministry, even becoming pastors in nondenominational churches.

A week ago, when he had prayed over the man in the back row, God had told him he had a very special purpose for this man. Of course, Chaplain Bill tended to forget that this was usually the case with each of the prisoners God had pointed out to him. He treated each prisoner as though he was someone special, somebody unique, and somebody that God would personally call upon. He did it because each man was in the process of becoming who God wanted him to be. He didn't see anyone else as being all that different from himself. He may have made different choices in life, but he was still on the same path—becoming who God wanted him to become.

Chaplain Bill opened in prayer. "Dear heavenly Father, thank you for each man here tonight. I pray, Lord, that you would touch each man's heart like only you can do. Stir in them a desire to know you better and better. Mostly, Father, I pray that each one may come to understand the unconditional love that you have for him. I also ask that what I am about to share from your Word would be received in the manner it is given. In love, Lord. In love. Amen.

"I'd like to read to you tonight from the book of John. If you have a Bible, open it up to John. If not, see me when we are finished here tonight, and I'll see that you get one. Jesus had been speaking to Nicodemus, a religious man, about being born again. Nicodemus was confused and did not understand the term 'born again,' so he had asked Jesus several questions, trying to understand. Finally, Jesus explained the phrase in a way that made it very easy to understand. That is what I want to read to you tonight."

Bill started reading from his Bible. "John 3:15–16: 'That whosoever believes in Him should not perish but have eternal life. For God so loved the world that He gave His only begotten Son, that whoever believes in Him should not perish but have everlasting life.'

"Do you believe in Jesus Christ? Do you believe that God sent his only Son to die on a cross for your sins? Do you believe that God could love the world so much that he would sacrifice his one and only Son? Let me tell you that he *does* love the world that much. I'll even narrow it down further. He loves me, and he loves you that much. Why? Sometimes I too wonder about that. I don't deserve to be loved. I know some of you feel that way too. Yet, he still loves us. There is nothing we can do to make him stop loving us. Isn't that good to know? God will always love you. It doesn't matter what sins you've committed. It doesn't matter how many times you've committed those sins. He still will open his arms wide and embrace us if we will allow him. Now, if you sit there with your arms crossed and a big old scowl on your face and tell him no, you won't accept his gift of love, even then, he still loves us. We just don't get all the goodies that go along with his gift. He's just waiting for you to love him back. I have a secret for you. You know all those people, the ones you think can do no wrong, God loves you just as much as he loves them."

Bill heard a few guffaws coming from the prisoners. Even those who had accepted Jesus as their Savior still had major issues with self-condemnation.

He continued on. "Yes, it's true. God doesn't discriminate. He loves us all the same. It breaks his heart when we don't love him back, though. I'm gonna read a little bit more.

"Verse seventeen, 'For God did not send His Son into the world to condemn the world, but that the world through Him might be saved.'

"Wow. I don't know about you, but I think that is awesome. Jesus did not come here to point fingers at me and remind me of all the sins I've committed. The Bible says he came here to save me. That's why he died on the cross. It's the best way he could show me he loved me. He doesn't bring up the past. Once you ask him to forgive you, it's all done. Those sins will never be brought up again. That's how much Jesus loves you guys. Once we accept Jesus's love and forgiveness, the hardest part sometimes is forgiving ourselves. He doesn't bring up our past, but more than likely we will. It doesn't always have to be that way. The first step is believing in the One who came to save you. Then we need to ask for forgiveness for the things we have done wrong. I promise you that once you do that and ask Jesus into your heart, Jesus will fill you up so much with love that you'll nearly burst with the joy of it. Is there anyone here tonight who would like Jesus to fill them up with his love?"

Bill didn't ask for bowed heads like some churches did. He figured if a decision was going to be made here, it was going to have to be lived here, out in the open for everyone to see. One of the guys he'd been talking with over the past few weeks raised his hand. Tears rolled down Bill's face as he asked Denny to come to the front and pray. As Bill prayed with him, Denny began to weep.

Mark wasn't sure why Denny was crying. He was literally bawling like a baby. He wanted to get a Bible from Chaplain Bill but wasn't so sure about hanging around for one. Things seemed kind of unpredictable, and he wasn't sure he wanted to be in the midst of whatever might happen next. What if he started bawling? Besides the tears that fell during the accident, he couldn't remember the last time he'd cried. He didn't even cry when his old man passed away. What was there to cry about? He wasn't the most caring father in the world. His kids were low on his list of priorities. He could never tell what his dad's first priority was. His work or booze. Anybody's guess was as good as his.

Mark saw a stack of Bibles on a side table and wandered close enough to the table to get one. As he picked it up, he made eye contact with Chaplain Bill, who nodded his consent with a small tilt of his head. Mark left with a plain black vinyl copy of the Holy Bible, the most precious book he would ever own.

It seemed as if it were just yesterday, yet here he was, on the outside looking back. Neither the years, nor the book in his pocket, could erase the painful memories of his past. Now it was time to face them.

5

Jessi breathed in deeply. The scent of blooming lilacs reminded her to get out her cutting shears and cut enough for every room in the house. Lilacs were one of her favorite early summer flowers now that she lived in Wisconsin. She didn't know if she would ever get used to the change of seasons that Wisconsin's climate provided. She had made the move north three and half years ago. She'd needed to make some changes in her life, so she decided a change of scenery was in order. The only thing she had to overcome was leaving Ethan's grave and leaving Aunt Merry. She finally decided to move, promising herself she would come back every year to visit his grave. She said her good-byes to Ethan on the third anniversary of his accident and moved north to a small community in southern Wisconsin where she taught second grade in the local elementary school. Each June when school got out for summer, she returned for her yearly visit. She called it her pilgrimage to her past. She had never fully recovered from his death, and if it hadn't been for little Olivia being born eight months after the accident, Jessi probably would have died right along with him. Getting pregnant right after Mark got out of rehab hadn't been the plan, but it saved Jessi's life. Olivia changed everything for Jessi. She gave her a reason to live. At five years old, almost six if you asked Olivia, she was the light of her mother's life.

Olivia knew that she'd had a big brother and that he had died and gone to heaven. Jessi had explained it to her when Olivia was old enough to question her mother about their annual trips. After that, the only time they talked about Ethan was when they were traveling to Oklahoma for their visit, which they were about to embark on. On their journey Jessi would tell Olivia all about the escapades that were a trademark for Ethan—riding his bike with no hands and jumping off the high dive when he was only three years old. He'd almost given her a heart attack.

Talking to Olivia was one way to keep all the memories alive. As the memories found their way to the forefront of her mind, so too did the pain and guilt. She had never forgiven herself for allowing such pain to come to her son. She doubted she ever would.

A week after school let out, Jessi and Olivia headed south on I-90. The trip would take them two full days of driving. To break things up a bit, they stopped at a hotel in Missouri. Jessi watched as her daughter immediately took off her shoes and climbed up on the hotel bed. "Olivia Jean, you be careful jumping on that bed."

Even jumping on the bed, something kids did every day, scared Jessi. *What if she fell off the bed? What if she hit her head,* were all thoughts that passed through her head. Every time she would come close to the edge, Jessi would cringe. Knowing that Olivia had to stretch out those growing legs, she managed to conceal her fear for a little while.

Jessi pulled her swimsuit out of her overnight bag. "I'm going to the pool." She knew that would put an end to the bed bouncing.

Olivia bounced down on her seat and leaped off the bed. "Me too, Mommy. Wait for me."

Jessi watched her daughter dig through her backpack and pull out her hot pink swimsuit with Dora the Explorer on it. She quickly put it on and waited by the door as Jessi changed. They smiled at each other and walked hand in hand to the swimming pool. After a full evening of swimming, they feasted on cheese pizza and watched television curled up in their pj's. It wasn't too long before Olivia fell sound asleep on the pillow next to Jessi. Jessi flipped through the TV channels once more before turning it off for the night. She watched her daughter's breathing, slowed by sleep. She couldn't help but push a dark tendril of hair back off her cheek. She was a beautiful child. She tried not to think of Mark when she looked at Olivia, but it was hard. She looked just like her father. While Ethan had looked more like Jessi, there was no mistaking whom this child came from with her dark blue eyes and that dark hair. What a striking combination. She was sure to break more than her fair share of hearts when she was older. Jessi smiled as she pictured her daughter's future, boys calling and hanging around the house. She could just see it now. Naturally, her mind drifted from one child to the other. Ethan was still very much alive in her heart and mind. If he truly were alive he would be eleven years old; her baby, almost a teenager. She still missed him so much. What would he look like? Would he wear his blond hair long or short? Would she constantly be on him to pull up his pants like she wanted to tell the kids she saw around town? She stifled a sob as she faced the fact that she would never know those things. On this trip she let the tears flow freely. She cried herself to sleep remembering the boy that was so engrained in her memory. The boy she still loved with all her heart.

6

Mark walked away from the prison with the clothes he had on, a small backpack, and the limp that would be a constant reminder of his failure for the rest of his life. His first goal was to find a job. He had a few leads from Chaplain Bill and had interviews set up for every day this week. The prison lined up a small furnished apartment for him. He would get his act together and then he would find Jessi. He knew she would never forgive him, but at least he could apologize and accept responsibility for what he had done. He realized now, after many hours of counseling, that he had pushed all the blame and all his guilt onto his wife. It wasn't right that she was still walking around with the weight of his actions on her shoulders. He had to make it right.

He shielded his eyes from the sun as he heard Chaplain Bill's car before he could see it. Everyone within a mile or two could hear Chaplain Bill's car. He threw his pack into the backseat and jumped into the front seat. "You were right about the car. I didn't need to know the make, model, or color. The sound completely gave it away."

Chaplain Bill threw his head back and laughed. "I told you so. I couldn't sneak up on a deaf person. They would be able to feel the vibration!"

After some polite chitchat, they rode in silence. Mark had given Bill, as he now insisted on being called, the address before he was released from prison, so Bill knew right where he was going. Bill realized that being released from prison was not the comforting experience that most prisoners expected. Most were unsure of themselves and the ever-changing world that they were now thrust into. He tried to ease into conversation with Mark on familiar comforting terms.

"Do you remember what happened after you took the Bible from the table?" Bill asked Mark.

Although Mark remained silent for a while, he did. He remembered reading for so long by the lights outside his cell that he was dropping over tired the next day. Every chance he had, he read. It took a couple of months to work up the courage to go back to chapel. When he did, it was his turn to weep. This time he hadn't been self-conscious of the act. He had felt utter relief. The peace that had accompanied his act of obedience to his Maker was indescribable. It had been too long since he had felt unconditionally loved by anyone. So much love filled his soul that he felt as if he would burst with the fullness of it. Never in his life had he felt such joy.

"Yeah, I remember. I can hardly believe it's been over five years. I don't think I ever cried so much as the night I finally surrendered my life to the Lord. The monotony of being in prison and following the same routine every day seemed to go on forever. The day Jesus entered my life will forever remain the most important day of my life and the closest to my heart. The desire to learn and grow in God hasn't diminished for me. I pray that it never will. I think our prayer times and personal studies helped me mature in a world where hope is a much sought-after emotion. Not too many men have hope when they are in prison. Even the idea of being released doesn't give them a reason to hope. Most have nothing on the other side to return to. A life of crime, maybe. A life of petty theft, robbery, abusive relationships, and all the other possible immoral acts sure don't give one the feeling of anticipation. I'm not sure what I have to return to, either. I have to see Jessi, just once, to convince her that I have changed. I know she'll never give me another chance, but I want her to see the difference that God has made in my life. I need to take full responsibility for the state my marriage was in and the death of our child. I just have to trust that God knows what he is doing. For all I know, I'll end up with a broken and bloody nose for knocking on her door. I'd deserve it too." Mark realized he'd been carrying on a one-way conversation for some time. "I'm rambling again, aren't I? Sorry, I seem to be thinking out loud lately, and it's usually about the same thing."

Bill made a right turn and scanned the row of apartments for the right address. As he pulled over and parked at the curb, he looked at Mark and felt true compassion for a man who had no idea what life was about to bring him. He was in a state of complete unknowing. For a man, any man, this was a very difficult place to be. "Mark, every day is a gift. Learn to treasure what it is God is showing you. Learn to make your days his days. When we follow his perfect will for our lives, we are walking in the direction he wants us to go. Each day, keep your Bible with you. It's your source of strength. The very words that Jesus spoke have tremendous power in our lives when we let them. When you feel weak, open the Word. When you feel helpless, hopeless, friendless, open the Word, and God will fill every place of emptiness inside of you. Lean on him for everything. If you put your trust in him, his plan for your life will come forth."

Both men opened their car doors and headed to the apartment. Mark opened the front door. It was small—a furnished galley kitchen and a small living area with a couch, chair, a table and two chairs, and a television. Off the living area was a small bedroom with a twin bed and dresser and a bathroom. He didn't have much room, but it was just him, and he really didn't need more than he had. It was a start. He now believed in fresh starts.

Bill left with the promise that he would be back to pick him up for church on Sunday morning. Mark walked to his bed, laid down, and stared at the ceiling. "What do you have for me, God? I don't know this world anymore. I'm not sure that I want to know it again. This is the place where I messed up. I'm scared. What if I mess up again? Help me, Lord."

Mark fell asleep talking with his Father and his Friend.

7

It was early June. Aunt Merry had looked forward to this month for the past three years. Jessi would be coming soon with little Olivia, although little Olivia wasn't so little anymore. She would be six come September and was growing like a weed. This was the visit that Olivia would give her heart to Jesus. She just knew it. The child was almost ready her last visit. But Merry didn't want to push her. She needed to be ready to make the most important decision of her life. If ever she'd seen a child with a Christ-like disposition, it was this one. She was gentle, compassionate, meek, and kind. Her spirit was always mindful of others and their needs, even at five years of age. It amazed Merry how God had had his hand upon this child from the day she was conceived. Often, beauty comes from tragedy, as was the case with Olivia. She brought an appreciation for life to every situation she was in, and many times it was very contagious. Oh, she had to quit dawdling. The women would be coming in less than an hour, and she still had to finish the dessert and pick up the living room. She'd busied herself in the kitchen first. Thank heavens she'd made a couple of extra strawberry rhubarb pies for the freezer. She'd planned on spoiling Jessi and Olivia with them, but no one would be the wiser. Once the pies were in the oven, she hurried to the living room and made sure all was ready. She wasn't one to be vain, but she did take a little bit of pride in her appearance. After all, cleanliness is next to godliness. So she made her way to the bathroom and combed through her hair and applied a little bit of cologne to her wrists. Merry pulled out the pies just as the doorbell rang, indicating the first of the ladies to arrive. She was in an especially festive mood today and could not manage to keep a lid on her excitement, so when she opened the door with an exuberance that went far beyond her normal countenance, her secret was out.

Betsy was the first to arrive and took notice immediately. "When are they expected, dear?" she questioned Merry without a proper greeting, not that Merry noticed.

"Oh, sometime tomorrow afternoon. I'm so excited I can barely sit still. I'm so jittery from a lack of sleep, and all this caffeine I keep drinking doesn't help much. Once a year just isn't enough, Betsy. I just miss them so much."

"I know what you mean. When my David moved to California and took my only grandchildren with him, I barely forgave him. Now I know not to wait for him to come to me; I go out there regularly. Have you considered a visit to Wisconsin? I hear spring, with everything turning green, and the fall's turning of colors are so very beautiful. I'm surprised you haven't been to visit yet. You could be there in a jiffy if you flew."

"You know, I really should consider it. I was kind of waiting for an invitation from Jessi, but I don't think one is in the making. I doubt if she's thought of it, to be honest. Between her duties as a teacher, being a single parent, and her mind still dwelling on the past, I'm surprised she remembers to breathe. Until the day she accepts Christ, I doubt that girl will ever get a moment's rest. She puts on a pretty good act; I'll give her that. But I can see through that act in a heartbeat. She can't fool me. It's been five years since the boy's death, and she is nowhere near done grieving. It's just not right." The doorbell kept Merry from continuing.

Caroline was at the door, with Mabel and Judy just behind her. Merry, somewhat settled from her conversation with Betsy, let them in. She greeted each one with a peck on the cheek. "Good afternoon, tea and pie are ready in the kitchen. Betsy, would you pour the tea, dear? I see Georgina just pulling up. I'll wait here for her."

Merry and an out-of-breath Georgina entered the kitchen. Everyone looked at Georgina with apt attention, knowing full well that she had news. She only came to meeting in this fashion when she had something good to report on one of their prayer subjects. Didn't matter much who it was; if the group was praying for the person and they found their Savior, Georgina was bound to find out. Everyone stopped chewing their pie, stopped drinking their tea, and stopped their individual conversations almost immediately. Georgina had the floor.

"You might want to sit down for this one, Merry." She waited until Merry found her stool before continuing on. "Mark, you know, Jessi's Mark, has been released from prison. He found Jesus in prison. It's real. He came to church this past Sunday with Bill, the chaplain from the prison, and I saw him myself. Talked with him too. He's a changed man. There's nothing about him that's the same except his looks. God is answering our prayers regarding your family, Merry. It's just taking a while for us to see it is all. Little Olivia will find Jesus while she's here, you watch. And I believe Jessi is going to find him in a most powerful way. That girl has a world of hurts that need to be healed. The only one that I know that can heal those kinds of hurts is Jesus. She's gonna find him. I just know it."

Merry wiped her eyes with a tissue. She knew she should be joyful over Mark's finding Christ, but she couldn't help but feel let down. It was Jessi that her heart yearned for, cried out for, and whom she paced the floor in prayer over. *Lord, why couldn't it have been Jessi?* She stood and went into the living room. Everyone abandoned their pie and tea and followed. What followed was a powerful prayer meeting on behalf of the "daughter" who occupied a large part of Merry's heart.

8

Jessi crossed the Missouri border into Oklahoma just before lunch the next day. She and Olivia took their time heading out on the road. They started their day with breakfast at the hotel, and then they went for another swim before getting ready to continue on their trip. If Jessi knew her daughter as well as she thought she did, Olivia would be sleeping right after lunch, especially with all the swim time this morning.

Upon seeing the first Sonic, Jessi exited the highway and stopped for a late lunch. This too was their special treat. There were very few Sonics in Wisconsin. Therefore, there were no cherry limeades. This could be a mortal sin on the part of Wisconsin, according to Olivia. Sure enough, after eating the last bite of her cheeseburger, Olivia couldn't help but yawn. This triggered a yawn in Jessi. "Hey, quit that, young lady. I can't go to sleep like *some* people I know. I have to drive the rest of the way to Aunt Merry's house."

Olivia giggled at the prospect of her mommy curled up in the backseat of the car, sleeping. "Oh, Mommy, you're being silly. Only little girls can sleep in backseats. Mommies have to sleep in beds. Their legs won't fit in backseats. You'd be all scrunched up!"

Jessi had to agree with the child's logic. She wouldn't be able to walk straight if she fell asleep in the positions she saw Olivia sleep in. Aunt Merry's guest bed would be a welcome sight tonight, after a long two days of travel. It was also the one time of the year when Olivia wasn't entirely her responsibility. Aunt Merry gladly took Olivia with her shopping, playing at the park, and to church. Anywhere Aunt Merry went, you were sure to see little Olivia as well. This gave Jessi a much-needed break in the day-to-day care of her child. Even though Olivia was a very well-behaved child, she was still able to get into mischief on occasion. The brief reprieve was a welcome benefit of making the journey each year.

Jessi did some basic stretches before getting behind the wheel for the last leg of the trip. Olivia buckled up in her seat, which was slightly reclined, and almost instantly fell asleep. It would be quiet the rest of the trip. They had made it to Tulsa before stopping for lunch, so they only had a couple of hours to go. Olivia would sleep until they pulled in Aunt Merry's driveway. It was a good thing too. She would be wired for the rest of the night. There was always a special present for Olivia to open. Last year it was a magical music box with Cinderella in a coach with the white horses. Olivia loved to shake it and watch the snow. Jessi had wound it up for her and showed her how the sound changed when she placed it on a solid surface. Olivia smiled when she heard the difference. It was a much fuller, richer sound. The child listened to it over and over. It was what she went to sleep to. Jessi couldn't wait to see her face this year. She had it on good authority that this year's gift was an extra special gift. Of course, they were each year.

At three thirty Jessi pulled into Aunt Merry's driveway. Olivia sat up and stretched. "Are we there yet?"

Obviously, she hadn't quite opened her eyes yet.

"Yep, we're there!"

With those words Olivia's eyes flew open. Almost in unison Aunt Merry came bounding out of the house, running toward the car. The very sight of her warmed Jessi's heart. She was home.

Olivia was the first to reach Aunt Merry. Aunt Merry bent down and gave Olivia the biggest bear hug ever. "Oh, Aunt Merry, I've missed you so much."

Aunt Merry wasn't sure if she would ever let go of the child. Finally, she rose up and turned to Jessi. "My dear Jessi, oh how I've missed you, child."

She let two tears escape her closed eyes as she breathed in the scent of the woman she'd practically raised as her own. Jessi returned Merry's hug with clinging desperation. This precious woman was her grounding, her sense of well being, and the sole source from which she felt loved. Each year it was the same. Her soul cried out in protest against the separation that was destined to come. Reluctantly, each woman loosened her grip, and they walked arm in arm to the house. It was at this time that Aunt Merry noticed how small Jessi had become. "Oh, honey, don't they eat in Wisconsin? You're nothing but skin and bones."

Jessi smiled in response. She knew this was coming. When she had unpacked her summer things and nothing fit anymore, she figured she'd hear it and hear it good from Aunt Merry. Upon walking in the house, she knew the situation would be rectified in no time. Something smelling awfully good was cooking in the kitchen. "Aunt Merry, if I came fitting into my clothes I would have to buy bigger ones when I leave. This way, they start out a little big, and I fit right back into them when I go back home. It's cheaper this way."

She gave herself a quick pat on the back and had to admit it was quick thinking, but it worked and that's all that counted. She laid it on even a little thicker when she walked into the kitchen and looked into the oven. "Aunt Merry, is this what I think it is? Olivia, I think we had better unload the car and get cleaned up for supper. It looks as though we are having Aunt Merry's famous pot roast with mashed potatoes and gravy for supper. Mmm… homemade biscuits too? Now this is heaven!" Jessi walked over and gave her aunt another hug. "Thank you. You always make me feel like I'm at home when I'm with you."

Jessi followed Olivia out the door to the car, and they started carrying suitcases into the spare bedrooms. Aunt Merry had a big two-story house that she had lived in since forever, at least it seemed that way to Jessi. There were four big bedrooms on the top floor, with a shared bathroom, and then another bedroom on the first floor, although Aunt Merry refused to move her things to the first-floor bedroom. She insisted the stairs did her no harm each day, and until she couldn't possibly climb them, she wasn't moving. Besides, she liked to eat as much as she liked to cook, and the exercise did her good.

Both Jessi and Olivia were set up for their visit on the second floor. Olivia's room would be in Jessi's old room, which was still done in her childhood choice of pink satin and ruffles, canopy still intact. And Jessi was in the guest room, which Aunt Merry had recently redecorated in a Victorian theme to please Jessi.

Jessi walked to the window and looked out at Aunt Merry's garden. There were flowers everywhere and a small pond with a waterfall. Even her little playhouse from childhood had been redone in pretty pinks and greens for Olivia to enjoy. There were new window boxes on the windows with real flowers in them. She remembered having tea parties with her dolls and stuffed animals in that playhouse. Aunt Merry always made little cookies for her to serve to her "guests," as she liked to call them. Saturday afternoons were perfect for her tea parties, as Aunt Merry could move dinner back a little to give Jessi time to grow hungry again.

Olivia would never want to leave. This part of her childhood reminded her of a time when she was still good and God still loved her. She hadn't been so wretched back then, so unlovable. This world would be Olivia's now, a small part of her childhood that she could share with her daughter. It was looking to be a wonderful, magical summer.

As she began putting her things away, she noticed small leather-bound books tied with ribbons in each dresser drawer. She picked up the first one just as Aunt Merry called her down to supper. She assumed the books were her aunt's journals but was quite positive they were left by mistake. Her aunt must have forgotten to remove them when she cleaned the dresser out for her to use. She would ask Aunt Merry about them at the supper table.

There was barely enough room on the table for all the food. Roast beef with carrots were on the large center platter. A big bowl of mashed potatoes with real butter melting on top and a dish of homemade gravy sat on one of the corners. There were hot biscuits piled high in a basket and bowls of homemade applesauce, freshly pickled beets, and cottage cheese. And anytime mashed potatoes and gravy were on the table you had to have her creamed corn that she put up in the freezer each year. Olivia couldn't believe her eyes. Jessi had to good-naturedly reprimand her daughter. "Olivia, please close your mouth and sit down at the table."

Olivia sat down in her designated spot at the table. "Is it Thanksgiving?" she asked, eyes still wide with wonder.

Jessi stifled a laugh while Aunt Merry answered her question. "I suppose it's a little like Thanksgiving. I'm very thankful that you and your mom are here with me, and I wanted to make a special supper to celebrate your being here. Do you think you can find something to be thankful for?" she asked, turning the question back to the child and into a prayer as well.

Olivia pondered the question for a moment. "Yes, I can. I'm thankful for you and Mommy, the two people I love most in the world, being here with me. I'm also thankful for all this yummy food you made for us," she replied as she eyed the food, sending the two adults at the table a very obvious message. She wanted to eat.

"Okay, then, all we have to do is thank Jesus for the food he has provided for us, and then we can eat." With that, Aunt Merry prayed over their meal. "Dear Lord, I thank you for providing this food for us. We are truly grateful to you. I also thank you for bringing Jessi and Olivia home safe and sound. In Jesus's name. Amen."

Olivia waited for the signal from her mom that she could dig in and started filling up her plate. It wasn't too long before she was stuffed and asked to be excused. She had opened her gift from Aunt Merry earlier, and it was exactly what she had asked for, for Christmas, an American Girl doll and some of the accessories that went with it, including a book.

After Aunt Merry told her about the special dessert she had made, she sauntered to the living room to play with her new doll.

Jessi sat back in her chair. "That was an awesome meal, Aunt Merry. Thank you. Olivia and I will clean everything up. You must be exhausted from all the cooking and redecorating you've been doing. Speaking of redecoration, I think you missed a few things when you were cleaning out the dresser for me to use. I found a few of your journals in the top drawer."

Hmmm... so she did find the journals. With Jessi, Aunt Merry was never sure what she would bring up and what she would file away on a shelf and never even let her know she had found. Curiosity must have gotten the best of the girl, just as she had hoped it would. Good. "Oh, no, dear. I thought you might enjoy reading through them sometime. Just like Olivia loves your old room and playhouse, I thought you might enjoy reading about some of my experiences while I was growing up. Kind of a family history lesson of sorts. And as for cleaning up, don't be silly. I look forward to your visit so much that I hardly even notice the work. I love having you both. You add so much life to this house."

Jessi looked at her with suspicion. "All right, I'll tell you what. What if you and I do the clean up together, and we'll let Olivia play with her new doll, which, by the way, she dearly loves. Thank you again."

Both Jessi and Merry rose from the table and began clearing the dishes. Aunt Merry filled her in on her mother and what little she knew of her father. Neither parent was particularly close to Jessi and only made contact with her on her birthday and at Christmas, by way of a Christmas card. She was surprised they even continued that superficial contact. For some time after the accident, her mother had called and had come around more than usual, but it wasn't long before things got back to normal. They cleaned up the rest of the dishes, making small talk as they went.

They sat in the living room for a while and watched Olivia play with her doll. Olivia started yawning and rubbing her eyes. Still being full from supper, they all decided to forego dessert and head to bed. Jessi tucked Olivia into bed and turned the nightlight on. She was surprised Olivia didn't protest and want to sleep with her. Instead, she fell asleep with a small grin on her beautiful face, the picture of perfect peace, while clutching her new doll, Samantha. Carefully, Jessi tucked her in and gave her forehead a kiss. She whispered, "I love you, little one. I don't know that you'll ever quite know how much." She quietly left the room and returned to her own.

After getting ready for bed, she sat in the sitting area and sorted through her aunt's journals. There were three journals. The first one appeared to start when Aunt Merry was sixteen. The first few entries were typical entries for a teenage girl. Which boys in her class were the cutest, who liked who, and what she and her friends did together. The last one she read surprised her, though.

> Sunday September 22, 1963
>
> I can't believe I'm writing this down for the world to see. I will keep this in a safe place and hope that no one dares to invade my privacy and read it. Last night Ella, Dorothy, and I decided to sneak out of the house and go down to the Jarvis Family farm. Lester was having a party, and he invited us, but our parents wouldn't allow us to attend. We decided there would be no harm in going for a little while, especially if we weren't gone long and were back in our beds before we were found out. What fun we had! We danced and drank punch, which was spiked—I could tell by the taste. I even danced a slow dance with Lester Jarvis. He is already eighteen years old. Why, he's a full grown man and so good looking. We stayed too long and had to hurry to get back in our beds. Of course, the alcohol in the punch had nothing to do with it! Ha! We were lucky we didn't get caught. Oh, how much fun we had, though. I'd do it again in a heartbeat if it meant I would get to dance with Lester again. That's all for now. Good night diary, Meredith.

Jessi could hardly believe what she had just read. Perfect Aunt Merry, sneaking out at night? Why, she did have a few sly bones in her body. That little sneak. If she ever caught Olivia doing something like that... and then she started laughing.

Aunt Merry saw the light on and heard the chuckling. She went to bed content that the line had been cast; the bait had been taken. Jessi was hooked. She trusted that God knew what he was doing when he gave her this idea. Jessi had too many illusions when it came to her Aunt Meredith. It was time she knew the truth.

9

Jessi's entire day revolved around her visit to the cemetery. She left at sunup and returned after sunset. This day was her special day. Olivia didn't accompany her. Aunt Merry didn't. It was hers, and hers alone. She drove to the cemetery in quiet speculation. She thought of all the times she had shared with her son. She remembered the day he was born. The long hours of painful labor were a distant memory with one look into his sweet face. She would do it all over again in a heartbeat. Even walking the floors with him at night and getting next to no sleep could not diminish the love she had for this child, the joy he brought into her life. He wasn't a perfect child, just perfect for her. How sweet and gentle he was. One lopsided grin could brighten her entire day. She relived his birthdays and Christmases. The times she had to kiss his owies when he was little and wipe away tears that were born of frustration from being a late talker. Everything that made Ethan, Ethan, she missed. All his good traits—the kindness and compassion, his willingness to share, his humor and humble spirit—would be remembered until the day she died. Even his stubbornness and his uncanny knack for saying the right thing at the wrong time would be never forgotten.

She couldn't understand why others questioned her on not getting over the death of her son. He wasn't supposed to die. What was so hard to understand about that? She missed him. She lived for him and breathed for him. Was it really a shock that she would continue to miss him after his death? "The grieving period should be over, dear." "You need to see a counselor, dear." She'd heard it all from good-intentioned people whose opinions were not asked for. She'd learned to stay away from them. That was part of the reason she'd moved to Wisconsin. Eight hundred miles separated her from the nearest do-gooder. She did get lonely at times, but she'd learned to live her life through Olivia, just as she had done with Ethan. She also learned that her memory of Ethan was with her no matter where she went. She didn't have to visit his grave every week like she had for the first year after his death. She had found many ways to keep him alive. She had all of her pictures and the mothering journals she had kept from his birth, all constant reminders of the boy who had been stolen from her.

Jessi pulled into the cemetery fully prepared for a day of work. She had stopped by the nursery and picked up plants that would decorate his tombstone for the summer. She did this each year, even knowing he would pooh pooh the idea of having flowers by his resting place. It made his space warmer and somehow a little more homey. She couldn't stand the thought of her son lying in the cold ground without any hints of home.

This year she chose wildflowers to plant. She pulled the car up near the row and opened the trunk. While carrying her supplies to his grave, she noticed someone else had recently visited. She couldn't for the life of her think who it might have been. Next to his tombstone was a potted plant and a baseball and a glove. She furrowed her brow and figured Aunt Merry would have mentioned this if she had done it. Maybe someone from church. Well, whoever it was, it was awfully nice of them to remember Ethan. Not too many people did anymore. She set the things to the side while she did her planting. She loved working in the soil. She loved watching what she planted grow. Lovingly, she started digging around the small tombstone. She placed one plant after another in the rows she had prepared. When she finished, she pulled the dirt in around the plants and tied blue ribbons around the sturdiest of the stems. Ethan loved blue. It was his favorite color. She scooted back and looked at her work. She began to weep. Regardless of the flowers, the ribbons, and all the care that she'd taken, it was still just a grave. It was cold and dark. She couldn't stand to think of her little boy in a box in the ground. The ground wasn't meant for a vibrant, wonderful little boy like Ethan. "Oh, Ethan, I miss you so much. I'm so sorry. Mommy's sorry, baby. Mommy's so sorry."

Every day she second-guessed her decision to end his life support. Every day she wondered, *What if I'd waited one more day? Would he have woken up?* The day of the accident was also a constant reminder of her failure. She forgot to make that phone call. If she had, would Mark have decided to stay home? If she'd only checked the answering machine, she would have been home, and Ethan would never have been in the car with Mark. Mark was right; Ethan's death was her fault. She had failed Ethan as a mother. All of this ran through her mind as she sat next to Ethan's grave and sobbed. She tried to make it through her visits to Ethan's grave without falling apart. So far she had not been successful. Time was supposed to be the healer of all wounds, but she wouldn't allow this wound to heal. It was her rightful punishment for what she did to Ethan. For the pain she sentenced him to, she would live in pain for the rest of her life.

Jessi sat in the grass for hours that day, reminiscing and wishing. A few times she tried to talk with Ethan. She just didn't know what to say except that she was sorry and she loved and missed him. She never gave praying a second thought. She no longer even considered trying to pray. Her whole attitude toward God had drastically changed when he refused to answer her prayers on behalf of Ethan. She used to feel unworthy of his love; now she wouldn't give him a passing thought. He didn't deserve it; he took her baby from her. She would never ask anything of him again. He may call himself God, but he certainly wasn't her God. He never would be. It would be a long time before she realized that by denying God she would never be reunited with Ethan.

She stood up and replaced the potted plant, baseball, and glove. They seemed right there somehow. Ethan had always asked Mark to play ball with him in the backyard, but Mark never had time. She had done her best to take his place, but it just wasn't the same. A boy needed his dad to play ball with him. It was just supposed to be that way.

She turned and walked to her car. If she had cared to glance about her surroundings, she would have seen Mark watching her from a distance.

Although he felt an extreme urgency to speak with her, he respected her privacy and her need to mourn her son. He could wait until another day to seek her out and ask her forgiveness. He had already taken his turn at the foot of his son's grave and given his son the glove and ball. It proved an unsuccessful attempt at assuaging his guilt at being an absent and non-attentive father. He had been in prison for over a year when he was notified of his son's death. He wept for days. He wasn't even permitted to attend his own son's funeral. Someday, in heaven, he would be able to apologize to Ethan face-to-face. What a glorious day that would be. As Jessi drove away, Mark looked into the heavens. "Thank you, Jesus. Without you I wouldn't have any hope of seeing my son again."

He turned and walked down a dusty trail that led through the cemetery. Occasionally, he would stop to read a tombstone. Mostly he just prayed as he walked.

10

Mark had been sitting on the park bench for over an hour contemplating what he had to do. He had been approaching Jessi's aunt's house when he saw Jessi and some little kid getting out of a car. It seemed like quite the reunion between Jessi and her aunt. He didn't know where she was visiting from or why she had moved away, but he saw her unload the suitcases from her car with the help of a little girl and move them into her aunt's house. He had been on his way to stop and talk with Jessi's aunt the day he had seen her unpacking the suitcases from her car and decided it was Jessi, not her aunt, that he really needed to talk to. The only problem was he hadn't been ready at the time. Now, after seeing her at the cemetery, he knew he could not put it off any longer. He had to see her and talk with her. He hadn't meant to eavesdrop that day, but he couldn't help it. He heard the guilt that was so evident in her voice. He had to relieve her of the burden that she had been carrying for so long. He'd rehearsed the conversation in his apartment until he felt he had perfected it. Prayer was the better solution, but it felt good to at least have a plan.

She was just as beautiful as the day he had married her. After all this time, he still loved her. He had known it the moment he had laid eyes on her unloading that car. He took in everything about her that day. She was wearing a pair of tan shorts, a white pullover t-shirt, and a pair of tennis shoes. He used to laugh at her because she always wore tennis shoes. She couldn't stand getting her feet dirty. Her hair was in a ponytail, the way she used to wear it when she was working outside in her garden. Was he ready to face her?

The temptation to fall back into his old ways had never been so great as it was at that moment. To have to face the woman that he loved and yet had hurt so badly would be the hardest thing he'd had to do since getting out of prison. But he knew it had to be done. God would not reveal more of his plan for Mark's life until he was obedient in this one thing.

A drink sure would help make it easier. No! He had to stop these voices in his head, tempting him. Mark quickly pulled out his pocket Bible and began reading. Slowly he felt the temptation slip away, and he felt a surge of God's power curse through him. *This is what Bill meant. When I feel weak, the Word of God will make me strong. Lord, help me be strong in you. No matter what comes of this visit, I know you will never leave me, nor forsake me.* While still in an attitude of prayer, Mark followed the leading of the Father and walked from the park to Jessi's aunt's house. He stood for only a moment before knocking on the front door.

Meredith stood at the door looking at her ex-nephew-in-law. Should she invite him in? She didn't really know what to do. Had she stopped to say a quick prayer, she would have gotten her answer, but she was too dumbfounded by his visit to even do that. She just hadn't expected this. So she said the first thing she thought of: "What do you want?" She sounded rude and extremely out of character, but it was what she felt at that moment.

Mark had expected this, so he didn't let it deter him. "I'd like to speak with Jessi, if I may?"

Merry eyed him cautiously but seemed to remember her manners. "She's not home right now. I'll let her know you stopped by. Although I'm sure that she doesn't want to see you, Mark. For the past five years she'd been trying to forget you. I don't think she's ready to face you."

"I don't have a choice, Meredith. This is something I have to do, whether she is ready or not. I'm thinking that if it were up to her, she would never be ready. It's just something that has to be done. The sooner, the better. I've changed, Meredith. I have to take the blame that I placed on her shoulders all those years ago and put it where it belongs. It's too much for her to carry, and it's not fair that she should continue. I have to let her know that everything that happened was my fault. I take full responsibility for everything. I blamed her for not being a good wife. I put all the blame on her. I have to rectify the situation. She was a wonderful mother, and I was jealous of the love she poured out on our son. I used that as an excuse for what I did. I have to get that across to her. I know I may end up with a broken and bloody nose. It's the chance I have to take. Can you understand what I am saying?"

For the first time in six years Meredith's eyes were opened up regarding this man. While she loathed him for what he had done, she realized that he was no more of a sinner than she was and he was just as forgivable as she was. God was not a respecter of persons. He forgave all those who asked forgiveness of him. Even Mark. She stepped back from the door and nodded her invitation to him to come into her home. She was pretty sure Jessi would not understand this when she found out, as she surely would. But she knew this was of God. And for once, she must be obedient to God where Mark was concerned.

She offered him a glass of iced tea, which he accepted and was grateful. She began to speak with a quiver in her voice. "Mark, I need to ask you to forgive me. I have allowed the pain I have felt over losing Ethan and the great love I have for Jessi to get in the way of doing what God has wanted me to do all along. I have prayed for you to find Christ, don't get me wrong, but I did it with a wrong attitude. I did it because it was the right thing to do, not because I truly wanted you to come to Jesus. I had heard from a friend that you came to know Jesus while you were in prison, and I was almost sad. I wanted it to be Jessi so bad that I couldn't find it within myself to be happy for you. That was so wrong of me. Can you ever forgive me, Mark?"

He looked at her with tears in his eyes, unable to do anything more than nod his head. She continued on. "The Bible says that when the least of these gives his heart to the Lord, the angels rejoice. When your name was added to the Lamb's book of Life, the angels literally had a whooping party. And here I am resentful, begrudging you the very salvation that God granted me so long ago on a day when I thought all hope was lost. I pray that I will never again forget the mercy and grace that I received at the hand of the Father. Oh, Mark, I am so sorry. I will stand by you in prayer and support. Jessi doesn't know Jesus yet. I'm praying that changes very soon. Until she does, she is not going to be very open to you being in her life. I pray that you will be patient with her. She doesn't know the heart of the Father like we do. She hasn't realized that she needs his forgiveness. She blames him for Ethan's death almost as much as she blames herself, and yet she still finds herself unworthy of his love, and therefore she rejects him to keep from being hurt again. She looks at the possibility of a relationship with him like she would an earthly relationship. Those have all added up to pain for her. Every man who has ever been in her life has rejected her. I know that causes you pain, and I'm sorry for that. But I'm also sure you have come to terms with it. That's also how she looks at a relationship with God. As if the Father would ever turn his back on her. She doesn't realize how precious she is to him. I'm trusting that someday she will. I have God's promise on that."

Mark too had felt peace regarding Jessi's faith. "I too know that someday she will reach out and ask for the forgiveness that God offers. I just wish it would be sooner rather than later. I know God is going to use me somehow in all of this. He made that painfully clear to me when he let me know in no uncertain terms that I had to come here to speak with her. I just don't know what I'm supposed to do or say. Does he always work this way? Give little glimpses into his plans but never let you in on the whole thing?" Mark went on, not giving Merry a chance to answer. "I know one thing for sure: he sure is growing my patience. Each time I'm not sure I can take anymore, I remember the words that my chaplain spoke to me the day I got out of prison: 'Take one day at a time, Mark. One day at a time.'" With that, he stood to go. "I would appreciate any and all the help you can give me, Merry. I treasure your prayers, and I value the wisdom of your words. I also understand your feelings about me in the beginning. I know you were honest about your reaction to me, and I appreciate that. I wouldn't have expected anything less. I also forgive you. Not because I believe you have anything to be forgiven for—I deserved everything I got—but because you asked for it. I respect you enough to give you what you ask. I too ask for your forgiveness. I have much more to be forgiven for."

Merry smiled and embraced Mark. "I forgive you, Mark. That much I can do. Forgive as the Father has forgiven me."

He turned as he walked down the front steps. "I'll be back every day until she speaks with me. I will be persistent about this. Tell her that for me, would you?"

She gave a slight nod as her assent, and he turned and walked away from what was to be the first of many visits to her home.

11

After Mark left, Merry spent the rest of the afternoon on the phone with her prayer group. She asked for each member to be in prayer today, as she would have to speak with Jessi as soon as she got home from her visit with her mother. She had taken Olivia to see her grandmother for the day and would be back this evening before Olivia's bedtime. After Jessi put Olivia to bed, she would have to tell her about Mark's visit, and she was afraid it would send her back to Wisconsin as fast as she could get there. Mark did not know about Olivia, and Jessi would do anything to keep it that way. Once she was sure all the ladies were praying, she sat on her back porch and read her Bible and prayed. Even though she knew a major storm was about to hit, she felt as if she were in its eye. It was a strange but peaceful feeling knowing that God was in control of the storms. She was still there when she heard the car pull up. She went to the front door and opened it for Jessi, who was carrying a sleeping Olivia.

"I see we have a sleeping beauty on our hands. A rough day?"

Jessi grinned. "Well, kind of. You know how Mom can be—absent most of your life, but when she decides to play the part she goes to the nines to make an impression. How long has it been since she's even contacted Olivia, let alone seen her? I just don't get her, Aunt Merry. Doesn't she understand that Olivia would just like her grandmother in her life?

She would benefit from the relationship too, even though she doesn't seem to think so. I thought things would get better since she stayed by my side at the hospital. I guess I was wrong."

Aunt Merry followed her while she carried Olivia to her bed and got her changed and tucked in. "Well, sweetheart, you know your mother as well, if not better than, I do. She has been this way since you were a little girl. That's why you had a bedroom upstairs at our house and a playhouse out back to play in. She gave you life and felt as if she had done her part as a mother. That was all she was willing to give. And I'm guessing she was feeling guilty today, like she did on a regular basis when you were small. I take it she was overdoing it a bit?"

"You wouldn't believe it, Aunt Merry. We went shopping, out to lunch, to the zoo, and then out to supper. I put my foot down when she suggested a movie after dinner. I suggested we go back to her house, where she could get to know her granddaughter a little bit. She reluctantly agreed, and when we did get back to her house she didn't even know what to say or how to act. Next year I don't think I am going to call her when we come. I just hate to rob Olivia of a relationship with her grandmother. You and I are the only family Olivia has. She needs more, Aunt Merry. She needs more."

"Well, why don't we head downstairs and have a cup of tea. There's something I need to talk with you about, and it has to do with exactly that." Aunt Merry prayed as she headed downstairs. *Father, please give me wisdom with what I'm about to say. Be my lips, Lord, and speak for me. Guide me, Father. I don't want to hurt this child that I love so much. Prepare her heart, Lord, so she is open to what she is about to hear.*

Merry put the tea kettle on to boil and took two cups down from the kitchen cupboard. She was purposefully slow at her tasks. She added a tea bag to each cup, along with a teaspoon of sugar. She and Jessi had shared so many cups of tea over the years that she didn't have to ask what Jessi wanted. She added the milk once the tea bag had steeped for a minute, carried the tea to the table, and sat down at the table with Jessi.

"Honey, I'm not going to pull any punches with you here, and you are not going to like what I'm about to tell you, but I don't have any choice. Mark came by the house today."

Jessi stood up and sucked in a sharp breath. "I have to go, Aunt Merry. I have to go tonight. He can't find out about Olivia. He'll hurt her. I know he will." Jessi was starting to panic. She was moving her feet but retracing her steps, trying to make sense of all the thoughts that were flooding her mind. "I didn't even know he was out of prison. I thought he had another year. When did he get out?" She didn't expect an answer; she didn't even realize she was speaking out loud.

Aunt Merry stood up and faced her niece. "Look at me, Jessi." She took Jessi's face in her hands and turned it so they were looking eye to eye. "We need to sit down and discuss this calmly. You can't be waking that baby up and taking off and driving in the middle of the night. First of all, you're too tired to drive all night, and you'd be putting yourself and Olivia at risk. I know that's something that you don't want to be doing. Second, he doesn't even know Olivia exists. He hasn't seen her, and I certainly didn't tell him about her. All he wants is to talk with you. Talk with him. Let him tell you he is sorry, and then you and Olivia can disappear. If you don't talk with him now, he will find you. He told me to tell you he won't give up. At least if you talk with him now, it will be on your terms. You can set the time and place. If you wait until he finds you, he might find Olivia first. Is that a chance you are willing to take? Do you want him asking questions about Olivia? One look at her, and he'll know she is his. This is the best way, Jessi. Think about it."

Jessi sat back down, closed her eyes, and put her head in her hands. "Oh my gosh, you are right. What am I going to do? I can't do this Aunt Merry. What did he say? What does he want?"

"That's the first thing I asked him, honey. He said he only wants to talk with you. That's it."

"About what? Why does he want to talk with me after all this time?"

Merry took a sip of her tea before answering. "Well, I think he may have wanted to speak with you for quite a while now. You never once opened one of his letters to see what he had to say, and you sent them all back. I'm thinking that may have been a mistake, but there is nothing we can do about it now. You will have to face him, Jessi. It's the only way he's ever going to leave you alone. You have no choice but to meet with him. It's the only way."

Jessi kissed her aunt good night and went upstairs. She went into Olivia's room and knelt beside her bed. She watched her daughter as she slept. Nothing could ever take this child away from her. She wouldn't allow it. She would protect her with all she had as long as she lived and breathed. She kissed her lightly on the cheek before heading into her own room. She didn't like the idea of meeting with Mark, but she could see the logic in what Aunt Merry was saying. She could always count on the wisdom of her aunt. Her first response would have been to run. Run fast and run far. But Aunt Merry was right. He would have found her, and when he did, he would find Olivia. She had to be smart about this. She had to think.

Jessi sat in her sitting area with only the moonlight shining through the open window for light. She would have to call the prison to find out where he was living. She would start there. She couldn't imagine they wouldn't know, but if they didn't, she would contact his sister. If he was out of prison, surely he would be in touch with her. Even with his drinking problems, the two of them had remained close. She could never understand why. During his trial, Julia had been there to support him. Each day Jessi slipped into the back of the courtroom to make sure Mark paid for his actions. She didn't want to face him, so she left before he could see her. Once, during a break, she had come face-to-face with Julia. Julia gave her a hug and told her she was sorry, and she wasn't there to try to keep Mark from going to prison. She knew he deserved what punishment he received. She just wanted him to know that someone loved him unconditionally. Mark needed to know that someone still cared about him, even though he'd messed up. Jessi had never understood Julia's way of thinking.

After coming up with a plan of action, Jessi stretched and went to bed. She had decided to get up early the next morning and go running. It was something she hadn't done in a while but used to do when she was stressed out about something and needed to think. She curled up in bed and eventually drifted off into a sleep that was full of dreams and nightmares. She woke up only once, though she tossed and turned most of the night. She arose at seven the next morning feeling as if she had gotten no sleep at all. She was out the door by seven thirty, running as if her life depended on it. She never would have guessed that her ex-husband had become an early morning person himself and was at that moment on his way to see her. If she had, instead of running, she would have been driving far from where she was, with her daughter safely strapped in the backseat.

12

Mark knocked on Merry's front door at quarter to eight. He had an interview at ten, and it would take him a good forty-five minutes to get across town by bus, so he'd had to start early. A little girl rubbing her eyes came to the front door and said hello.

There was something about this little girl that had been bugging him since he had seen her the first time unloading the luggage from the car. Up close, he knew exactly what it was. She looked just like him. This was his daughter. She had to be. He could see it as plain as day. "Is your mommy home?" he tested her.

"No, she went running. I saw her leave a little while ago. She didn't know I was up," Olivia spoke through the screen.

At that moment Mark heard the back door slam. Aunt Merry must have been out in the backyard. The child must have just come down from sleeping. When he saw the expression on Aunt Merry's face, he knew he was right. She was his. This was the reason Jessi had moved away. She didn't want him knowing about his daughter. Even though he was disappointed, he couldn't blame her. In her eyes, he would have no rights to a child. Not after Ethan.

When Aunt Merry reached the door, she simply said, "Oh, my."

Mark smiled. "I just was making the acquaintance of this little girl. May I come in?"

Aunt Merry opened the door and let Mark come in.

"I was hoping to catch Jessi, but her daughter told me she is out running. It would seem I have missed her again."

Mark had seen the understanding cross Merry's face. She knew that he knew. How could he not after seeing her face-to-face?

Well, she might as well introduce the man to his own daughter. "Mark, this is Olivia. Olivia, this is Mark. He used to be a friend of your mommy's."

She made it clear that this was to be the boundaries of the relationship. He had no problem with that, at least for now.

"Olivia, is it? Well, that's a beautiful name. How old are you, Olivia?" he questioned her, wanting to know how long he'd been a father to this little girl without knowing it.

Olivia smiled at him. "I'll be six in September. I'm going to kindergarten this year. I'm a big girl now."

Mark returned her smile, and his heart swelled. "Wow, you *are* a big girl. Almost six years old and going to kindergarten. Who would have guessed? Are you here visiting with your mommy?" He couldn't help but ask the question. His original plan had been to speak with Jessi and somehow convince her that he was sorry and he was responsible and then walk away and let her begin healing. That was going to change now. There was no way he would walk out of this beautiful girl's life now that he found her. He needed her love too much. And he could sense she needed his. He would have to convince Jessi; he just didn't know how.

Aunt Merry spoke before Mark received the answer he was hoping for. "Olivia, why don't you run upstairs and get dressed." She was still in her nightgown.

"Mark, why don't you and I sit down and have a cup of coffee." Olivia took off at a full run toward the stairs. "Olivia, walk please," Merry called after her.

Soon they heard the pitter-patter of small feet going up the stairs.

Merry placed the two cups of hot coffee on the table and sat down next to Mark. "This is going to be very hard on Jessi, Mark, you knowing about Olivia. Don't expect too much out of her too soon. You are going to have to let her get used to the idea for a while. Even then it's going to take persistence on your part to be able to have a role in that child's life. You are going to have to decide what role you want that to be. She thinks her father is dead, Mark. My advice to you would be to wade in very slowly, if you don't want a battle on your hands, that is."

Mark chose his words wisely. He still needed and wanted this woman's prayer and support. "I have to admit, seeing her, looking at a reflection of myself, was quite a shock. I knew she was mine. I just knew. She looks too much like me not to be. Did Jessi know before the accident that she was pregnant?"

Merry knew what he was asking. "No, she didn't find out until after the accident. She was having symptoms but didn't think anything of it, as she was running herself ragged between the school and the hospital. It wasn't until she got into a regular routine that she realized something else might be wrong. It was what saved her, Mark. I don't think she would have continued on if it hadn't of been for this baby. Her life revolved around Ethan. She needed something else to love desperately enough that it gave her back her will to live."

He shook his head. He knew exactly what she was talking about. While God had become the driving factor in his life, Olivia had replaced Ethan as Jessi's. "I don't know what I'm going to do yet. I can tell you I won't be able to walk out of Olivia's life. If that is what Jessi is expecting, then she will be let down. I will take her to court for visiting rights if necessary, although I hope it won't come to that. Knowing her hatred for me, though, it is a possibility."

Olivia, fully dressed, chose that moment to walk back into the kitchen. "Aunt Merry, can I have some cereal? I'm hungry."

The three of them sat together at the table, making small talk, while Olivia was chomping on Cap'n Crunch. All three of them heard the front door open and shut.

"That would be Jessi."

Merry closed her eyes and said a quick prayer just as Jessi walked through the kitchen door. She started to say good morning, but the words got caught in her throat. As she looked at the scene before her, she suddenly felt lightheaded and fell to the floor. Aunt Merry and Mark rushed to her side. Mark helped to get her to a more comfortable chair in the living room then returned to the kitchen to sit with Olivia. Aunt Merry washed her face with a cool washcloth while quietly beckoning her back to consciousness. Jessi slowly opened her eyes and drank from the glass of orange juice that her aunt was offering her. She questioned Merry with her eyes. Aunt Merry nodded her head, and Jessi closed her eyes while a few tears slipped down her cheeks. She knew she should have left last night. None of this would be happening right now if she had.

Once Aunt Merry figured Jessi was over the worst of the shock, she voiced what Jessi already knew to be true. "He knows, Jessi. One look at her, and he knew. How could he not? She looks just like him. We knew this would happen if he saw her."

Jessi sighed. "I should have packed up last night and headed home. I had a feeling this was going to end up badly. I never listen to my gut. What is wrong with me?"

"Nothing is wrong with you, Jessi. You are a normal human being created by God to be just who you are. I love you. Olivia loves you. And whether you want to hear it or not, God loves you. As far as Mark knowing he has a daughter, it is best to be open and truthful about these things, anyway. He does have some rights as far as she is concerned. You need to listen to him, Jessi. He would have found you anyway, even if you had left. He would have come after you. I have talked with him now a couple of times, and I believe this to be true. He wouldn't have given up until he found you. Deal with this now. Come to some agreement with him, or you may not like what the courts have to say if it comes to that."

Jessi could hear what her aunt was saying, but she just couldn't comprehend it. Mark having a part in Olivia's life? How had it come to this?

Jessi looked up at her aunt. "Could you put him off for just a day. It would give me a little time to think and come to terms with this. Let him know I will meet with him tomorrow morning at the park around the corner at eight. We'll talk then."

Jessi picked up the glass of juice and headed upstairs to her room. She should have checked in on Olivia, but she knew Aunt Merry would have everything under control. Things would be okay. She just had to believe that.

Mark had been waiting in the kitchen, talking with Olivia, while Merry was tending to Jessi. He had learned that Jessi and Olivia lived in Wisconsin and Jessi was teaching there at a local elementary school. That was the one bit of information he had been hoping to learn: where his new home was going to be if he was to remain in Olivia's life, which he fully intended to do. The rest of the time they talked about Olivia—what she liked to do, what her favorite foods were. She took horseback riding lessons, a convenient hobby, as they rented a house on a horse farm. She loved pizza and fruit. Vegetables ranked pretty high on her list as well. She seemed to be a well-rounded kid. Jessi had done a good job with her. They were just talking about her horse, Mr. Ed, when Merry walked through the kitchen door.

"Are you finished with your breakfast, Olivia?" she asked as she started putting away the cereal and milk.

"Yes, I know. Go and brush my teeth." Olivia looked at Aunt Merry with concern. "Is Mommy okay now? Mark said she is tired and needs to rest."

Merry gave Mark an appreciative glance. "Mark is right. Your mom is tired, and she went to her room to lie down. Why don't you go and give her a kiss before she goes to sleep?"

Olivia looked to Mark before leaving the room. "Will you still be here when I come back down?"

Mark looked to Merry for some indication before replying. She gave a little shake of her head.

He looked at Olivia and frowned. "No, I will have to say good-bye for now. I have an appointment in a little while, and I would hate to miss it. But I hope to visit with you again soon. Is that okay with you?"

The corners of Olivia's mouth turned up. "Yes, I would like that. Maybe I could show you my new doll and playhouse. Bye." She turned and again ran up the stairs.

Mark looked at Merry, afraid of what Jessi's response was. "She said she will meet you tomorrow morning at eight at the park down the street. Try to be understanding of why she did what she did. It will help you empathize with her feelings and be more open to a solution that will satisfy both of your concerns. And, Mark, remember to pray tonight. Pray like you've never prayed before."

"I will." Mark stood and headed through the living room and out the front door. He said his good-byes to Merry and walked to the bus stop that would take him to his appointment in the city. If everything worked out, he thought to himself, he would be looking for a job in Wisconsin pretty soon. He'd never been to Wisconsin. Other than getting pretty darn cold in the winter, he didn't know too much about it. But he was more than willing to find out.

13

Mark arrived at the park fifteen minutes before Jessi. He was nervous and didn't know what to expect, even though it was he who had requested this meeting. He knew what he originally wanted to talk with her about, but once again a wrench had been thrown into his plans, albeit this time it was a good twist. He had spent most of the night praying and asking God for direction and wisdom. He didn't feel any more knowledgeable regarding the whole situation, and he wasn't given some great words of peril to share with her. All he felt was to share his heart; be honest with her for once and let her see the difference in him for herself. It would take time to win her trust; he knew that. But in the end, if he had a relationship with his daughter, he would be the happiest man in the world and that would make it all worth it. The only thing that could make it better was if he actually was able to reestablish his place next to his wife as her husband. He wasn't sure at first if that was what he had wanted. Now that he'd glimpsed into her heart and had seen all the love she was capable of giving, he knew he wanted to be loved by her and to return that love as a husband was supposed to love his wife. Mark sat thinking and praying while waiting for Jessi to enter the park.

Jessi started jogging at seven thirty. She took the long way around the block to the park but didn't care that she would leave Mark waiting on her for a few minutes. She still needed more time to think, and running always helped clear her head. She knew from her conversation with Aunt Merry that he wanted to be able to visit with Olivia. He wanted to spend time with his daughter. She also knew that she didn't want him to have anything to do with Olivia. They would have to find a happy medium that she could agree with if she was going to be able to control the outcome of all this. The courts would probably grant him shared custody with visitation rights if she couldn't come up with a plan that would suit both of them. She was hoping that her living in Wisconsin would ward him off. He was never fond of cold weather. Maybe he would be happy with seeing her for a little while when they visited Oklahoma. She would start there and work her way up. One thing she would never permit was Olivia riding in a car with him. That was out of the question. She had jogged around the back entrance of the park and approached him from behind. He had figured she would come from the direction that faced Merry's house. He didn't pay any attention to the steps he heard from behind him until she spoke his name.

"Mark." She approached him cautiously. Besides yesterday morning, the last time they had faced each other was in Mark's hospital room, and that meeting hadn't gone so well. She didn't think this one would go too much better. "So you met Olivia, I see."

She sat down next to Mark on the bench, keeping as much distance as possible between the two of them.

Mark spent a moment in prayer before he answered. "I understand why you didn't tell me about her. I would have done the same thing if I were you."

"You didn't give me much of a choice, Mark. I couldn't take a chance of something happening to her. After Ethan, I didn't dare put Olivia at risk. I don't think I would have survived if she weren't part of my life. She means the world to me. What is it you want from us?"

"I'm not sure I deserve anything from you. At first, my only intention was to apologize to you for all I have done, but now I also have Olivia to consider, and my relationship with her. And I do apologize from the bottom of my heart. I don't expect you to forgive me, at least not yet. I was so wrong, and I treated you horribly. I accused you of being a poor wife, and nothing was further from the truth. I lied to you. I did have a drinking problem. I still do if I rely on myself, which I have learned I can't do. I have not touched alcohol in over six years, not even since getting out of prison, and I never will, not even a sip of wine. I can't imagine how hard it was for you to live with me for all those years. Always providing for our family because I couldn't keep a job long enough to bring in a decent paycheck would have been more than enough stress, let alone everything else I put you through. You have nothing to feel guilty about, Jessi. I take full blame for everything—our failed marriage, my drinking problem, the sadness that I always found in your eyes, and mostly, Ethan's death. I was so stupid. I don't want you carrying the weight of the world on your shoulders anymore. When I was in prison, I realized what kind of burden I put on you. It wasn't fair of me. I was trying to justify my actions instead of taking responsibility for them. I won't be doing that anymore. If I am going to change, it has to start with accepting myself and changing as God gives me strength."

Mark had been looking down while he spoke. He was afraid if he looked at her he would break down and not be able to say all he wanted to say. He looked up and glanced at her to see if she was reacting somehow to what he was saying.

Jessi wasn't sure how he wanted her to respond. She'd never heard him take responsibility for his actions before. He sounded like he might actually mean it, but she'd heard so many lies that she wasn't sure what to believe. What was she thinking? She didn't even want to believe him. He killed her son. Did he really think she would just forgive him and make him feel better?

"Mark, why are you telling me all this? Do you really think I could just forgive you and pretend nothing happened? And then I suppose you want me to just hand Olivia over for visiting rights, huh? I don't think so, Mark. Ethan is dead because of you. For once you could have done the right thing, but no. You had to drink and drive while our son, no, my son, was in the car. A real father wouldn't have purposely put his son in danger like you did. I can't trust you with Olivia. What is wrong with me? Why would I even consider this. What am I going to do?" She'd stopped talking to Mark and started arguing with herself.

Mark knew this was going to be hard. He knew she was going to blame him and accuse him, and he knew everything she said was going to be true. He just didn't realized how much the truth was going to hurt. Knowing that time hadn't healed her at all and that she still harbored just as much resentment toward him as the day of the accident crushed him inside. He'd come so far in realizing God's love for himself that he wasn't ready for the fresh attack of guilt that hit him.

"Jessi, God has forgiven me. Society says I have paid my debt, and I'm free to go. But do you think for one minute that I will ever forgive myself? There's not a day that passes that I don't see Ethan's face and hear the plea in his voice as he cries 'Help me, Daddy.' And I was completely helpless, no, make that useless, to help him. I know I am nothing, Jessi. But I loved him too. I still do." Through tears, he whispered his last words. He wiped his eyes and looked up at her. "I want to spend time with my daughter, Jessi. I need her too. In the little time that I have spent with her, she has filled a huge hole in my heart. I will do whatever you ask. I will sit in your living room a couple of hours a week if that's all you want. I just need to spend time with her. I don't want to go to the court system, but if I have to, I will. I would like us to be able to work this out on our own. I need her, Jess. Please don't make me fight you on this."

Jessi knew that he would get more than what she was willing to give if he went through the court system for visitation. She offered him what she quietly begged he would accept. "You can come over to Aunt Merry's a few times when we come to visit. I'd be willing to give you that much."

"No, Jessi. I want more than that, much more than that. I will be moving to Wisconsin to be near her. I need her in my life as a constant. I would be willing to compromise because of my past and visit with her once a week. We can finalize the details when I am all settled and have a job there. I'm assuming they build houses in Wisconsin. I'll need to make arrangements, and I'll let you know when I do. I'm sorry that this has been so difficult for you. I can't say I never meant to hurt you, because at one time I did. There is so much that I would undo if I could, but I can't. I told Olivia that I would come to see her sometime. I'd like to see her again before you leave, and maybe then I will have some information for you." He apologized once more. "I'm sorry, Jess. I'm truly sorry." He turned and walked away toward the bus stop.

Jessi couldn't believe her worst nightmare had just come true. Mark was going to move to Wisconsin. He was going to be a part of her life whether she liked it or not. It didn't look as though she was going to have a choice in the matter. She had always known this would be a possibility. She'd just hoped it would never become a reality. Jessi turned and walked home.

14

Jessi walked in and slammed the door. Since leaving the park she'd thought of a hundred responses to Mark and his solution to being with Olivia. Why she couldn't come up with one quick enough to counter him before he walked off, she'd never know. Now she had to face the possibility of Mark actually moving to Wisconsin and being a constant in hers and Olivia's lives. She walked through the kitchen and out the back door, where she watched Olivia and Aunt Merry playing in the garden. Neither noticed her presence in their land of fairies, castles, princesses, and frogs. Olivia was dressed up in the princess costume that her grandmother had bought her. She had to admit that it was a good gift, even if it was purchased out of guilt. Olivia loved it. Maybe that's all that counted. The memories Olivia would have of her grandmother may be few, but at least they would be special. Mom always saw to that. Jessi could hear Olivia talking to Aunt Merry from her perch outside the back door.

"Mr. Frog, you need to kiss the princess, and then you can be a real prince. The princess needs a real prince, right, Aunt Merry?"

"Yes, sweetheart, the princess needs a real prince. She certainly can't marry a frog, you know."

Olivia giggled. "How silly. Who would want to marry a frog?" Olivia continued. "I think Mommy is a princess. She's pretty like one. Don't you think so?"

Merry played along. "Yes, I do think she is pretty like a princess. We should ask her to play castle with us when she gets home."

Olivia thought about that for a moment. "Who would be her prince?"

Merry knew the child was a sensitive one and wondered just how much she understood in regard to her mother and father. "Well, I don't know, Olivia. Who do you think should be her prince?"

"Well, that nice man who came over yesterday would make a nice prince. And he did say he was going to come back and see me. Maybe he would like to be Mommy's prince?"

Merry sighed and looked around. "Well, you could certainly ask her. I don't know if your mommy wants a prince right now."

An incredulous look crossed Olivia's face. "Why wouldn't Mommy want a prince? Mommy reads me stories about princesses, and I know that all princesses want a prince. Ask Mommy; she'll tell you. Cinderella wanted a prince. And Snow White wanted a prince. In my story, Mommy wants a prince."

Jessi figured this was a good time to interrupt their play, and she walked to where she would be seen.

Olivia saw her first. "Mommy, tell Aunt Merry that all princesses want to have a prince. Tell her."

Merry looked at Jessi with a look that said, "I tried."

Jessi sat down in the grass next to her daughter. "Olivia is right. A princess definitely wants a prince."

Olivia raised her chin a little and looked at her aunt. "See, I told you. Mommy wants a prince."

"Whoa, what makes you think Mommy wants a prince?" Jessi waited for Olivia's reply.

Olivia, with tears forming in her eyes, defiantly crossed her arms and again lifted her chin before replying, "Because, Mommy, I want to have a daddy!" She then turned and ran from the garden, through the house, up the stairs, and into her room.

Jessi rested her head in her hands. Her daughter was missing her father. She was going to have to find out if anything Mark said was true about the past six years. While she wanted nothing to do with him, Olivia needed her dad.

Jessi got up and followed Olivia to her room. She knocked on the door and entered to find Olivia lying facedown on her bed, crying. It broke Jessi's heart to see her daughter in pain. She sat down next to Olivia and rubbed her back. "Honey, I want you to have Daddy too. I really do. Mommy needs you to forgive her for something. Do you think you can do that?"

Olivia sat up in bed. She and her mother had a pact. When one of them did something wrong or hurt the other one's feelings, they asked for forgiveness. "Mommy, why do you need me to forgive you?"

Jessi was hoping she wouldn't regret this decision. "Because I told you something that wasn't true. I thought I was doing the right thing, but now I know that it wasn't the right thing. Telling the truth is always the right thing to do."

"What wasn't the truth?"

"Well, I told you that you didn't have a daddy. But that wasn't the truth. You do have a daddy."

Olivia's eyes were dry and open wide. "I do? I really do? Where is he, Mommy? Where is my daddy?"

This was the tough part. "Well, do you remember that man who was here yesterday?" Olivia nodded her head. "He's your daddy, sweetheart."

Olivia threw her arms around her mother's neck. "Oh, thank you, Mommy. I've always wanted a daddy. All my friends have daddies, and I wanted one too. Now I have a daddy." Olivia stopped talking and became pensive. "Mommy, didn't Daddy want to be my daddy?"

Jessi knew this was coming. Olivia was too smart to just accept that she had a father. She would have a lot of questions over the next few days. "No, honey, it's nothing like that. Your daddy had to go away for a long time, and he wasn't able to come and be your daddy. Now that he is back, he wants to be your daddy real bad. He loves you, Olivia. As a matter of fact, he is going to move to Wisconsin just so he can live by you. What do you think of that?" Jessi smiled at her daughter.

"Will he live in our house? Like all my friends' daddies?"

Jessi breathed out. "No, he won't live with us. He will have his own house, and he will live there. But he can come to our house and visit you. How does that sound?"

"Well, I think he will live in our house with us. Mommies and daddies should live together with their children. Aunt Merry told me I can pray to God anytime I want, and he will listen to me. She told me it's okay if I ask God for things as long as I'm really really sure I'm thankful and thinking of others first. I am thankful for having a daddy, and I am thinking of you and Daddy first. So I'm gonna pray and ask God to let you and Daddy and me live all together in our house. That's what I think."

Olivia hopped off the bed. "I'm going to tell Aunt Merry about my daddy. I just knew he was your prince." And with that she ran out the door.

Jessi opened her mouth and then shut it again.

15

Mark walked around for a while before stopping at a bus stop. He had to think about what had just happened with Jessi. He couldn't believe she'd tried to put him off with seeing Olivia once a year while she visited her aunt. That was no way to be a father. He wanted a real relationship with his daughter. He'd never done anything right in his life, and this was his chance to prove that he could be a good father, even better than good.

His daughter needed him. He had heard about girls who had no relationship with their dads while he was in prison, both from the guys who took advantage of young girls and the fathers who taught the guys who took advantage a lesson. He didn't want his little girl looking for approval and worth from physical relationships with guys who didn't love her. She needed to develop her own sense of self-worth so she wouldn't need the approval of others. For that, she needed a father who would love her and encourage her. She needed *him*.

Now, convincing his parole officer that this would be a good move for him was next. He stopped at a payphone and made an appointment for the next day. Mark headed home and read his Bible while he ate macaroni and cheese for supper. He read in Romans, and when he got to 8, verse 28—"And we know that all things work together for good to those who love God, to those who are called according to His purpose"—he repeated the verse to himself several times and waited for God's peace to envelop him, praising his Father with his lips.

That night Mark went to church with Bill. There was a men's Bible study he had been looking forward to taking part in. Bill picked him up at six fifteen, and on the way to the church Mark told Bill what was happening.

"Bill, I don't know what came over me. I went to meet her with Meredith's words specifically in mind: 'Go slow; take it easy,' she said. 'It will take her time to get used to the idea.' But when she suggested I see Olivia once a year when she visits her aunt, I just blurted out exactly what I had been thinking. I told her I would be moving to Wisconsin to be closer to Olivia whether she liked it or not. I didn't even give her a chance to comment. Then I left the park and called my parole officer. Do you think I acted too rashly? Do you think I actually have a chance?"

Bill had seen many different scenarios in his days of working within the jail system. "I'm not sure how the system will react, Mark. I've seen some guys with totally crazy ideas who have actually been given the go-ahead, and some others with relatively tame ideas who have been turned down. It depends on who you talk with and whether or not they decide to take up your cause. Have you prayed about this? Is this God's will for your life?"

Mark thought about all the hours he'd spent in prayer. He mostly thought about the instant bonding he had felt with the little girl he met at Meredith's house, his little girl, and the desire to be with her, teach her, and learn from her. There was so much they could give each other.

"Yes, I have, Bill. I have prayed and read my Bible for hours. I can't sleep at night. I can't concentrate during the day. I just can't imagine doing anything else. Oklahoma doesn't even appeal to me anymore. All I can think about is Wisconsin. I went to the library and looked up all I could about the state. I want to be near her, Bill. I just can't imagine the alternative."

By the time they reached the church, Mark had Bill's word that he would find out all he could for him, as well as put in a good word for him if possible. Bill pulled into the parking lot, and both men entered the church. Bible study was exactly what Mark needed. He met some men who agreed to pray for him. He even found a job with a business owner who needed a janitor. The Oklahoma job market was down, and he'd had a hard time securing a position in the construction field. Mark gave a shortened version of his testimony and walked away with a whole support group. Things were looking up.

The next morning, Mark entered the county complex where his parole officer was located. At ten he was ushered into an office and was sitting and explaining his situation. "I'm not asking for the probation period to end. I'm just asking for a transfer into the Wisconsin system. My ex-wife had a child while I was in prison and didn't tell me, after which she moved to Wisconsin. Now I have a five-year-old little girl who lives eight hundred miles away from me, and I would like to live near her. Is there something I can do?"

Terrance Clark—friends called him Terry—had been a parole officer for twenty-two years when Mark Jensen entered his life from within the system. He liked the guy. He wanted to help him. Mark had been through some rough times, had done some pretty heinous stuff, but underneath he was a pretty decent guy. Terry dealt with all types, and Mark was pretty much the exception when it came to rehabilitation. Most of the guys he supervised went through all the hoopla, said all the right things, and then ended up back in prison for doing the same thing, if not something worse. He would bet the farm that Mark would never see the inside of a prison cell again.

"Mark, I'm not making you any promises here, but I'm going to see what I can do. I'll make some calls and talk to some people who can make things happen. I'll do my best."

Mark left Terry's office feeling pretty hopeful. He had to call him back in a week to see where things were at. If all went well, he would be moving to Wisconsin within a couple of months.

Mark decided to head to his sister's house, as he would be starting work and wouldn't have much time for a while. The company he was going to work for had been without a reliable janitor for so long that Mark was going to have to work some extra hours to help get them in order. Between that, spending time with Olivia, and going to church, he'd be pretty busy. He'd not seen his sister since he'd been released from prison, and he wanted her support. Her support had made all the difference while he was in prison.

Mark called from a payphone before he took a bus to her neighborhood. She was excited to hear from him, and yes, by all means, he could come over. She had a direct selling business that she operated from her home and was usually pretty flexible with her schedule. Today she had been making phone calls and doing paperwork. She was glad for the break.

As soon as Julia hung up with her brother, she closed up the office and headed to the kitchen. *I bet he hasn't had a good meal since before he went to prison*, she thought. Right away she set to work making lunch. Chicken fried steak with mashed potatoes would hit the spot. She was just finishing up when the doorbell rang. She had worried that Mark would fall back to his old ways once he was out of prison. She would know as soon as she saw him if her worries were in vain or with good cause. She made her way to the door and broke out in a huge grin when she looked at him. He looked better than she'd seen him look since the accident. He looked healthy and vibrant. He actually looked happy. She knew that he had made a complete turnaround while in prison. He'd come out a completely different person. She threw her arms around his neck in a big hug. She stood back and looked at him. "It's so good to have my little brother back. I've missed you. I have lunch ready."

Mark inhaled a deep breath and said, "Something smells delicious," and followed his sister into the kitchen. She had the table set for two with a salad already on the table. She dished up the rest of the food and set it on the table.

"Sis, I believe I need to say grace. I have a bunch to be thankful for." They bowed their heads. "Lord, I want to thank you for all you have been doing in my life. Thank you for my wonderful sister and all she has put up with from me. I pray that somehow I can be a blessing to her, Father, as she has blessed me so much. I thank you for the food that you have so graciously provided. In Jesus's name, amen." Mark dug in with gusto.

After lunch, Mark and Julia discussed all his options. Julia felt as though she was losing her brother again. Wisconsin was a long ways away. "When do you think you will be moving?"

Mark sensed his sister's mood. "Well, I can't leave until I get the go-ahead from my parole officer, and even then I won't be leaving until Jessi and Olivia return to Wisconsin. You know, sis, you could come with me."

Julia hadn't given the possibility a thought, but now that Mark had brought it up, it was worth looking into. She didn't have much to remain for in Oklahoma. They had family that lived in the area, but she'd never felt particularly close to them like she had felt to Mark. For some reason, probably their nearness in age, they had always been close. Even during the hard years, they could help each other out. Her husband had died several years before in a work-related accident. They had always planned on having children someday. He died before they got around to it, and she'd always regretted waiting. The idea of living near her niece was very appealing. "Mark, what do you say we drive over and see Olivia? I'm dying to meet her."

"I already planned on going over today, so you are welcome to come with me. There's just one thing; she doesn't know I'm her dad yet. So we can't say anything. I want to make this as easy for her as possible. She thinks her dad is dead."

"That's gonna be hard to explain. What does Jessi say about it?"

"Jules," Mark said, reverting to his childhood pet name for her, "I understand completely why Jessi did what she did. It's easier to tell a kid that her father is dead than that he's a loser who is in prison for killing her older brother. In some ways, I want her to think I'm dead. I'm going to have a real hard time answering her questions honestly as she gets older and still retain her love and respect. I would have probably done the same thing. I better call and make sure they're home before we head over."

Mark picked up and dialed while Julia thought about the possibilities. She could sell her place and buy something up north. She'd have Mark around to help with the stuff she didn't know how to do or didn't have time for, and he'd have a place to live and decent food to eat. Her business could be operated from anywhere in the world, so that wasn't an issue. She did have her church and friends, but she would find a new church, and she didn't seem to have a problem making friends. This was worth praying about. Her thoughts were interrupted when Mark addressed her.

"Julia, did you hear me?" Mark grinned at her. "I didn't think so. I said we can go over, but Jessi wants to talk with me first. It seems she has found her tongue since we last spoke. I'm sure she is going to give me a hundred reasons why I can't move to Wisconsin, now that she's had time to think about it. I think I caught her by surprise when I told her my plans."

They headed over to Aunt Merry's house in Julia's car, a two-door Corsica that badly needed replacing. She had planned on going and looking at new cars—she had the money set aside—but if she was seriously considering this move, it would make more sense to wait until she got to Wisconsin. It wasn't long before they were pulling up in front of the house. Julia turned to look at her brother. "I'm nervous, Mark. What if she doesn't like me?"

Mark started laughing. "Julia, she is a five-year-old little girl. You don't have to impress her. Just be yourself. Besides, what's not to like." He leaned over and gave her a kiss on the cheek.

They approached the house and were let in by Aunt Merry. She led them into the living room and offered them some cold iced tea. It was an unusually hot day, even by Oklahoma's standards. A hundred and five in the shade made cold sweet tea go down pretty well. Aunt Merry was about to go get Jessi when Olivia screamed what sounded like "Daddy" and took off for Mark at a full run.

She reached her dad and threw her arms around his neck. "Oh, Daddy, how I've missed you. Why didn't you tell me you were my daddy?" Leave it to Olivia to get right to the heart of the matter.

Mark's eyes were overflowing. He didn't think he'd hear her calling him daddy for a long time. The sound of his name coming from her lips brought a surge of emotion that emerged and erupted from the center of his being. Before he could speak, Jessi interrupted.

"Olivia, I would like to talk with your daddy for a little while, and then you can ask him all the questions you want, okay?" Jessi gave her a look that said "it better be okay," so Olivia shook her head in agreement.

Jessi led Mark out to the garden. "As you've noticed, I told her about you."

"Yeah, wow, what a surprise. I wasn't expecting that. Thanks."

Jessi raised an eyebrow. "It wasn't for you, Mark. It was for her. She's a pretty perceptible little girl. She's realized something's going on, and she's been asking about you, I mean, her daddy, so I had to tell her about you. I had no choice. I had to apologize for lying to her. She hasn't yet begun the great inquisition, but when she does, she's going to have a million questions. We have to tell her the truth. If we don't, she'll just be hurt later. I need your word that you will be honest with her, no matter what the consequences. No lies, Mark. We both have to learn to be truthful."

Mark remained hopeful. This wasn't going nearly as bad as he thought it might go. "I can live with that, Jessi. I don't want to lose her right after I've found her, but I can't lie to her either. I just can't lie anymore to anyone, including myself. I've changed, Jessi. I will spend my entire life proving that to you if I have to."

Mark went back into the house and spent the rest of the afternoon playing dolls with his daughter, while Merry and Julia looked on. It was the most fun he'd had in a long time. Jessi, not willing to take part in the happy reunion and yet not wanting her sour mood to ruin everyone else's afternoon, left.

16

Jessi drove with no destination in mind. She drove on automatic and was surprised at the places that her subconscious led her to. She first drove to her old neighborhood and parked outside the house she'd lived in with Mark. The sight of the small home brought back many memories, both good and bad. Her counselor had been suggesting she make this journey for years now. She didn't intentionally set out to do his bidding but unwittingly found herself doing just that. She watched four boys tossing a football around. Surprisingly, she did not feel the pain she once would have. All around her were familiar sights. Her old house still looked the same, but she knew if she entered it there would be little left that would remind her of home. Even its smell would have changed, reflective of the current inhabitants. Nothing changed, and yet nothing remained the same. Strange.

Continuing on her drive, she once again passed the old houses that she used to covet. Now, instead of desiring the brick and columns, fireplaces and wide porches, she yearned for what was inside of them—the family that actually made the house a home. They were what really counted. She knew that now. Her desire was loved ones that would love her unconditionally, whom she could love with all her being in return. She pulled into the parking lot of her old school and walked around. She visited the playground and looked into the windows of her old classroom. Her replacement had made the place her own, just like Jessi had when she first started teaching there. The basic setup was the same, yet everything was different. Again, memories—both good and bad—flooded her being. She had friends here. She wondered what ever happened to them. Did they still teach? Did they move away like she had, or did life simply go on without her, with them barely even noticing she was gone? She didn't know. Except for her visits to Aunt Merry's house and Ethan's grave, she never once reconnected with any of her friends from before the accident. They tried, she knew. She'd received plenty of cards and meals. Many tried to stop by and comfort her, but she wanted nothing from anyone. It was as if she had died right along with Ethan. Eventually everyone gave up and went their own directions, not knowing what else to do or try. She didn't even write out thank-you notes; her guess was Aunt Merry had taken care of them. Again, she just didn't know.

Her next stop was in front of Aunt Merry's church, the place Jessi had attended Sunday school as a child. This was where she learned that she was different from everyone else, where she heard the grownups whisper about her when they thought she wasn't listening. They gossiped about the little girl whose parents abandoned her to live a life free from encumbrances that the little girl inevitably brought to their lives. Not thinking through their actions, the adults reinforced the feelings of worthlessness that Jessi had already felt. No one knew that while she seemed preoccupied, she was actually listening to everything they said. She learned the art of being invisible at a very early age and therefore heard many things that were not intended for her ears. Only after the damage had been done—and Jessi would hold a grudge against the church for many years to come—did Aunt Merry explain that eavesdropping was not a proper thing to do, and in most cases what people had to say wasn't worth listening to anyway, especially when they spoke in hushed tones.

When she was little, she had listened in to her parents discussing the accident of her birth and how neither her mother nor her father were happy they had a young child in tow. Later, when they finally decided to hand her over to Aunt Merry to raise, she hated them for not loving her. She took her anger out on her aunt, who loved her regardless, unconditionally. It was a long and difficult process for both of them, yet neither would change a thing. She also learned about Jesus in this church. He was someone that neither her father nor her mother ever spoke of. He was all Aunt Merry talked about, though. She tried to teach Jessi that Jesus loved her. Jessi had already come to the conclusion that she was unlovable and therefore, not worthy of Jesus's love; the conversations she overheard confirmed this in her mind. She decided to move on.

    The next drive Jessi took was the route that Mark had taken the day of the accident. She drove past the grocery store and the bar. She parked by the tree that still bore the evidence of being hit. She ran her fingers over the indentation and looked for little pieces of glass that might still be there. She walked down the road to where a flower cross stood, still reminding all who passed that someone who was loved dearly died in this very spot. Each day, it seemed, she forgot some little detail, something she never thought she would forget. She pictured the accident happening, as she had done a hundred—no, a thousand—times before, and found that while she was still very much affected by the memories she held on to, with or without her, time forged on; and somewhere along the way, she decided she wanted to move on as well and live. When that happened, she did not know. Sometimes she caught herself remembering the good times and laughing out loud, like the time she was playing catch with Ethan and threw a crazy ball, which of course he dove after and ended up with a black eye from when it swerved back toward him. At the time she felt horrible because she was the cause of his pain, but later, when they looked at that big shiner, they both started laughing. To this day she couldn't tell you how to throw a curveball. Maybe that was when her healing process started, when she started remembering Ethan for who he was and not because he was hers to lose. She was confused by her own thoughts, unsure if she should be thinking this way. She decided to go to Ethan's grave.

She sat cross-legged in front of Ethan's tombstone. Jessi found some peace in the fact that this visit didn't start out in tears like all her other visits had. She began to tell him about her day. "Hi, Ethan. It's me, Mom. I just wanted to stop today and talk with you. I know you won't answer me, but I'm hoping that you can hear me and that maybe if you talk with God, he will help me find peace and healing so I can be a better mom for your sister. You would love her, Ethan. She is so different from you, yet so much like you. She doesn't look anything like you and me; she's the spitting image of your dad. Crazy, huh? Same dark hair and bright green eyes. She's got a temper, too. You wouldn't believe it. Says exactly what she thinks before she thinks. Sometimes that can be a good thing, sometimes not, but it's your sister, and we love her for it. Lately, she's been making me think about how I've been living. I've been living in our past, Ethan, and that's not fair to her. She needs a mom who's not afraid to live in the present. She has so much passion and enthusiasm for life that I feel sometimes I'm smothering her with my pain. It's not that I want to forget you; I could never do that. It's just that I need to start remembering the good stuff and letting the bad stuff go. I need to be able to share all those great times we had with her so she can get to know you. I think that's what you would want me to do anyway, but I thought I better check with you on it. I know that you've forgiven me, Ethan. I can sense it in my heart. I'm learning to forgive myself. I don't know that I will ever fully forgive myself, but at least I'm trying. It's already the end of June, and we'll be heading back to Wisconsin in a few weeks. I'll come back to say good-bye before we leave. I love you, son. Until forever, always remember that."

17

Some say that God is easier to find in the rich colors of the north, Merry thought as she looked around at the dry, red earth around her. Personally, she'd never had a problem finding him here in her little corner of earth. Everything around her spoke of God's love, mercy, and grace. In a woman down on her knees coaxing flowers to grow out of stubborn, fruitless soil, she saw God's patience when dealing with all the humanness of his children, painstakingly wiping their tears and holding their hands while helping them back on the path from which they wandered. In a father and his son playing ball outside, the father teaching the boy the art of catching the ball, all evidence of our heavenly Father molding and teaching his children in ways of righteousness and wisdom. Finally, looking west, she saw insurmountable beauty as the colors of the setting sun blended perfectly with redness of the earth, creating a memory in her mind that could never be saved to canvas. This was God. Only God could take something that looked so desolate and lifeless and make it more beautiful than anything she'd ever seen.

Merry had taken to walking lately. It wasn't very far from her house to Mabel's house, where prayer group was being held this evening. Along the way, she prayed, ever mindful of seeing God in all she passed. She considered this time her quiet time, even with all the things going on around her. Today she passed a young mother pushing a stroller with a child propped up to see the sights. The obvious bond they shared reminded her of God's love for his children. They smiled and said hello as they passed.

Things had been a bit noisier than usual at home with a five-year-old girl in the house, not that she would have it any other way, but it did limit the amount of quiet time she could spend in prayer. Walking was the perfect answer. She could be in her surroundings without having to pay particular attention to them. She could stay focused on the Lord and his will for her family, directing her in prayer.

Mark had been a regular part of life here lately, and she saw the difference he made in Olivia's life. Olivia needed a father as much as Jessi needed a husband, only she would never say that within Jessi's hearing. No telling what the girl would do. Time would tell what part Mark would play in all their lives. God had given her a measure of peace regarding the situation, but sometimes God's solutions were not in line with his followers'. Of course, if Merry got to choose the outcome it would be a relatively short one. Jessi would accept Jesus, and then she and Mark would remarry, giving Olivia both a mother and a father to love and raise her. Tada! But she knew it wasn't wise to second-guess God.

Merry continued on her walk, letting her mind wander to and fro. There still was no word on whether Mark would be able to move to Wisconsin. He'd been uptight at his last visit, thinking he should have had an answer by now. She told him to wait on the Lord; he would provide the patience needed to do so as well.

Jessi was coming along. Though still not ready to accept the Lord, she had come to terms with Mark being in their lives, just barely.

Maintaining an attitude of worship and prayer, Merry fluctuated between humming a worship song and giving voice to bits and pieces of prayers that overflowed from her heart. "Oh, Lord, wouldn't it have been so much easier if you had created us to love and worship you? Oh, just ignore this old woman, Lord. I'm just trying to do your job for you again."

Merry knew that the joy in being loved was in the willingness of the lover; otherwise it wouldn't be love. Practicing patience was still on her daily agenda, a virtue that she hadn't perfected in the twenty-six years since becoming a Christian, and didn't think she would perfect this side of heaven, a place she would not see until everyone she loved was safe and had security in spending eternity alongside her, praising the Father.

She looked up and realized she had been so engrossed in her thoughts she had passed Mabel's house. She backtracked half a block and entered into a place set aside for prayer. The women had already finished their snack when Merry had arrived and were heading to their prayer closets. Merry joined right in and remained in the attitude of worship and prayer, the sole reason for coming.

18

It had been two weeks since Mark had talked with his parole officer, and still he hadn't heard a word from him. He had called and left a message inquiring about things a week after the meeting, as he'd been instructed to do, but still hadn't heard whether or not he'd be able to move. He was running out of patience. He finished sweeping the break room and headed toward the time clock. Another day of work done. It felt good to have and hold a job. He'd been working six days a week for the past two weeks, and he was about to get his first paycheck. He decided to celebrate and buy a little gift for Olivia, not that there would be much left after paying rent and buying what little groceries he could survive on. But in case he couldn't move until his probation period was done, he wanted to give her something to remember him by. He picked up his check and walked to the little gift shop that was across the street. He had just enough time to make his purchase and still catch his bus. He bought a four-by-six picture frame that had "Me and My Dad" written across the top. He bought a disposable camera and was going to ask Aunt Merry to take a picture of the two of them together, and then he'd put one in the frame and give it to her. He would buy himself a frame later. Hopefully she would like it. Mark made it to the bus stop just in time to catch the bus.

When he got home there was a note taped to his door. His next-door neighbor had volunteered the use of his phone for Mark's work and for his parole office to be able to reach him. The note read, "Terry called and wants you to call him at home as soon as you get this message. Come on over, and you can use my phone. I should be home. Brian."

Mark sat down in the chair in the living room, not knowing if he would be ecstatic in a few minutes or depressed, praying to God that it would be the former. Not wanting to put it off any longer, he walked to Brian's apartment and knocked on the door.

The door opened, "Oh, hey, Mark; come on in." Brian stepped aside and let Mark in the door. "You got my message, then. Good."

Mark walked to where the phone rested, took a deep breath, picked it up, and dialed the number. On the third ring, he heard a familiar voice answer the phone. "Hello."

"Hi, Terry. This is Mark Jenson."

"Hey, Mark. Good to hear from you. How is your new job going?"

Even though he wanted to hear the answer Terry had for him, he answered his question quickly, trying to be patient and end the small talk. "It's going good. I've really enjoyed the work." He decided to get right to point. "Have you heard anything yet about my move to Wisconsin?"

"Well, that's why I called. I have some good news for you. After looking at your prison record and talking with all your references, the judge has granted you permission to move to Wisconsin, with the understanding that you will be transferred to the Wisconsin parole program. Your parole period will remain the same, and you will be given a parole officer in Rock County, the county you have requested. Your paperwork should be finished and the transfer completed by the end of July, just a few weeks away. You got your wish, Mark. I'll let you know when everything is in order. Good luck. I'm happy for you."

Mark hung up the phone, and a huge grin spread across his face.

"Good news?" Brian asked, watching him from the living room.

"Better than good. An answer to prayer, that's for sure. Looks like you'll be losing a neighbor. I'll be moving to Wisconsin at the end of the month." Mark let out a whooping, "Yes!"

Brian knew a little bit of what Mark was going through. "Hey, man, I'm happy for you. There's not much else worth having if you don't have family to share it with. Let me know if you need anything while you're still here."

Mark walked out of Brian's apartment and into his own with a contagious grin on his face. He walked around for all of five minutes with a nervous energy before he headed to the bus stop and over to Julia's. He couldn't wait to tell her. He really couldn't wait to tell Olivia. Even though Jessi would be unhappy about the whole thing, he was more than sure Olivia would be thrilled.

As Mark rode the bus and waited for his stop, he watched people get on and off and wondered where they were going and what the story of their lives was. A few looked happy and sad, while most looked like it took everything they had to just exist, like he used to look. To think, so many didn't know the joy of salvation. Everything changed when you had a relationship with God. It wasn't circumstances; it was how you looked at things. The real changing took place inside, deep in the heart of a man, which, in effect, changed the circumstances, making them more bearable. These people needed hope. They needed Jesus. Mark was beginning to get a glimpse of God's will for his life. He had a passion for the souls of the lost. Would God use his failures to help others? Only time would tell.

At the next stop, Mark got off the bus and started the short walk to his sister's house, praising and thanking God the whole way for the miracle he had performed on Mark's behalf. He had to use Julia's phone to call Bill and the guys from the men's prayer group. They would want to know how God had chosen to answer their prayers. Mark had been forewarned that God might not choose to answer his prayer the way he wanted it answered. He'd prayed for understanding if that was to be the case but was very glad it wasn't.

Julia opened the door, surprised to see Mark standing before her smiling like an idiot. "Thank you, Jesus!" came out through tears as she hugged her brother, ever thankful for him being in her life.

She hung on for a long moment. All the years of worry he'd put her through seemed to be fading into the past, gone like a bad dream with the first rays of morning. She'd prayed hard for him during those years. Sometimes she had to separate herself from him physically, but she never left him in her prayer life. She was thankful to find out that Aunt Merry had been praying during those years too. Now she joined Aunt Merry in praying for Jessi. The final ending had yet to be seen.

Mark pulled away first. "We have to celebrate, sis. I'm taking you out to dinner. No amount of protesting is going to work. It's final. You've cooked for me so much lately; it's your turn to be treated. Where do you want to go?"

"Well, since you put it like that, I want a chimichanga. How does Mexican sound?"

"Mmm...great. I haven't had that in ages. Can I use your phone before we leave? I need to call Bill and some of the guys from prayer group. They are going to want to know how everything turned out."

"Sure, go ahead. I need a few minutes to get cleaned up, anyway." Julia disappeared down the hallway to change.

Mark made his phone calls, letting the guys know his good news. They offered all sorts of encouragement, and everyone seemed genuinely happy for him. He and Julia made their way downtown to her favorite authentic Mexican restaurant. They talked mainly about the future and how they envisioned things to come.

Julia had her own good news. "Mark, I've decided to go with you to Wisconsin. I've done nothing but pray since we first discussed it, and I have a positive feeling about it. I believe it is God's will for me to move on. This place holds so many memories for me, both good and bad. I feel like I too need a fresh start. Do you think you could handle being so close to your sis?"

"Do you really mean it?" he went on without waiting for her answer. "This keeps getting better and better. Yes, yes, I can more than handle it, sis. I wasn't sure how I was going to make it on my own. At least here I have you, Bill, Aunt Merry, and the church supporting me. There I'm going to have no one, and the only adult I will know doesn't want to be in the same room as me."

They planned their move to coordinate with Julia selling her house. It might mean moving a couple of weeks later, but it would also be the answer to how he was getting to Wisconsin, seeing as he couldn't drive, and where he would live once he got there. Until Julia found a house, they would share an apartment. They went on for a couple of hours, talking and finalizing their plans.

Jessi curled up in her room with Aunt Merry's journals. Aunt Merry was at Mabel's house, and Olivia had been invited to spend the night with a friend from church, so Jessi had some free time to sit and read. She had been looking forward to reading them again and had just been too busy to do them any justice. She picked up where she had left off. The next entry was dated Tuesday, October 8, 1963:

> Lester and I went walking after church on Sunday. He held my hand, and we walked down by the creek. I loved having him close to me. We talked about all sorts of things. He told me what he wants to do with his life. He's hoping to go to college in the next year, if he saves enough money. His dad wants him to stay and work the farm, but he doesn't want to. He wants to be an engineer and work and live in the city. It sounds so exciting. I haven't given much thought to leaving our little country town, but given the right circumstances, I'd do it in a heartbeat, especially if they would include Lester. I think of Lester every night before I go to bed. I think I'm in love. Meredith.

"Who is Lester, and why haven't I ever heard of him?" Jessi asked herself out loud. She continued reading through the entries, some of which were just normal day-to-day events of a teenager, and then others, like this one, really surprised her.

>Wednesday, December 11, 1963
>
>I can't believe my dad said yes. Lester and I are going to the movies on Saturday night. Of course, we're really not going to the movies. Lester was invited to this really groovy party, and he's taking me. Of all the girls Lester could ask, he asked me. I can't believe my luck. I must be the luckiest girl in the world. I found a great hiding place for my journal now, as I dare not let anyone see it.

...

>Sunday, December 15, 1963
>
>I had to pretend being sick today for church. I felt so sick after last night. I got in late, and mom and dad were already in bed, thank heavens, because one look at me and they would have known that I had managed to get into something bad. As it was, this morning I had to make up an excuse as to why I couldn't go to church. I told them Lester bought me something to eat after the movie and it must have been bad. They believed me. I thought for sure I was found out. Nope. They completely believed me and told me to just rest and it would probably pass. Yeah, it'll pass. I'm not sure that I'll ever try that again. A guy at the party had some joints that his cousin brought when he was visiting from California. At first I didn't want to try the joint that was being passed around, but Lester told me he wouldn't have invited me if he thought I'd still be acting like a baby. So I gave in, and for a while it was great. We were drinking beer and passing around the joint. I felt so grown up and cool. Then my

stomach started hurting, and I started throwing up. Yuck. Lester took me home right away. I can't believe I acted like such a baby. No one else was sick at the party. He probably won't ever ask me out again! I'm so mad at myself. Why can't I just be more grown up? Ugh!

Jessi closed the journal, not sure how much more she could take for the night. This was a side of her aunt she could never have imagined. Why was her aunt letting her read these? Why would anyone want someone else to read about the skeletons in her closet? Jessi headed downstairs and put tea water on and waited for her aunt.

When Merry walked through the door, she could tell that Jessi had something on her mind. She bent down to give her niece a kiss. "How are you, dear?"

She started busying herself with the tea, knowing that whatever was on Jessi's mind would come out when she had sorted it out herself.

"I was reading your journals. For what reason could you possibly want me to read them? I'm just surprised by what I'm reading, and even more so that me reading them is okay with you."

Jessi looked downright troubled.

Merry sat down opposite Jessi and took her hands in her own. "Sweetheart, I want you to know firsthand that the perfection you see in me is just not so, and if reading about my past is going to help you do that, then so be it. I've tried to tell you that I too have made mistakes in my life, but you refuse to believe me. This way there can be no question. Oh, don't look so down. There isn't all bad in those journals. Some very good things happened too. You'll just have to keep reading to find out what."

Merry gave Jessi the best "wouldn't you like to know" look she could muster up and hoped it worked. They continued to talk a while until they both started yawning. Each woman closed her bedroom door, lost in her own world of thought, Jessi wondering if she really even knew the woman down the hall, and Aunt Merry on her knees, desperately

until forever   113

praying that Jessi would continue reading. It would be a long time before sleep came to either woman.

19

Olivia woke up and looked at her surroundings, startled, until she remembered she had spent the night with Bethany, her friend from church. Today was going to be a fun day, and she couldn't wait to get started. She could smell breakfast, and it smelled really good, so she nudged Bethany, who was sleeping in the twin bed next to her own. Bethany's mom, Mrs. Bowers, had promised to make homemade waffles with strawberries for breakfast. Bethany had a beautiful bedroom. She had two beds in her room, both decorated with pink and white polka dots, a white nightstand in between, and pretty matching curtains. She even had a seat that had a pink cushion on it by the window. She had a big white dollhouse with lots of furniture and dolls to play with, and there were pretty pictures on the walls of ballerinas. As far as Olivia was concerned, it was a dream bedroom, kind of like the one she slept in at Aunt Merry's house, her mom's old room. Olivia pushed Bethany even harder. "Hey, come on; wake up. I'm hungry, and I can smell breakfast."

Bethany's eyes slowly opened, and she rubbed them with the backs of her hands. "I don't want to get up." She groaned before slowly swinging her legs to one side of the bed.

Olivia had always been the type of kid who would take off running the minute her feet hit the floor. Bethany was clearly not like that. Olivia walked over to her and looked closely at her friend. "My mom wakes up looking like you do, all grumpy. Do you need to go downstairs and drink some coffee before we can discuss our day?"

Bethany looked at Olivia like she was a crazy person. "Are you kidding? I'm not allowed to drink coffee. I'm just a kid, like you."

Olivia stood and walked to the door then turned and looked at Bethany. "Well, you need it, just the same. Can we go downstairs now?"

Bethany grumbled and followed Olivia downstairs to the kitchen. Mrs. Bowers, who was used to Bethany's morning moods, was surprised to see the girls awake and entering the kitchen. "Wow, you mean I don't have to go up and drag you out of bed? I thought for sure, as late as you two were up, I'd be dumping cold buckets of water on you."

Olivia laughed.

Bethany scrunched her face and said, "Not funny."

Both girls sat down at the table, and soon Mr. and Mrs. Bowers and Bethany's little brother joined them. They bowed their heads, and Mr. Bowers said grace. After breakfast, they headed off to church in the family's minivan.

Olivia had never been to church so much in her whole life. She had been going with Aunt Merry every Sunday since they came. Now she was going with her friend and her family. Did everyone here go to church? She wondered why they never went to church in Wisconsin. She'd have to ask her mother about it.

Olivia liked being with Bethany and her family, even if Bethany was a grump in the morning. It was easy to pretend that she was a part of a real family with a mom and a dad and even a brother and sister. She hummed all the way to church thinking about the things she'd learned so far, things about Jesus. She would have to ask Aunt Merry about him. She would know about Jesus, since she talked about him so much. She sat and listened to a man talking up front. Bethany called him "pastor." She wasn't sure if that was his name or what. It seemed odd to not call him Mr. Pastor, but Olivia did as she was told and just called him pastor.

After "pastor" got done talking, everyone stood up and sang some songs. Olivia didn't know the songs they sang, so she just looked around at the people. She was looking for Aunt Merry but hadn't seen her yet. Maybe when everyone sat down again she would find her. After the singing it was time for her and Bethany to go to class; this was her favorite part. She liked her teacher and liked listening to the stories. They always made something fun and had cookies for a snack. She followed Bethany out of the big room and into the hallway to their class. On the way out, she saw Aunt Merry and waved to her. Aunt Merry smiled and waved back.

Ms. Shelly, as she liked to be called, taught the five- and six-year-old girls' class at the First Christian Church of Oklahoma City. She had twelve girls in her class and enjoyed teaching them both Bible stories and the lessons that could be learned from them, and lessons for everyday life, like how to be a good friend. The past few weeks, Olivia Jensen had been in her class, and she was glad to see her again this morning. The child had such a thirst for the knowledge of Jesus, and she wasn't shy about asking questions. She had yet to give her heart to the Lord, but if her quest for knowledge was any indication, it wouldn't be long. Shelly knew her aunt well and liked her immensely, as she was one of her mother's best friends and praying partners. Her mother, Judy, didn't talk much about their prayer meetings, but she did give Shelly the good news if someone they were praying for found faith. Shelly, like Judy, rejoiced with the group.

Shelly greeted the children. "Good morning, class."

"Good morning, Ms. Shelly," the children responded, not quite in unison.

"Before we get started, I have a question for you. Who remembers what tomorrow is?"

Everyone's hand but Olivia's shot up in the air. One of the girls couldn't wait to be called upon, so she answered out loud, "Vacation Bible School starts tomorrow!"

Shelly smiled. While trying to get the children ready for real school and reinforcing the simple courtesy rules from school, she oftentimes found their excitement too much for them to contain. "Yes, that's right.

Tomorrow we start Vacation Bible School. How many of you are going to be coming?" Once again all the hands but Olivia's shot into the air.

Shelly decided to talk to Merry about Olivia attending Vacation Bible School as soon as church was over. With everything else going on in her life, and the fact that she didn't work in the children's department anymore, Merry might not be aware that it was starting tomorrow. "I'm so glad that so many of you are coming tomorrow. Remember, it starts at nine thirty and ends at noon. Don't forget to tell your moms and dads, okay?"

All the kids eagerly said they wouldn't forget, and Shelly started in on the Sunday school lesson. "Okay, girls, it's time for our story. Today's lesson is about friends in the Bible. The first friends we are going to talk about are David and Jonathan. Before I tell you about David and Jonathan, I wonder if some of you could tell me what you think makes a good friend? How do you know if someone is your friend?"

The girls began raising their hands one by one. Emily thought that being nice was important. Bethany looked at Olivia and said that a real friend would let you sleep as long as you wanted. Chelsea said that sharing was very important. All the girls gave very good virtues of a friend.

"Those are all very good answers. I have friends who are all of those things—they are nice, they share, and another thing they do that is very important to me is they love me, and I love them very much. I know they love me because when I am sad they try to make me happy, and when I laugh they laugh with me. They care about me and my life. Not everyone cares about our lives like our friends do, do they? That's what was special about David and Jonathan in the Bible. They were very best friends who loved each other very much."

Ms. Shelly went on and told the story of David and Jonathan before David became king, including the times Jonathan saved David's life from King Saul, Jonathan's father.

"I'm going to tell you about someone else in the Bible who wants to be everyone's friend. Can anybody guess who that might be?"

Most of the girls, having been in church most of their lives, guessed whom Ms. Shelly was talking about.

"That's correct. Jesus wants to be everyone's friend. But there's something that makes him very sad. Can anyone tell me what that is?" The girls were pretty silent on this one. Ms. Shelly continued. "Jesus gets very sad when people don't want to be his friend."

Krista, a very sensitive child, was close to tears. She couldn't understand why someone would not want to be Jesus's friend and asked, "Why wouldn't someone want to be friends with Jesus? He's my very best friend."

"Well, there are different reasons that people don't want to be Jesus's friend. First, they might not believe in Jesus because they haven't ever seen him. They don't have what we call faith. Faith is when you believe in something that you can't see. Like Jesus. We can feel in him our hearts, and we can feel his love inside us, but we can't see him, right? But we believe in him because we have faith. Another reason some people don't believe Jesus is because of pride. Pride is not being able to accept help, and there are people who don't want any help from Jesus or anybody else. Do you think there are things that you can do to help people believe in Jesus?"

All the girls nodded yes.

"That's right; there are some things that you can do. First, you can tell people about Jesus so they can learn to have faith and believe. Second, and this should be very easy for all of you, you can do something nice for someone. This shows them that it's okay to be helped, and it will quietly lead them to Jesus. I want each of you to think of something nice you can do this week for someone who you think might not know Jesus. Have you thought of someone yet?" The girls each nodded. "Okay, I want you to do something nice for them, like take them cookies you baked or pick some flowers for them or anything nice you can think of. There are many things you can do, and I want you to tell me next Sunday who you picked and what you did for them. Okay?"

All the girls got excited and started talking among themselves about their assignment for next week as they headed to the work table to make their art project.

It wasn't long before the bell rang and church was over. After all the kids were picked up from class, Shelly found Merry talking with her mother and asked if she would be bringing Olivia to Vacation Bible School. Merry didn't make any promises but said she would ask Jessi and do her best to get Olivia there.

The next morning, Ms. Shelly found Olivia sitting at the table, ready to learn more about having a friend like Jesus.

20

Monday after work Mark headed to Merry's house to visit with Olivia. He found her sitting on the front steps with her face cradled in her hands. "Hi there. Penny for your thoughts?"

Olivia looked up at him. Not recognizing the phrase, she asked, "Penny for my what?"

Mark smiled at his daughter. "It's just a different way of asking what you are thinking about."

"Oh." Olivia was quiet for a moment, thinking about how to answer her dad. She'd had a lot to think about lately with Sunday school being yesterday and Vacation Bible School today. She was learning a lot about Jesus and how good he was, but she didn't understand how he could be in her heart. How did he get there? She felt like she was missing something but didn't want her friends to make fun of her if she asked. Maybe her dad would know.

"Well, we are talking about Jesus in Sunday school, and I don't understand how he could live in my heart. Everybody at church has Jesus living in their hearts." She looked down at her chest and back at her father. "I want him in my heart too, but I don't know how he gets in there."

Mark almost laughed with joy but held back because of the seriousness with which Olivia asked the question and the tears that already threatened to pour down from her frustration. "I believe I can help you with that. All you have to do is ask him to come in and live there. You can't see him, but once you ask him, he'll come right in and live in your heart too."

"Really? Just like that? But how will I know that he came into my heart?"

"Well, you will feel really happy on the inside. And you'll know that Jesus is the one who is making you feel that way. It's like he's smiling inside of us, and it makes us smile too."

"Can I ask him now?"

"You sure can. Do you want me to pray with you?"

Olivia nodded her head.

Mark began to pray with his daughter. "Jesus, we thank you for being here with us today. Thank you for living on earth and loving us so much that you would die on a cross for us so we can live with you forever in heaven. You came back to life so death couldn't keep us, your creation, from you any longer. Olivia, you can ask Jesus to come into your heart now."

Olivia continued in her childlike way. "Jesus, please live in my heart. I want you to smile in me 'cause sometimes I'm sad, and you will make me happy. I want to live with you in heaven forever, Jesus. Please come into my heart and live there."

Olivia looked up at her father, who smiled back at her and nodded his head. Both ended the prayer at the same time. "Amen."

Mark hugged his daughter tight, and when he pulled away she had a huge smile on her face.

"It's true, Daddy. I can feel him smiling inside me, and it's making me smile too!" Olivia jumped up and ran into the kitchen. Mark followed close behind. "Aunt Merry, Jesus is living in my heart. I prayed, and now he is in my heart."

Merry looked from her great-niece to Mark and back again. Tears of joy filled her eyes. Another prayer answered. She wouldn't be able to wait until she and the others met to let them know. If the angels in heaven were rejoicing, then the prayer partners would want to be rejoicing too.

Merry bent down to Olivia's level and gave her a giant hug. "Oh, baby, you have made me the happiest aunt in the world today. I'm so proud of you."

Olivia ran to find her mother.

Mark and Merry looked at one another, both instinctively wanting to follow Olivia to find out what Jessi's reaction would be. She wouldn't dissuade Olivia from her newfound faith, Merry was quite certain of that, but she probably wouldn't exactly be jumping for joy either. Neither she nor Mark wanted to intrude, so they patiently waited for Olivia to return. The look on her face would tell them all they needed to know.

Olivia found her mom upstairs in her room with one of Aunt Merry's journals. She knocked on the door like her mother had taught her to do.

"Mommy, can I come in?"

Jessi looked up from her reading. "Yes, sweetheart. I was just doing some reading. What have you been up to today? I thought your dad was coming over?"

"He's here now. But I wanted to tell you something." Olivia wasn't sure if her mother would be excited for her like her dad and Aunt Merry were, but she wanted to tell her anyway.

Jessi couldn't tell if what she was about to be told was good or bad. At first glance, she'd thought Olivia was excited, but now she looked a little apprehensive. "Why don't you come over here and sit on my lap. Then you can tell me whatever you'd like, okay?"

Olivia walked to her mother and climbed on her lap. She looked up at her mother and couldn't contain the smile any longer. "Oh, Mommy, I asked Jesus to come into my heart, and he did! I'm so happy inside." Olivia was grinning broadly at her mother as she looked up in expectation of praise.

Jessi managed to create the expected response to the news her daughter had just shared. "Oh sweetheart, that's such good news. I'm very happy you have Jesus living in your heart." Not wanting to say any more than was necessary, Jessi reminded Olivia that her father was downstairs waiting for her.

After Olivia returned to the kitchen, where Aunt Merry and Mark were waiting for her, Jessi sat back and closed her eyes. It was hard to ignore God's existence while she was in Aunt Merry's house. When at home, she could stay busy and remain a loner, therefore keeping most everyone at arms' distance, especially those who believed God was good and only wanted what was best for his children. No matter what Aunt Merry or Mark and now Olivia believed, Jessi could never understand or love a God who could take a small child from his mother. Every time she faced the God issue, she also faced Ethan's death. Not getting over and finding forgiveness in the latter would keep her from finding true peace with the former. She stayed in her room for most of the afternoon. Mark and Aunt Merry were sure to be celebrating with Olivia, and she didn't feel like taking part in a celebration.

Upon returning to the kitchen, Olivia found Aunt Merry busy making a special dessert for supper. She said today was a very special occasion and she was making Olivia's favorite treat. Mark and Olivia made their way to the living room, where Mark told her stories of Jesus and the disciples. Olivia had five years of Bible stories to catch up on, and Mark was more than willing to be the one to educate her. They started out with Adam and Eve and the garden. Each time they met thereafter, there would be a new story for Olivia to learn.

As Merry put the chocolate-filled cupcakes in the oven to bake, she hummed a joyful song of thanksgiving to the Lord, praising him for his faithfulness.

21

Jessi walked through the grocery store, wanting to pick up something for she and Olivia to make for dinner. Aunt Merry was going to be gone most of the evening, and Jessi wanted to surprise her with supper to thank her for having Olivia and her for the majority of the summer. She had also invited her mother, as their relationship was improving although still strained at times. She and Olivia would be leaving for home on Sunday, right after Olivia returned from church, so it was time to start getting things packed and ready. The return home would be much harder on Olivia than it would be on her. Olivia enjoyed the excitement that being among friends and family brought. In fact, she almost thrived on it. Jessi could see that Olivia had never looked better, but there was nothing she could do. It was the end of July, and school would be starting in few weeks. She had to get back and get ready for the new year. She was deep in thought, not really putting anything in her basket, when she heard a distinct voice from her past.

"Well, hello there. Fancy seeing you here."

Jessi looked up and right into the eyes of Doctor Phillips.

When she didn't say anything, he continued. "I was surprised to see you wandering around here looking lost. Last I heard you were living in Wisconsin."

She realized he was talking about the empty basket that she'd been carrying around when she followed his gaze to her hands. She smiled. "Hi. It would seem that way wouldn't it?" She'd always liked Doc as a person, and he'd gotten to be her friend over time. "And yes, you're right. I did move to Wisconsin. Olivia and I are just here visiting, and we'll actually be going home in a few days. I thought I would make my aunt supper tonight to thank her for having us this summer. I obviously haven't found anything yet. The other problem is she's such a great cook. What could I possibly make that would in the slightest way impress her?"

Eric Phillips laughed. He had come to respect the woman standing before him. For the longest time, she had given him a reason to get up in the morning. Yes, he had his work, but it usually didn't put a smile on his face like she did. Each time he would schedule some time with her to talk about her son's condition, or in later days in passing, she would give him something good to think about for the day. He was hoping she might do that again. Of course, she had mentioned she was leaving, but an evening with her would be nice.

"Well, you could take her out to eat instead. For those of us who are not culinary experts, it's usually the best way."

Jessi pondered the idea. "You know, I didn't think of that. She rarely goes out to eat, and she's always cooking. That's a good idea." Jessi smiled at him.

Eric decided this was the best possible moment to ask, and if he didn't it would be his own fault. "Speaking of going out to eat, would you like to go to dinner with me Friday night? I know this great place, and I would love to see you again. Especially since you are leaving soon."

Jessi had never considered dating in the years since Ethan's accident, and then with Olivia, there just hadn't been time, not that she would allow herself to get close to anyone else ever again. But what harm could come of this? She respected this man, and there would be nothing wrong with having dinner with a friend. Anyway, in five days she was leaving for her home, which was eight hundred miles away. Nothing could ever come of it, and it would be nice to have some male companionship.

"Yes." Jessi felt a little jolt, like she was coming back to life. "I'll go with you to dinner Friday. Should we meet?"

"No, I'll pick you up. Just write down your address. It can't be too far away from my place if we're shopping at the same grocery store."

Jessi wrote down her address and phone number in case something came up, and Eric promised to pick her up at seven o'clock on Friday night. Since Jessi's cooking for Aunt Merry had turned into taking her out to eat, she bid Eric good-bye and left. She definitely had a little spring to her step. She was going out on a date with a doctor, no less. Wow! Not that she really considered it a date. Just friends. But it still felt good to be asked. It made her day.

Aunt Merry thought it particularly odd when Jessi actually entered the house whistling. "You seem to be in a good mood. Anything happen that I should know about?"

"Oh, nothing much. I went grocery shopping to make you a thank-you dinner, and I ran in to Dr. Phillips. Do you remember him?" Without waiting for her answer, Jessi continued on. "Well, I was having a hard time deciding what to make when he suggested I just take you out to dinner. I thought it was a great idea, so tonight, instead of Olivia and I cooking, we'll be taking you out to thank you. That will keep you out of the kitchen, even when it comes to clean up."

"Oh, phooey, Jessi. You don't have to do anything to thank me. I love having you two here. You know that."

"Don't try to talk me out of it 'cause it isn't going to work. Is there anything special you would like?" Jessi poured her a tall glass of tea and waited for Aunt Merry to answer.

"Oh, I don't know. I don't go out to eat often. Surprise me; how about that?"

"Be ready to be surprised. By the way, will you watch Olivia Friday evening? I have been asked to go out to dinner with Dr. Phillips." Jessi turned to Aunt Merry, grinning like a little school girl.

Aunt Merry opened her mouth to speak but had no idea what to say, so she closed it again. She just couldn't comprehend Jessi going out on a date.

Jessi watched her aunt's reaction to her news and couldn't help but chuckle to herself. She came to her rescue. "It's only as friends, Aunt Merry. He knows I'm leaving this weekend to head home. Don't make anything of it. It means nothing."

Still in a state of "wow," Aunt Merry finally responded. "Sure, I can watch Olivia. That will give us a little bit of alone time before you guys head home. What time are you leaving?"

"He's picking me up at seven. I have no idea where we're going or what time I'll be back. I hope that's okay."

"That's not a problem. You just go and have yourself a good time. Olivia will be just fine with me. It's about time you get out with other people your age and have some fun."

That night when Aunt Merry returned from her church planning committee, Jessi took the three of them out to eat. They had a wonderful time all dressed up, and since they all loved Italian, they went to a nice Italian restaurant, where Aunt Merry made a fuss about the prices. "Jessi, this is going to cost you a fortune. We could have stayed at home, and I could have made spaghetti. I should have put my foot down about this."

"Aunt Merry, here I am trying to thank you properly, and all you can do is complain. Is that how you show gratitude?"

Aunt Merry had the good manners to stop fussing over the cost of things and just enjoy the evening. "All right, you win. How can I argue with that? I've never eaten at this restaurant, and I have no idea what to get. Everything looks so good."

Jessi was glad her aunt was enjoying the evening. She'd have to thank Eric on Friday night for his suggestion. If it weren't for him, she'd be home trying her hand at some new dish, probably burning it and then ordering pizza. This was so much better.

The evening ended with tiramisu and coffee for the adults and ice cream for Olivia. They all went home full and ready to relax. Olivia put on her pajamas and headed to her room. Jessi followed to tuck her in, but when she entered she found Olivia kneeling beside her bed, praying.

"Jesus, thank you for this day. Thank you for giving me a mommy and a daddy. Also, thank you for Aunt Merry. Aunt Merry and Daddy say it's best to be thankful before I ask for stuff, so I have more to thank you for. Thank you for my new doll and my friends. Thank you for Sunday school and Vacation Bible School, where I learned about you. Do you think that is enough now? I'm just going to ask for two things. First, can you make my mommy love my daddy again? I want us to be a family. If you could do that I would thank you for it afterward. Also, and most important, can you make Mommy love you? She would be happy inside like me if she loved you, 'cause you would smile inside her, and then she would be happy too. Thank you, Jesus. Amen."

Jessi quietly watched her daughter climb into bed and then walked over to tuck her in. She sat down on the edge of the bed and bent down to kiss her good night. "Do you know how much I love you, Olivia?"

Olivia nodded and replied, "I love you too, Mommy."

"I know you do, sweetie. I heard your prayer, and I want to thank you for praying for me."

"You mean you're not mad at me? I thought you might be mad at me if you heard me pray. That's why I didn't wait for you to come. I didn't want you to be mad at me."

"No, Olivia, I'm not mad at you. How could I be mad at you when I love you so much, huh? But yet, I don't want you to be disappointed when you don't get what you prayed for. I'm not going to love your daddy like a mommy is supposed to love a daddy. Can you understand that?"

"No, Mommy, I don't understand. Why don't you love Daddy anymore. Did he do something to make you not love him?"

"Oh, sweetheart, sometimes things happen that make mommies and daddies stop loving each other. Grown-up things that little girls don't need to know about."

"Am I the reason that you don't love each other anymore? Did I do something?"

Jessi pulled her daughter in for a close hug. "No, baby, you didn't do anything. What happened with me and your daddy happened before you were even born. So see, it doesn't have anything to do with you. We both love you very much, so how could it be you?" Jessi smiled to reassure Olivia that her and Mark's problems were their own and had nothing to do with Olivia. She hoped it would answer, at least temporarily, the questions Olivia had about their divorce. She wasn't ready to sit down and tell Olivia about Mark's part in Ethan's death. She had hoped that Olivia would be older when they had to have that discussion. She'd put her off as long as possible.

After reading Olivia a story and tucking her in, Jessi made her way to her own room. She wasn't done with the journals yet and wasn't sure if Aunt Merry would let her take them with her to Wisconsin. Wearing a light pink summer nightgown, Jessi settled into the easy chair to read the next entries. It seemed Aunt Merry led a very busy and at times, a very rebellious life. Jessi wanted to know more about this side of her aunt, the side that Jessi would never have guessed existed.

> Friday, January 3, 1964
>
> Lester bought me a beautiful necklace for Christmas. He said I was his girl. I couldn't believe it. I was so happy I cried. We spent the whole day together at Lester's house New Year's day, and Lester said it was time I start thinking about becoming a real woman. I didn't know what he was talking about, but if it means Lester will love me, I'm more than willing to be a real woman. Ha! Me? A real woman? Yeah, right. Lester said he wanted to show me something, so we left and went for a drive. He took me to the lookout, and he parked. I was a little scared. I'd heard of

this place, but I'd never been to it. Lester told me not to be afraid. He just wanted to spend a little time with me without anyone else around. He held me, and he kissed me... a lot! I was a little nervous when his hands started roaming around a little too much for my comfort, but he said that was part of becoming a woman. I suppose if it's what Lester wants, I should at least think about it, especially seeing I'm supposed to be his girl and he is a grown man. A grown man wouldn't want to be with a baby who was afraid. He told me to decide if I want to grow up or not. I'm not sure what to do. Good night, diary.

Jessi closed the journal and went to bed, not quite sure what to think about what she had just read. Confused, she'd opened the curtains to her bedroom window and lay in bed looking at the stars. Did God really create all of this? How else could all of nature come to be? Chance couldn't have a part in any of creation. The stars in the skies were an accident? She could never believe it. They were too beautiful. Jessi fell asleep thinking about God and his hand in the lives of those around her. If only she could find out why he didn't love her and answer her prayers. What was wrong with her?

She slept fitfully and tossed and turned. She dreamed of a big, bad, ugly, supreme being who was chasing her with a big stick and whipping her with it whenever he felt like it. Her perception of God was changing; at least she was starting to acknowledge him again.

22

Mark entered Merry's house on Friday afternoon to find Olivia sulking on the couch. "Hey, what's up with the long face?"

"Mom is going out on a date tonight, that's what."

Mark took in a sharp breath. He didn't know Jessi was dating someone. He'd have thought Aunt Merry would have told him if she was. "She's going out on a date tonight? With who?"

"Her doctor friend. He's taking her out to dinner. I don't want her to go on a date with a man. I want you and her to be my mommy and daddy together. Why can't *you* take her on a date? This isn't fair. I asked God to make all of us a family. Why isn't he doing that?"

"Sometimes when we ask God to do something, he has a different plan in mind. We have to learn to trust him because he knows best for us. I know it's hard to trust him sometimes, but we have to try. Can you do that? Can you try to trust him?"

"Why would God want something different? If he wants what's best for me, then this would be it. I just know it would." Olivia started crying in earnest now, her sobs breaking Mark's heart.

"Can I tell you secret, Olivia? You have to promise that you will never tell anyone, okay?"

Olivia nodded.

"I pray for the same thing as you. I want us to be a family again too. But we have to patient with your mom, okay? And we can't give her a hard time for going out on a date. Deal?"

"Deal!" Olivia jumped up and hugged her dad. "You want us to be a family too? Now I know God is going to answer our prayers. I just know it!"

Jessi had just gotten out of the bath when she heard Mark's voice downstairs. He wanted to see Olivia before they headed out on Sunday. She would never have thought he'd have kept any of his promises, but he had. It still amazed her to see the changes in him. She wasn't ready to admit it to anyone that he'd indeed changed, but she knew it to be true. You don't live with a man and be his wife and not know when the man changes. She remembered the uneasy feelings she had had with Mark when he'd want to be alone with Ethan. Those feelings were nowhere to be found now when he was with Olivia. She actually trusted him. He loved Olivia; that was obvious. He was giving up everything he'd ever known to be close to her. She just hoped that his wishes didn't go further than spending time with his daughter. He would have to eventually realize that there was no chance that they would ever be together again. Those days were over. She'd come to tolerate him in her life and even appreciate him for being a good father to Olivia, but she didn't think she would ever forgive him for taking Ethan away from her. She would never be able to get over that.

Jessi set about the task of getting ready for her first date since she had divorced Mark. True, it wasn't a real date, but it didn't hurt to dream a little either. She chose the nicest outfit she had hanging in her closet—cream-colored slacks with a turquoise shell patterned blouse. She wore pumps to match and pulled her long hair into a French knot, tied up to keep the hair off her neck. In this heat, she didn't care for her hair sticking to the back of her neck. She carefully applied her makeup. After putting on a coral shade of lipstick, she made her way downstairs.

Mark and Olivia were sitting at the dining room table playing a game of Sorry. Mark stopped midsentence when she walked into his view.

"Wow, you look great." A deep feeling of jealousy swept over him, one he did not expect. He knew she was preparing for her date; he just had no idea until he saw her how strongly he was opposed to the idea. He tried to get his feelings off of display and back into hiding, where they were supposed to be. "Olivia said you had a date tonight. Have fun."

The lightheartedness with which he spoke belied his true feelings. She was his wife. "Till death do us part" was the vow, and as far as he could tell they were both alive and well. Especially Jessi. She'd never looked so good to him. Then again, his past life never allowed him to appreciate her to the fullness, the way a husband was supposed to love his wife. If ever he had the chance, he would show her just how much she was loved.

The doorbell rang promptly at seven. Dr. Phillips was courteous to Mark but a bit reserved and not overly friendly. Mark supposed the good doctor knew all about him and his past sins. He had it coming. How people treated him would be an issue all his life. He had no illusions about that. Mark watched his ex-wife walk out the door. It took all the control he could muster, but didn't let his jealousy show. In this world she wasn't his anymore. He lifted his concerns to the Lord. *Lord, please protect her. She's mine, Lord, I know this is your will. It's taken me a long time to know your will in this area of my life, and no matter what I have to endure until your will is accomplished, I will stand fast. Lord, help me in preparing to be her husband once again. Help me to love her as I should and be all she needs me to be. Father, I ask that you show her all your glory. Let her find her peace in you, oh Lord.*

Mark turned his attention back to his daughter and the game they were playing. She had become the light of his life in such a short time. Soon, she would be leaving, and he wouldn't be able to see her until he moved to Wisconsin at the end of the month. He would miss her. It would only be a month. He'd make it.

Eric had the door open for Jessi as she made her way to his car. She couldn't help but wonder if this was the good life, the life that she was intended for—riding in a Jaguar with the top down to a restaurant that she would never be able to afford on her own. She'd never known this kind of life, although she'd always wanted to. Going on a date with someone who was successful and prosperous was as foreign to her as traveling to the four corners of the world. She liked the feeling.

Eric watched Jessi and couldn't help but think she was missing out on her intended life. She was beautiful and classy without the hard edges that the wealthy oftentimes possessed. She could fit into his world nicely. While he loved the finer things in life, he didn't treasure things above people. That was the one thing that had always kept him on the ground with everyone else. He guessed that Jessi would be able to keep her head about her, even in a state of advantage.

"Nice car." Jessi felt the leather interior, how smooth it was. Did people really live this way? She'd been driving her used car for so long she didn't even know what it felt like to sit in the lap of luxury.

"Thanks. One of the tradeoffs for working thirty-hour shifts, not getting much sleep, and having absolutely no time for a social life. Although I have to admit, since I'm getting older, things have calmed down from what they used to be. I used to catch a couple hours' sleep at the hospital then start another long shift. Now at least I'm on a regular schedule. The only thing that throws that off now is unplanned emergency surgeries. They can last a while, and if it's toward the end of my regular day, well, it can get to be a long day. But enough about work. We're here to relax and enjoy the evening. I've made reservations for us at NIKZ at the Top. I was thinking a nice night out on the town would give you a nice ending to your visit."

Eric pulled up to the entrance of the building and opened Jessi's door for her before handing the keys to the attendant. They entered and took the elevator to the top floor, where the rotating restaurant was located. Jessi had never dined here, although she'd heard it was a beautiful way to see the city night lights. They were seated by the window. As she looked out over the city, she was amazed at how darkness with a touch of light could make even the dirtiest, seediest parts of the city look beautiful. Those who recommended the view were correct; it was stunning.

The wine steward appeared with their finest house wine. Before he could ask, Jessi spoke up. "Eric, I am fine with water. I would rather not have any wine." While never caring for alcohol to begin with, Jessi was adamantly against it since the accident. She was even uncomfortable being in someone else's presence when they drank. Knowing the circumstances surrounding her son's death, Eric was comfortable ordering bottled water for both of them. He then dismissed the wine steward.

He apologized, "I'm sorry, Jessi. I should have thought about that beforehand."

The waiter appeared with the menus and also told them of the house specials. They both took a few minutes to look over the menu. Eric asked if she was ready to order, and when she was he nodded to the waiter. The waiter approached the table, and Eric ordered for both of them. "We'll start with the baked Brie, then the lobster bisque. For the lady, grilled salmon with rice pilaf and garlic-sautéed vegetables. I will have your nine-ounce filet mignon, medium rare, with mushroom demi-glace, risotto, and asparagus."

The waiter collected their menus. "Very good choice. The salmon was flown in fresh this morning, and the filet has been aged to perfection. I'm sure you both will enjoy your meals." He left them both to their conversation and the constantly changing view of the city.

Eric watched Jessi. This environment suited her. She seemed very comfortable. "You were meant for this kind of lifestyle, you know that, don't you?"

Jessi had always dreamed of the perfect life, and yes, she had to admit it included being well enough off financially to never have to worry about anything. She smiled at Eric. He'd given her a taste of what it would be like to fulfill those dreams. "This is like another world for me, Eric. So different from what I am used to. I'm used to five-year-olds and their issues. I can open a great jar of spaghetti sauce and toss a mean salad. I have no idea what half the items on the menu are. Although, even *I* have to admit this is nice." She didn't want to give him any kind of hope, but it was hard to pretend she had no interest when on the inside she yearned for what she was seeing. The couple sitting closest to them was obviously very successful. The woman was dressed exquisitely and was wearing an absolutely beautiful necklace with a matching bracelet and earrings. She realized her interest was just a little too obvious when the woman looked over at her and smiled. Jessi could feel her face burning. Eric had watched the whole thing with amusement.

"Don't worry. She likes being looked at. That's why she wears what she is wearing. For the attention. You did not offend her."

So Eric had noticed too. Great. "I'm sorry. She just captured my attention. It would seem she has everything."

"You can never tell how happy a person is just by looking at them. You should know this, Jessi. She may look like she has it all, but what's going on inside of her or behind closed doors may not be all that pleasant. The clothes and the jewelry don't make the person. What's inside makes the person. It's a funny thing with people of wealth; oftentimes they use fine things to cover up everything that is not perfect in their lives. For some it may be a marriage held together by a Band-Aid, or a family torn apart by drugs or alcohol. Things are rarely what they appear to be, only a façade."

"I guess when you have been without money most of your life, you tend to see it as a fix all. But you're right. It just makes it easier to cover up everything that's not right."

"Oh, don't get me wrong. I'm not saying that it's wrong to have money. Obviously, I have spent a good deal of money on my vehicle, and I enjoy it. I work hard, and I enjoy nice things. Used properly, money is a great tool. We can't live in today's society without it. I'm just saying it's easy to get caught up in the trap of needing to personify perfection to everyone if money becomes the fix all in a person's life. What other people think becomes very important, and sometimes how people feel gets pushed to the wayside. Humility is often not a character trait of the rich." Eric laughed a little. "You know, this is not the conversation I planned for this evening."

The waiter appeared with the baked Brie and apples.

Jessi smiled and thanked the waiter. "Oh, really, and what conversation did you plan for this evening?" She helped herself to some of the appetizer.

"Well, I was hoping to convince you that you missed Oklahoma City way too much to live eight hundred miles away. I mean, look at all the ambiance that you are missing."

"Are you referring to the restaurant or the company?"

"Guilty. I guess a little of both. How does that sound?"

"Honestly? A little scary. This is the first time I've gone out with anyone since the accident and divorce, and I'm not ready to commit to anyone. I don't know that I'll ever be ready. Going with you tonight was a huge step for me."

Eric reached for her hand and squeezed it. "I'm sorry to pressure you, Jessi. That wasn't my intent. I truly am thankful for your friendship. I have missed you all these years. You were a bright spot in my days. I enjoyed talking with you. It's not often you meet someone who is just who they are no matter who they are around. I didn't feel the need to be anything but myself with you. I just miss your company. No strings attached." Eric couldn't help smirking and adding, "Although, if you ever change your mind, you know where to find me."

Jessi pushed her plate away, completely stuffed. The waiter appeared with the dessert menu, and Jessi just groaned. "You would have to carry me out of here on a gurney if I took another bite."

"I guess that means no. But thank you." Eric paid the bill and took Jessi's hand to help her to her feet.

"It was wonderful. Thank you." Jessi couldn't help but add, "I really enjoyed the ambiance, and not just the restaurant."

"You do have a sense of humor, Jessi. You also have a beautiful smile. I wish I could see it more often. Let's go, shall we?" The drive home was spent mostly in silence.

Eric walked her to the door and bent slightly and gave her a light kiss on the lips. "Thank you for a most wonderful evening, and I hope that you'll think of me once in awhile. Good night, Jessi." He turned and walked away, not giving her a chance to reply.

Jessi quietly slipped into the house. She made her way to her room and realized she'd had her fingers pressed to her lips, not moving them. Tears smeared her makeup and left a path down her cheeks. In all this time she'd not realized just how lonely she was. Except for a young child and an aging aunt, she was truly alone in this world. Not only alone, but lonely.

23

Jessi spent Saturday doing laundry and packing her and Olivia's things. It was the end of July, and it was time to go home. They were going to spend the day here with Aunt Merry, and after much begging and pleading by Olivia, Jessi promised they wouldn't leave until after supper on Sunday. Mark had said his good-byes the day before, promising that he would contact them as soon as he arrived in Wisconsin. He told Jessi that he would make up all the money he owed for child support. He wouldn't have been able to do anything about it while he was in prison, but he would help her as soon as he got a job, giving more than would normally be required of him.

Jessi was humming while she took all but their overnight bags to the car. Aunt Merry had wanted to ask Jessi all day about her time with Doctor Phillips. Finally she got up the nerve. "I take it from all the singing and the smiles that your date went well last night."

Jessi turned and grinned smugly at her aunt while continuing to hum as she worked.

"What kind of answer is that?" Not expecting a reply, Aunt Merry went to the kitchen to prepare a light lunch of grilled cheese and tomato soup. She'd already started a special good-bye supper, and she didn't want lunch ruining their appetite for supper.

When the sandwiches were ready, she called both Jessi and Olivia to the kitchen. Olivia asked for permission to eat in the garden with her dolls, which Aunt Merry quickly granted. Now she would have Jessi's undivided attention and get some answers. They both sat down at the table, Jessi still with that smirk on her face. "All right, that's it. My patience is running out. Tell me about last night."

Jessi almost burst out laughing at her aunt. "Okay, I'll tell you, although there really isn't much to tell. Nothing can come of it anyway. It just felt... well, nice." She continued on. "We went to NIKZ at the Top, and I ordered the fresh salmon. It was a very pleasant evening. I realized how much I've missed adult companionship. We talked for what seemed like hours, and then we came home. End of story."

Aunt Merry looked at her with skepticism. "Are you sure that's it?"

Jessi took the last bite of her sandwich and stood up and headed to the door. "What else could there be?" She grinned and walked through the door. She opened the door just enough to look around the corner to Aunt Merry sitting at the table. "Oh yeah, did I mention he kissed me good night?"

All Merry heard after that was laughter emanating from the living room. He kissed her good night? What did that mean? What was she thinking? Surely she wasn't seriously considering this relationship, was she? *Lord, this was not in my plan. What are you up to?* Merry continued with her supper preparations. The meat was marinating and the rolls were rising by the time Jessi came back into the kitchen for a drink.

"I just finished making some fresh iced tea." Aunt Merry nodded toward the pitcher sitting on the kitchen counter. "How are things going? Are you going to be able to fit everything in the car?"

Jessi grabbed a glass from the cupboard and filled it with ice and tea. "Yeah, I've got the front seat and the floorboard behind the driver's seat to fill up yet. Mom bought her way too much stuff. I won't have anything to get her for Christmas."

"I'm sure you'll find plenty. They have so much out in the stores these days. I really have no idea how we survived when we were kids.

No gadgets and television games. It was simple toys for us: a few board games and dolls. Boys were still able to play cops and robbers without being chastised for playing with guns. I remember Ethan would use anything that even remotely looked like a gun and use it. We didn't have to buy them for him. He came up with his own."

Merry smiled at Jessi. She rarely, if ever, brought up Ethan to her, but it seemed like the right time to do so. There were memories she didn't want to forget, and if she didn't talk about them or record them somehow, she would.

Jessi sat down at the table with her tea, and Aunt Merry poured herself a glass and after peeking in on Olivia, who was still outside, sat down with her.

"I still miss him, Aunt Merry. But I feel like I'm starting to move on with my life. Not just for my sake, mainly for Olivia's. She needs a mother."

"I'm thinking this is a good thing, Jess. You've given yourself more than enough time to mourn. He wouldn't want you to only remember the bad. He was too happy of a child for that. I remember he always wanted you to be happy. He hated to see you cry, and he'd try to make it all better."

Jessi smiled at the memories. "Yeah, he would stand in front of me and use his little chubby fingers to wipe the tears off my cheeks. Then he would ask where my boo-boo was and if he could kiss it and make it all better. He was so tenderhearted."

"Unlike some kids, he was always mindful of others and their feelings. You did a good job with him, Jessi. Just like you are doing with Olivia. You have a lot to be proud of."

"Thank you, Aunt Merry; that means a lot coming from you. It's been hard. I've raised Olivia as a single parent, and I was very close to being a single parent with Ethan. I always tried to make the decision that would be best for them, no matter how hard or painful it was. I've never understood how some people can be so selfish with their lives when it comes to their children. I mean, why do they have kids if they don't intend on doing their best by them?"

"Well, I'm glad your mom chose to have you. Even though she was a selfish person and didn't give you the time and energy that she should have, I wouldn't have you in my life if she hadn't had you. Maybe the fact that she did have you was the one unselfish thing she's ever done for you. Have you ever thought of it that way? It's always easy to see the negative. Sometimes it's not as simple to see things in a positive way."

"I guess I've never thought of that. I suppose if everything she'd done had been selfish, she would have aborted me. Then I wouldn't even be here." She didn't notice the painful look that crossed her aunt's face.

"I'm just glad that God brought you into my life, Jessi. He has given me the joy of my life, and that was you. You will always be the daughter I could never have. So never, ever think that you were unwanted. You were the most desired child in this world. You gave my life meaning. I've always felt that God's purpose or plan for my life was to be here for you. He loved you so much, and he knew that you would need me, so he made us family and bound us together with love. I love you, Jessi, more than any other earthly thing. I hope you know that."

"I do. I don't know what I would have done without you in my life. You were always there for me, even when I first came and was so angry at my parents for not wanting me. I took out all my anger on you, and I'm sorry for that. It didn't take me long to realize that things were going to be different. You never left me to my own care, and you did things for me that no one else had ever done. Even your simple motherly acts of making cookies for me after school were foreign to me. I'd never had anyone think of me or what I might like first. It was a different concept. I expected you to be like my parents. I never dreamed you would be more like my parent than either one of them would ever be. Thank you. I love you too."

Olivia came bounding in the door. "Mom, do we have to leave tomorrow? Why can't we stay? We could stay a little bit longer."

"No, Olivia, I need to get home and get ready for school. I have a lot of planning to do, and we also have to get you ready for school. You will be going to kindergarten this year, and we have to shop for school clothes and school supplies. We have a lot to do, and if we're going to get it all done, we have to get home. Now run upstairs and look under your bed to see if you got everything out to be packed. I'm sure there are some things hiding around here that you haven't found yet. If you don't look real good, they'll be left behind, and then you'll miss them."

Olivia ran out of the room and up the stairs. They could hear her traipsing around her room opening doors and closing them, looking for items that might be hidden.

Jessi started to head out to finish her own work but turned back to her aunt. "I've been meaning to ask you about the journals. I haven't finished them yet, but I know you probably don't want me to take them with me. I can finish them next summer when I come down if you'd like."

Aunt Merry shook her head. "No, you take them. I myself have something to talk with you about. I've been waiting all this time for an invitation to come to your house, and frankly, I'm tired of waiting. So I'm inviting myself. I'd like to come for Christmas. It gets to be so long between visits, and I miss the both of you so much that I've decided I can come your way once a year, so I get to see you more often. Not only that, but you are the only family I have, and Christmas gets to be so lonely without you."

"Oh, Aunt Merry, I'm sorry that I haven't thought of it myself. Of course I want you to come. We miss you too. I don't know why, but I thought you wouldn't want to come to our house. It's a lot smaller than here, but I'm sure we could make you comfortable. This will make leaving tomorrow so much easier on Olivia. She will be so happy. I am too, for that matter. We can have a real family Christmas. Can you stay for a while?"

"I was thinking three to four weeks. Would that be all right, or do you think you would get sick of me for that long?"

"That would be perfect. You will be there while I'm off for Christmas break, so we will have plenty of time together. You might not like the snow. It'll be pretty cold by that time of year. Do you think you can handle it?"

"I'll buy myself a nice warm coat and some new boots. You did say you have a fireplace, right?"

Jessi nodded yes.

"Then I'll be just fine tucked away in your little cozy house spending time with my two favorite people. I'm sure you'll be done with the journals by then, and I'll just bring them back home with me. How does that sound?"

Jessi wrapped her arms around the older woman's neck. "Perfect, just perfect. I can't wait."

Jessi went and changed the laundry one more time. One more load, and she was finished with that part of the packing. Tomorrow would be much easier on all of them now. Aunt Merry was coming for Christmas. She would tell Olivia at suppertime.

As she was checking the rolls, Aunt Merry was very pleased with how things were progressing. The hurt conjured up during their conversation was totally unintentional by Jessi, but it didn't change the pain it brought forth. They would be having a very different kind of talk when she came for Christmas. Jessi would be done with the journals for sure by then, and she would have some explaining to do. She never meant to hurt Jessi with the information she was giving her, but she would definitely feel a letdown and some disappointment in her aunt. But it had to be this way. She had to know that God loved the unworthy and that no one, no matter who they were, was worthy of God's love on their own.

Everyone continued to work through the afternoon. Jessi left to run some last-minute errands. She also stopped by the cemetery on her way to the store, her last good-bye until next year. She brought flowers and set them by his grave. "Hey, buddy, it's Mom. Olivia and I are headed home tomorrow, and I just wanted to come and say good-bye. Things are going good. Better than they have in a long while. I'm sure you'd be happy for me. I feel better, Ethan. I'm going to share everything about you with your sister. I'm even going to put out your pictures so she can get to know you too. She doesn't have any memories, so I will share all mine with her. I love you, Ethan."

Jessi spent a little more time sitting there reminiscing before she headed to the store to get the things she needed for the trip. Even these visits were getting easier.

Back at home, Aunt Merry and down-faced Olivia set the table and got everything ready for supper. "I'm going to miss you, Aunt Merry."

Jessi walked into the house smelling hot, baked rolls and teriyaki beef with roasted vegetables. It smelled wonderful and made her stomach rumble. She'd not realized how hungry she'd gotten while getting all her work done. Olivia looked so cute she had to laugh. As she walked in the dining room, Olivia, in a pint-size apron, was carrying a bowl of fresh green beans to the table. The sight of it reminded her of her own childhood and the meals that she used to help with. She'd end up with flour in her hair, on her face, and all over her clothes. It was more work to have her help than to have her play on her own, but Aunt Merry insisted she'd rather have her helping. It was no bother. She did have some wonderful memories, things she wouldn't trade for the world.

"It smells like it's time to eat. I hope so, 'cause I'm so hungry I could eat a horse."

Olivia, always the practical one, started laughing. "Mommy, but we're not having horse for supper. Aunt Merry made a different supper. It looks really good."

Sniffing again, Jessi commented, "It smells really good too! Is it time to eat?"

Aunt Merry walked into the dining room carrying a large platter with the beef and vegetables. "It sure is. We started putting everything on the table when we heard you pull in. I'm glad you're hungry, 'cause I'm sending you off with a good meal to hold you over till I come."

"You won't hear me arguing. You are the best cook around."

Everyone took their places at the table, and Aunt Merry asked Olivia to say grace. "Dear God, thank you for all this good food that Aunt Merry and me made. Thank you for my mommy and my daddy, and thank you for letting us be a family again. Jesus's name, amen." Olivia looked up and grinned at her mother. Jessi just shook her head.

While Jessi was filling Olivia's plate, she told her the news. "Guess what, Olivia? Aunt Merry is going to come and spend Christmas with us."

"Really? Is it true? Oh, Aunt Merry, you've never come to visit us before. This is going to be so much fun. If there is snow, do you want to go sledding with me? It's really fun. We can go really fast down the hill. We can build a snowman too. Have you ever built a snowman before?" Actually giving Merry time to answer, she plopped a bite of beef into her mouth.

"Yes, it's really true. But I don't think I would make a very good sledding partner. I can watch you, though. How does that sound?"

Olivia smiled in response.

"As far as the snowman is concerned, we'll have to see. I've never built one before, and I have to admit, it does sound like fun. When I was little we always lived in the south, and I never did get to play in the snow. A few times it would flurry a little bit, but there would never be enough to play in. I think I missed out, don't you?"

"Yeah, I love playing in the snow. Someday Mom is going to take me skiing. Right, Mom?"

"Yep, that's what I told her. We'd go skiing together. It may be cold in the north during the winter, but there sure are a lot of fun things to do. You don't have to go too far outside of the house to make a snowman, and you can take plenty of breaks for hot chocolate, so you might want to take her up on her offer. A well-built snowman is an accomplishment to be proud of, that is for sure."

Olivia looked hopeful, and Aunt Merry took the bait. "Okay, I'll make a snowman with you; that is, if your mom has hot chocolate ready for us when we're done."

Jessi and Olivia spoke up at the same time. "Deal." Everyone started laughing. It was a pleasant evening for everyone, and before heading to bed, Jessi tried to talk Olivia into leaving first thing in the morning. "Olivia, you know if we wait to leave after church, then we're not going to have much time to swim when we get to the hotel. Is that what you really want?"

"Mom, we've already talked about this. You said we could leave after church. You promised. I want to say good-bye to my friends, and I like my class. My teacher is having a special class tomorrow because I am leaving. We can't leave early. We just can't."

"Don't go all dramatic on me. It was just a suggestion. I know what I said. I just wanted to remind you about the swimming thing. So, no complaining if we don't get there in time to swim, all right?"

Olivia crossed her arms rather stubbornly. "I'd rather go to church."

Jessi dreaded it because it also meant she had to go, that was if they were to take off right after the service. She'd planned on driving through Sonic and eating on the go since they were getting such a late start, that way Olivia could get her last fix of cherry limeades for the year. "Then to church it is. It's time for bed. Come on; I'll read you a story and tuck you in."

Olivia looked a little sheepishly at her mom. "Mom, do you think it would be okay if Aunt Merry tucked me in tonight. Seeing it's our last night and all?"

"Oh, sure. Why don't you head up and brush your teeth and put on your jams, okay?"

Olivia took off for the stairs, smiling all the way. Before Aunt Merry headed up, Jessi went toward the kitchen. "Do you want a cup of tea before we turn in?"

"Yes, that would be nice."

"I'll put the tea water on while you are upstairs."

Aunt Merry entered Olivia's bedroom just as she was getting into bed. She had one small gift to give her before she left and wanted to do it when they were alone. She took the package from behind her back and handed it to Olivia. She had it wrapped at the gift shop in pretty pink paper with pink ribbons. There were parts of Olivia that were pure tomboy, and other parts that were all girl.

Olivia looked from the package to Aunt Merry. "A present, for me?"

Merry looked at the child with pure adoration and nodded her head.

Olivia tore open the package. Inside was a brand-new children's Bible with gold edging and a picture of Jesus on the front. She'd seen some of the other children at Sunday school with this type of book and knew it was a Bible. Her teacher had also read stories from this book. She liked it a lot. "Thank you, Aunt Merry. Just think, my very own Bible. When I learn how to read, then I can read it all by myself."

"That's right. You can. But until then you'll have to ask your mommy to read to you." Merry felt a little guilty for being so sly, but if this was the only way to get that girl to read the Word, then so be it. She'd live with the guilt. "Tonight I will read to you. How does that sound?"

Olivia snuggled deep into the covers. "I'm ready."

Merry read her the story of "Daniel and the Lions' Den," one of her favorite stories from her childhood. She spoke of obedience and explained that God wants us to obey him, even if it means other people won't like what we do. Then she told her all about how God protects his children and keeps them safe. "No matter what else happens in life, God is always with us. He will never leave us, just like he didn't leave Daniel and his friends in the lion's den."

After tucking Olivia in, Merry turned on the night light and walked toward the door.

"Aunt Merry?"

"Yes?"

"I'm really glad God won't leave me. Even if bad things happen, like being thrown in the lions' den, God will be with me. Thank you for reading me that story."

"You're welcome, Olivia, and I am glad too. Good night. I love you."

"I love you too."

Merry turned off the overhead light and went downstairs to drink her tea and spend a little time with Jessi before bed.

"I was beginning to worry about you. I thought you might have fallen asleep as well."

"No, just spending a little alone time with my great-niece before she ups and leaves me tomorrow. Before I know it she will be all grown up and have a family of her own. Time passes so fast. I just want to cherish each moment I have. You are so blessed; you know that, don't you? She's a beautiful little girl, Jessi. She reminds me so much of you when you were that age."

Jessi remained quiet and listened to her aunt's memories.

"Before your mom and dad left you here for good, you loved to come and visit. It wasn't until after they left you and you felt the pain of being abandoned that you didn't want to be here. At Olivia's age, almost six, you relished coming here to visit. You would sit with me, and we would read Bible stories. Do you remember 'Daniel and the Lion's Den'?"

Jessi nodded her head yes.

"That's what we read tonight. I remember when I first read that story to you. You ran around for days pretending to be a roaring lion. Then you would pretend to be a lion that couldn't open his mouth. You were always so dramatic about everything; Olivia is just like you. She's going to want to go to church; you know that, don't you? She has a thirst for knowledge just like you did when you were her age. I hope that you will consider taking her. She needs this from you, Jessi."

Jessi didn't want this evening to end on a sour note, but she wasn't able to make promises she wasn't sure she could keep. "I'm not sure I can do that, Aunt Merry. I mean, it's not like God and I are exactly on speaking terms. I'll think about it, though. I'll give you that much. It's all I can offer right now."

"Then I will have to accept that, now won't I? Now where is that tea you were making?"

"I turned off the water when you didn't come down right away. It will only take a minute to heat back up. Do you want some honey in your tea tonight, or sugar?"

Both women enjoyed their tea while talking about school and Aunt Merry's upcoming visit. It was decided that she would make the flight arrangements and then let Jessi know when she was arriving so she could pick her up. It had been a long time since Merry had been on any kind of trip, and she was really looking forward to it now that the decision had been made. They finished their tea and went to bed—one anticipating morning, and one dreading it.

Service wasn't nearly as bad as Jessi remembered it. She didn't notice a single person staring and whispering about her, although she was certain a few did comment to one another when she wasn't looking. Pastor Pruitt spoke to his congregation in soft tones; he didn't yell at them like her memories of childhood. And he spoke about love and forgiveness like it was something he really believed in. She wasn't sure, but it almost seemed as though he also loved the people who were seated before him. He wasn't like anyone she'd ever met. After service she stood in line and shook his hand, like everyone else. When he reached for her hand, he held it in one and covered the top with the other and smiled warmly at her, like he knew her. "I'm so glad you could be with us today. I hope you enjoyed the service."

"I did, thank you." Jessi didn't know what else to say, so she continued to move forward. At the car there were hugs all around and promises of the upcoming visit. Jessi and Olivia drove off in their fully loaded car to go home. It would be a long drive with too much time to think. Maybe leaving for home right after service wasn't such a bright idea. She had no illusions of what she would be thinking about, a soft-spoken man with gentle words of a loving God.

24

Mark carried the last box to the U-Haul. "Well, this is it." He sure was glad his sister sold half her stuff to the couple who bought the house, or else they would never have fit it all in the truck. "You are such a pack rat."

Julia looked at the loaded truck and couldn't believe the amount of stuff she'd collected over the years. Yes, Mark was right. She had become a pack rat, but the contents of these boxes held more than stuff; they held memories. She had donated a considerable amount to the church for their annual rummage sale. They would have plenty of knickknacks and kitchen items for their sale this year, that was for sure. She would never forget the look on the youth's face when he came to pick up her stuff in his truck. He'd had to make three trips to the church in order to get it all. Her guess was he would think twice before volunteering his time and his truck again. She knew it was a lot when the pastor called and thanked her for making this year's rummage sale a successful one. They both had had a good laugh. Now, by the sight of things, maybe she should have given a little more. Even with selling half the furniture to the new owners and with what she gave to the church, she still filled a U-Haul.

Mark left his sister alone with her memories for a moment before interrupting her. It was already the end of August, and they were leaving for Wisconsin. "Hey, sis, you ready to go?"

She looked at him as he placed his hand on her shoulder. Together they stood looking at the house. She had too many memories, both good and bad, to walk away quickly without much thought. "Yeah, I'm ready. I mostly said all my good-byes; I just wanted one more look. I'm gonna miss it, you know?" She turned and linked her arm with her brother's. "This is for the good. I know that, Mark. I've had time to adjust and get used to the idea of creating new memories. I know we wouldn't be moving if it weren't for Jessi and Olivia being there, but I can't help but feel God has a plan for me there too. I am actually excited to see what he has in store for me. I feel peace about making this move. This will be good for both of us, you will see."

Julia got in behind the wheel of the U-Haul and started the truck. She had decided to sell her junker and buy a new car once she got to Wisconsin. It made more sense in the long run to not pull a new car behind the truck, especially seeing she would be doing all the driving, as Mark didn't have his driver's license yet. They would be making the trip in two days to give her plenty of time to relax and stretch out her legs. Mark would ride shotgun and control the map. Both were excited and a bit nervous to be venturing past their comfort zones, although neither regretted their decision to make the move.

Mark watched his sister get comfortable behind the wheel. "I can't believe it's finally happening. We're doing it, sis. We'll be in Wisconsin tomorrow night. I feel like we're scoping out the promised land, only we are going to conquer the giants and live in the land. I wonder if this kind is the kind of excitement that Caleb and Joshua had when scouting Canaan. A kind of excitement mixed with nervousness, yet you know it's a good thing and can't wait to get started. You know what I mean?"

Julia pulled out of the driveway. "I hear you. I'm a ball of nervous energy and feel like I could drive straight through to Wisconsin. Don't hold me to that when I'm ready to stop after eight hours of driving."

. . .

Olivia sat outside on the front step for the better part of the day. She watched and waited for her father to pull up in a big truck. Today was the day he was supposed to come, and she couldn't wait to see him. She had waited so long to have a daddy, and then once she had found him she had to go home and leave him back in Oklahoma. Now he was coming here to live by her. She couldn't wait to show him her school and the farm and the horses.

Jessi popped her head out the door. "Olivia, it's time for supper. You need to come inside now."

Olivia scowled. "I want to wait here for Daddy. Why isn't he here yet?"

Jessi gave her the "do what I said" look. "He'll be here soon enough. For now, I want your hands washed and you sitting at the table ready for supper, understand?"

"Yes, Mom." Olivia followed her mother into the house. She guessed she was hungry, and something sure did smell good. Might as well eat while she was waiting.

Julia exited the highway at the Highway Twenty-six exit in Janesville, Wisconsin. Their first stop was to see Olivia. Then they would check into the hotel for the night. Tomorrow would be soon enough to unpack the truck. It would just be her and Mark doing the unloading, so a good night's sleep and a cup of strong coffee would be just what they needed.

Julia turned onto a country dirt driveway. "I think this is the place."

She smiled at Mark and motioned to the front porch, which was now empty, as Olivia was running full speed toward the truck. "Daddy. You made it. I was waiting for you." She ran straight into his arms, and he swung her around while hugging her close to him. She pulled her face back from him. "What took you so long? I was waiting all day long."

"Well, it takes a long time to drive from Oklahoma to Wisconsin. You know that. It takes even longer in a big truck like that one. But I'm here now, right?"

"Right."

Mark put her on the ground and walked toward the front door where Jessi stood watching. Julia was still stretching her sore leg muscles but soon caught up. It felt good to be out of that truck. "How about a hug for your aunt?" She bent down on one knee, waiting for Olivia to give her a hug.

Mark continued to the porch. Jessi greeted him somewhat cautiously, although she'd had time to get used to the idea of him coming and living near her and Olivia. Maybe it wouldn't be such a bad thing. He definitely was good for the girl, and as long as he kept his word and stayed away from the bottle, she would let him maintain his relationship with Olivia. "Hi, Mark. How was your trip?"

"Long. I didn't realize just how long eight hundred miles could be, especially in a U-Haul, where you can't stretch out your legs. We stopped where you told us to, in Rolla, Missouri. We were ready for a break."

"Yeah, stopping helps break the trip up. Besides, if you traveled at night you would miss the great scenery. There is too much pretty countryside for that."

"I would have to agree with you. The foothills in Missouri were breathtaking. We left early enough that we watched the sunrise over the hills. Illinois was a bit boring, but that changed as soon as we hit Wisconsin. You couldn't have picked a prettier place to live."

Jessi nodded in agreement. She looked at Julia giving Olivia a hug. Julia coming with him certainly didn't hurt matters any. It might be nice to have a friend around. Even through the trial and divorce, Julia had proved she was a friend, never judging Jessi for what she was doing. Jessi had decided to make changes in her life, and that was one of the areas she'd decided to change. She needed friends. She needed someone she could call or go out to lunch with. It would be nice to have Julia around, even though Mark was part of the package. Somewhere she was finding some forgiveness in her heart for him. She didn't know when it took place, but she found she was less critical of him each time she saw him. Maybe it was the way he interacted with Olivia, treating her the way she'd always hoped he would treat Ethan. He'd never taken a true interest in his son's activities or cared about his son's feelings. Things were different now with Olivia. Everything Mark did showed that his concern for Olivia was first in his life, even above his own needs and wants. Jessi didn't quite know what to make of this Mark. It was hard to believe this was the same person she was married to so many years ago.

Gathering that his conversation with Jessi was over, Mark walked down from the porch and joined his sister, who was sitting in the grass with Olivia. "Hey, what are you two talking about, huh?"

They both started giggling and looked at each other. Julia spoke first. "Should we tell him?"

Olivia tilted her head. "Hmm ... I don't know. What do you think?"

"Well, maybe we should tell him. We are going to need his help, and if he's going to help us, then he needs to know."

"I guess you're right. Aunt Julia told me that next week is Mom's birthday, and I think we should have a party for her. Just the three of us. Do you think you could come over and we could have real family birthday party for my mom?" Olivia looked at her father with a hopeful expression. It wouldn't do for her to know that with one look, any resolve her father might have had would melt away.

There was nothing more he would like to do than help with Jessi's birthday party. It would give him the opportunity to do something nice for her. Without expectation of something in return, she might be more willing to accept his kindness. "Yes, I will help you plan a wonderful birthday party for your mom. We'll have to talk about everything when she isn't around, though, 'cause she'll know we're up to something if we try to whisper around her."

Olivia was so excited she couldn't sit still. She remembered all the things she wanted to show her dad. "Come on, Dad; I want to show you the horses." She pulled him along as she ran to the barn. She yelled over her shoulder toward the house as she went, "Mom, I'm gonna show Dad the horses." With that, they both headed to the barn.

Julia, obviously tired, walked up to the house where Jessi was standing. "And you make this trip every year, huh?"

Jessi laughed. "Yeah, come on in. They could be a while. Do you want some iced tea? I have a fresh batch made."

"Sounds heavenly. Thanks." Julia looked around the open parts of the house. She noted all the artsy touches here and there that were so typical of Jessi—the painted kitchen walls with stenciling, border wallpaper with picket fences and bird houses. The art breathed life into each room, letting a person glimpse a part of Jessi that she usually hid behind her veneer. Moments like these were rare. Julia had learned to identify them by always looking for the good in each person she met. Even the hardest of shells could be penetrated with a glimpse if you looked hard enough. Jessi's came through expressing herself through her surroundings. A gentleness and an appreciation for life were evident in her décor. Julia took a long drink of tea. "Mmm, this is good. I haven't found one place that can make a good iced tea since I hit the Illinois border."

Jessi agreed with her. "You won't find one around here, either. It seems that the northerners don't appreciate their tea sweetened like southerners do. Good thing we know how to make it at home. It's a favorite around here, especially during the summer months."

Julia wiped the perspiration from her brow. "Speaking of summer, I thought it was supposed to be cooler here. It's not only hot, but it's humid too. What's with that?"

Jessi drank from her own glass. "I tried to tell you. You just assumed since Wisconsin was so far north that it would be cooler all the time. Not so, as you'll soon see. It can reach the low one hundreds here during the summer. It doesn't happen that often, but it does happen. As far as the winters go, you will see temperatures drop to below zero, with the wind chill reaching to the negative double digits." Jessi watched Julia's face for her reaction, which registered complete disgust.

"Okay, I'll quit complaining about the summer heat. Just thinking about this winter is already making me cold. I'm going to need a new coat, that's for sure. Any suggestions?"

"I didn't mean to make it sound all that bad. It's really not, you know. The changing of seasons here is refreshing, and it's always different. After the cold winter, you'll see all the spring flowers coming up. It's positively wonderful. I think the main differences are the length of the seasons. In Oklahoma we would start to see warmer weather sometimes as early as February. I remember golfing once when I was on Christmas break; it was in the seventies. Here, you generally won't see the seventies until early June. One of the first differences you will see is when the weather changes from winter to spring, people will be wearing short-sleeve shirts when it is fifty degrees out. You won't believe it. At first, I thought they were crazy. Now I can appreciate the warmth after a cold winter, and I join right in with them."

"At home I would have the heat on, a fire lit, and a warm afghan over my legs at fifty degrees. I can't imagine running around like a lunatic in a short sleeve shirt, not even indoors, let alone outdoors."

"You wait, two to three years from now you'll be joining the rest of us crazies."

Julia just shook her head.

Mark and Olivia returned from visiting the barn and horses. "Hey, sis, we better get going so we can check into the hotel. I bet you're pretty tired. I know I am."

Julia sighed. "Yeah, I am pretty tired. It's been a long two days."

They all headed outside toward the truck. Mark explained their plans. "We are going to head into Janesville for the night, and then we'll be moving into the house tomorrow. Neither one of us has the energy to unload the truck tonight. I'll give you a call once we get everything done, okay?" He bent down to give Olivia a kiss and hug.

Olivia didn't want to let go of his neck. "You'll call me tomorrow, right, Daddy?"

"Yes, I'll call you tomorrow. I promise." Mark pried her arms off his neck by tickling her onto the ground. "I'll talk with you tomorrow." Mark nodded to Jessi before joining Julia in the truck.

They had a lot to do tomorrow before they could return the truck. Julia needed to find a car so they would have some sort of transportation. The utilities should be turned on in the house they had rented, but there would be groceries to get and the house to clean before anything could be put away.

Julia glanced at her brother while she was driving. "I'm very proud of you, Mark. I think that this is the single most unselfish thing you have ever done in your entire life. You must love that little girl a whole lot."

Mark continued looking straight ahead. "Not just her, sis; I still love my wife too." Mark looked to his sister to gauge her reaction. She remained expressionless.

"I figured that much. She's a good woman, Mark, but she's been hurt a lot. You'll have to give her plenty of time to warm up to you if you are to have a ghost of a chance at winning her back. I'm not sure I approve, only because I'm not sure that she will ever be able to completely forgive you for your part in Ethan's death, and I don't want that to be an issue hanging over your head for the rest of your life. It would be hard for any marriage to survive such a devastating trauma, let alone one with your set of circumstances." Julia realized she'd been talking too much; running off at the mouth without thinking or praying was sometimes a major failing in her life. "I'm sorry, Mark. I didn't mean to sound so negative. I just don't want to see you hurt anymore. You're my brother, and I love you. I care about what happens to you. I will pray about the situation, okay. God is in control. Always has been and always will be. Someday I'll remember that." Julia offered her brother an apologetic smile before turning back to the road.

25

Julia looked at her snoring brother. They had decided to share a room during the trip to save on money. It worked out pretty well. It was still early, but if they were going to get everything done that they needed to, they'd have to get an early start.

"Mark, time to get up. We have to get going."

Mark opened one eye and scrunched his face. "What time is it?"

"It's six thirty. You've been sleeping for a full eight hours. Besides, we have a lot to do today. Come on; you can sleep in tomorrow."

"Do I have to?"

Julia raised her eyebrows and didn't say a word.

"Okay, I'm getting up. You don't have to go all big sister on me here."

He rolled out of bed and headed to the bathroom. He would have to take another shower to wake up, albeit a quick one. He muttered, "Be right back," before the bathroom door shut behind him.

Julia took the time to finish getting herself ready for the day. Today was the first day in the past few that she actually felt human. She had gotten a good night's rest and was looking forward to seeing the house they would be living in until she found a house to buy; not only that, but she had to car shop today. The truck should be returned today if possible, and that would mean finding and purchasing a vehicle today—

a big job, to be sure. It was another ten minutes before Mark came out of the bathroom. "I thought you might have fallen in."

"Funny, sis. At least I'm alive now. So, what's the plan? I hope we get to start with breakfast and coffee."

Yes, breakfast will do us good. We've got a lot to do today. First, let's go check out the house. I've only looked at the pictures the rental agency sent me. He did mention the fact that it was for rent with option to buy. Who knows, maybe I'll love it and want to buy it. We can unload the U-Haul and then come back into town for lunch and to visit the dealerships. We'll return the truck then pick up the new car. If it all works out, we should be set."

After a light breakfast from the hotel breakfast bar, they headed to their new home. The house was in a quiet, older, residential area in Milton. It was too far to walk to Jessi's, and they didn't have a bussing system in Milton. He would have to apply for his license. He was sure they would make him use the ignition interlock device, but if it meant he would be able to drive, it would be worth it. It would also make it possible for him to work outside of Milton. He was getting the idea that if he wanted a job, he would have to look outside of the small town in which he was now living. There wasn't much to be had in a town this size.

Julia followed Mark's directions and went into Milton following Highway Twenty-six. After a series of turns they pulled into the driveway of a two-story white house with a lovely front porch. It even had a porch swing. Someone had lovingly tended the front yard, for there were still flowers and other plants growing along the walk and the front of the house. The paint on the house was peeling a bit, so that would take some work if she were to buy the place. They walked up the front steps and used the key that the rental agency had sent her. The front door was a full beveled glass pane surrounded by natural wood. So far so good.

They entered the house and were surprised by its loveliness. It would need a few updates, but overall the place was in good condition. The original woodwork was still intact, and under the carpet were hardwood floors. With a little elbow grease they would be beautiful. The living room ran the entire length of the front of the house. Behind it were the dining room and the kitchen. The kitchen was a bit smaller than she was used to, but with a few minor changes she wouldn't notice the difference. There was a room in the back of the house that would be perfect for an office and a half bath. Upstairs there were three bedrooms and a full bathroom. After touring the upstairs, she and Mark headed to the basement. She didn't have a basement in Oklahoma; most people didn't. This was new to her. Her laundry hookups were downstairs, along with a storage area and a craft or hobby room. The house had a one-car detached garage, and the backyard was fenced in. It had lots of charm and warmth. She attributed that to the natural wood. Quaint, that's what it was. Her previous home had been a ranch. She fell in love with the uniqueness of this home. If her new rental was given a good report card by a professional inspector, she might just go ahead and buy the place. By the time that happened, she'd know more about the neighborhood and the town.

Mark recognized the look on his sister's face. She was already planning. He could tell by the way she was looking around and muttering to herself. "Well, what do you think?"

"It definitely has potential. Well, I guess it's time to get to work if we're going to get it done. At least we don't have any big stuff except the beds. We'll have to be on the lookout for a used furniture shop. I bet Jessi knows right where to shop."

They headed outside and spent the next two hours unloading boxes. Both were winded and coated in perspiration by the time they finished. They were also extremely thirsty. Mark grabbed a couple of Cokes from the cooler they brought and handed one to Julia. "That was the easy part. Later, we have to put it all away if we're going to be able to survive here."

Julia looked around at all the boxes. Most were marked as to where they were going, and some had even ended up in the right room, but most were just scattered around the living room, barely leaving a pathway to get through. "We'll start with the obvious stuff first: bathroom and then kitchen. The rest will happen. You ready to head back into town? I saw a couple of car dealerships when we were driving around. I'm thinking a broken-in SUV. What do you think?"

"I think that is a good idea. This is snow country, and it couldn't hurt. I would also suggest looking at a General Motors product. This is a GM town, you know."

"Good idea. Wouldn't want to offend the locals right off the bat. Let's get going."

After test-driving several vehicles, Julia made her decision. She chose a 2005 Chevy Equinox. It was just broken in enough for her with fourteen thousand miles. As part of the sale, she talked the salesman into following her to the U-Haul rental shop so she could return the truck. After dropping the salesman off at the dealership, they got their first true taste of the SUV. "I like it. I'm going to be spoiled, though. This is nice."

"You deserve it, sis. This will be nice to drive in the winter. It should help to keep you safe on winter roads. I'm happy for you."

"Me too. Now let's get some lunch; it's almost suppertime, I suppose. You must be starved."

"I am getting hungry. It's nearly four o'clock. I'd say it's a little late for lunch."

After eating, they headed to the grocery store and got enough groceries for a couple of days. Later they could get more. When they got back, Mark dug out the phone and called Olivia. She answered on the first ring.

"Are you moved in yet?" She didn't even wait to make sure it was him. She had already answered the phone that way three times, and each time the caller had no idea what she was talking about. This time she was right on.

"Yes, we are all moved in. Nothing is put away yet, though. We just got back from Janesville where your aunt bought a new car. Exciting, huh?"

"Brand new? I've never rode in a brand-new car before."

"No, it's not brand new, but it's almost brand new. She is only a year old."

"Why did you call the car a she?"

Mark didn't realize he'd used the common endearment for cars while talking to Olivia, but it only made sense that she would call him on it. "A lot of people think of their cars as she's. I'm not really sure why or when it started happening that way, but I guess it's just a habit."

"Oh, do you like your new house. I wish you were living here with me and Mommy. I'm going to have to pray harder."

Mark didn't want to give her false hope, but he also didn't want her giving up. He needed her on his side praying alongside him. She gave him the strength to believe this was all part of God's plan. Time would eventually tell, but he had to stay strong in his faith and trust God no matter how long it took, or even if it wasn't in his plans at all. "We both will pray harder. How does that sound?"

"That sounds good. Can I come over tomorrow?" Leave it to Olivia to jump from one subject to another with virtually no warning.

"Well, I don't know. Your mom and I haven't talked about that yet. I think it would be best if you give us a day or two to get unpacked and settled. Then I'll come over and talk with your mom about our visits, okay?"

"Do I have to wait? I haven't seen you in so long, now I have to wait."

Once again, Mark felt the pull of his only daughter on his heartstrings. He was going to have to get a handle on this if he had any hope of not spoiling her to death.

"Tell you what. Maybe tomorrow I will come out to visit you again. I could bring some sandwiches, and we could have a picnic outside. And after our picnic I could talk to your mom about when you can come here to our house to visit."

"Yeah. We're going to have a picnic, Mom. Tomorrow Daddy's bringing a picnic."

Jessi took the phone from Olivia. "Hi, Mark, it's me, Jessi. What's up?"

"Olivia asked me if she could come here tomorrow, and I countered her offer with me coming over to your place instead. Maybe afterward we could sit down and talk about visitation now that I'm here."

"I think that would be wise. What time are you coming?"

"How does noon sound? Or would evening be better? It really doesn't matter."

"Well, Olivia and I were supposed to go over to her school around eleven to meet with her kindergarten teacher. Then I was going to take her school shopping. With everything else we haven't gotten to the school shopping yet, so how about evening? I think that would be best."

"Okay, let Olivia know I'll be over at six o'clock sharp for a picnic."

The rest of the day, Julia and Mark worked together at getting the house organized; she put the kitchen together while Mark set up their beds. Things were starting to come together. At least they were able to find the basic necessities. Julia noticed that Mark had been out of sorts since talking with Jessi on the phone. "Hey, little brother, everything is going to be all right. You know that, don't you?"

She could always read him. "You know me so well, you know that, sis? I just can't help but think that something is going to come along and ruin everything. I know it's my old way of thinking, that I'm not trusting God to follow through on his promises, but I can't seem to help it. I need to spend some serious time in my Bible and prayer before I hit the bed tonight. I haven't been spending my alone time with God like I had been. I guess I've made excuses to myself that I've been too busy with everything going on, and I've been too tired because of it."

Julia had known only too well how easy it was to fall into old habits, and she didn't want to see Mark begin to go down that road. "I hate to be the one to remind you of this, Mark, but God wants our firsts, not our leftovers. We always think of giving our first in our tithes, but he also wants our firsts in other areas of our lives, like our time. I know how busy life gets, and it's easy to put God on the backburner. It shouldn't, and doesn't, have to be that way. I fail in this area too sometimes. I have to continually remind myself that I have to take my time with God to survive my days. Without him I don't know what I would do. I don't think I want to know."

Mark gave his sister a hug. "Thanks, sis. I really don't know what I would do without you. I appreciate you being honest with me. I need to hear truth, and sometimes that truth might hurt. But it's worth it. I love you." He picked up his Bible and smiled at her. "It's time to spend some time with this. Good night."

After he headed to bed she found her own box marked "books" and pulled out her well-worn Bible. She rubbed her hand over the cover and traced the words *Holy Bible* with her in index finger. She carried her favorite book to her bed, and she too spent some alone time with her Savior.

26

Jessi watched her daughter get her clothes ready for the next day. They were going to see her kindergarten teacher and then go out to lunch and school shopping. It seemed as though she'd grown out of everything when they'd taken the box of fall clothes out of storage. Nothing fit. Not her socks, shoes, pants, shirts, underclothes—you name it, she needed it. It sure was expensive raising kids. It seemed as though she just got caught up and the rollercoaster started over again. "You ready, kiddo? It's bath time."

"I'm all ready. Let me get my jammies." Olivia followed Jessi into the bathroom and jumped into the water her mother had prepared for her.

"You need some help? I can get your hair if you want."

"I think I can do it. Maybe you could help me rinse it."

Jessi couldn't believe how independent her daughter was becoming. She used to have to hold her head out of the water to gently bathe her, and now she barely wanted help to wash her hair. It wasn't fair. They grew up way too fast.

"Okay, but you have to wash it really good, or else it'll still be dirty and I'll have to wash it over again. I'll just check it over when you have all the soap suds on and make sure you got behind your ears good. Then I'll help you rinse it."

Olivia started humming as she was washing. Jessi took the time to straighten up the bathroom a little bit. "You ready for me to check your hair?"

"Yep. I'm all done."

Jessi knelt beside the tub and looked over Olivia's head. "You sure did a good job. I don't have to rewash anything. Let's get it rinsed. Do you want to lay back, or should I just pour water over your head?"

"I'll lay back this time."

When bath time was over, Olivia paddled back into her room. After her mom had brushed her hair, Olivia pulled her Bible off her bookshelf. "Mom, would you read to me?"

Jessi looked at the Bible and wanted with all her being to tell Olivia no. Unfortunately there wasn't a good excuse she could use to keep from reading the Bible to the child. She had to wonder if Aunt Merry bought her the gift with an ulterior motive. It sure seemed she was reminding herself of lots of Bible stories since they'd been back from Oklahoma.

Jessi took the Bible from her daughter. "What story do you want to read tonight?"

Olivia pondered the question for a moment. She already had her favorites, but she was thinking a new story would be good tonight. "Mommy, how about we read about Jesus dying on the cross. We haven't read that one yet, and I remember it from Sunday school with Aunt Merry."

Jessi flipped through the children's Bible until she reached the story that Olivia wanted read. With each word she read, she felt an emptiness inside of her that just seemed to get bigger. Was this the answer? Were Aunt Merry, Mark, Julia, Olivia, and Ethan right? Did God truly love her and die for her?

"That's all for tonight. Maybe tomorrow night your dad can finish reading it to you." Jessi closed the Bible without finishing the story. Olivia looked as though she was about to cry, but Jessi couldn't help it. She didn't want to think about the possibilities any more tonight. She gave her daughter a kiss and turned out the overhead light. "I love you, Olivia. Maybe someday Mommy will be able to read you a whole story."

She tucked her daughter in, knowing full well by the tears shining in Olivia's eyes that she had hurt her daughter. She didn't mean to hurt her, truly she didn't. She'd have to find a way to get through those stories without letting them affect her so. She hated to see her daughter in pain, especially by her own hand.

Olivia watched her mom go out and close the door behind her. She kept a small light on by the bed so she could see real well. She crept out of bed and got her Bible off the shelf where her mom had put it. She opened the Bible and turned to the story that was left unfinished. She slowly sounded out the words and finished reading the story to herself. She hadn't told her mom that she could read. For some reason, she felt she wasn't supposed to tell her mom yet. Each night she was able to finish the story that her mom left unread. Olivia was very proud of herself. She'd tried real hard to learn to read, and the games she and her mom played helped a lot. She didn't feel like she was lying to her mom, because that would be wrong. So she prayed about it, and she felt like she had to wait to tell her, like a surprise. Just like her birthday party would be surprise. She finished her story and then knelt by her bed.

"Jesus, would you help my mommy love you? I know that sometimes she's sad, Jesus, and I don't like her sad. If she loved you, she wouldn't be sad anymore. I also told Daddy that I was going to pray real hard that Mommy and Daddy would be together so we could be a real family. I hope you don't mind that I keep asking you the same things over and over again. Sometimes Mommy doesn't like that either. But I really, really want us to be a family and live in the same house just like families are supposed to. Will you help us be a family, Jesus? Please? That's all I'm going to ask for right now so you don't feel like I'm being greedy. In Jesus's name. Amen."

Olivia climbed back into bed and covered herself up. She fell asleep thinking about being a real family.

Jessi changed into her nightgown and settled into her rocking chair with Aunt Merry's journals. It had been a while since she had taken the time to read any of the entries. Tonight seemed like the perfect night to take some time to read. She opened the journal and found where she left off.

> Saturday, February 15, 1964
>
> I'm so scared. We have driven back to the lookout several times, and I did things I am so ashamed of. I don't know what to do. Lester will barely even talk to me now. Yesterday was Valentine's Day, and I didn't even hear from him. When I called him to tell him I had a gift for him, he said he'd been busy and wouldn't be able to come over for a few days. He did say he had a gift for me too. That does give me some hope.
>
> I'm late for my period, and I'm afraid. I don't know who to talk to. I haven't talked to my friends in so long that they barely even acknowledge me anymore. It's all my fault. I thought if I had a boyfriend like Lester nothing else would matter. I thought it wouldn't matter if I still hung out with my childish friends. I'm beginning to think that turning into a woman wasn't such a good idea. I already miss being a girl. Gotta go; Mom's calling me for dinner.

Jessi couldn't believe what she had just read. Aunt Merry, promiscuous? Never. She wouldn't believe it. She couldn't believe it. It went against everything she'd ever thought about her aunt. She had to keep reading.

> Thursday, February 20, 1964
>
> I am so relieved. I got my period. Thank you, God. I promise I will be good from now on. I won't do that again ever, at least until I'm married. The other good news is Lester called and asked me to go to dinner next Friday night. I told him it was so far away, and he said he would explain then. He told me he missed

me. I'm so happy things are working out for me. Lester misses me. I love him so much. Maybe he's going to ask me to marry him. Maybe that is what he wants to talk about. That's it. He's been working real hard to save up for a ring, and now he's saved enough. I can't wait until next Friday. I called up the girls to see if they wanted to go and see a movie, and they said yes, so I have to go. We're meeting tonight at seven. Everything's great, just like it should be.

Jessi closed the journal. She couldn't take any more for the night. The idea of her aunt, the one she cherished and held up on a pedestal, doing the things this journal suggested just wasn't sitting well with her. She made her way to the kitchen and drank a hot cup of tea before going to bed. She needed something to calm her mind down before she could attempt going to sleep.

The next morning she and Olivia slept in a little bit before having breakfast and dressing for their day out. Olivia would be attending school in Milton, and Jessi taught school in Edgerton, one town away. They made their way to the classroom where Olivia would be spending a good portion of each weekday for the next year. Her teacher, Ms. Benedict, was fairly new to the school system, having only graduated from college two years prior.

Ms. Benedict greeted them warmly when they entered her classroom at their appointed time. "Hello, you must be Olivia. I'm Ms. Benedict, and I am going to be your teacher this year. Would you like to look around the classroom for a few minutes while I talk with your mom?"

Olivia nodded her head and walked around the room, looking at the pictures hanging on the wall. Ms. Benedict had a real bird in a cage. She stood next to the cage for a long time, trying to cajole the bird into speaking to her. She even tried to bribe it with some candy she had in her pocket.

While Olivia was familiarizing herself with the room, Ms. Benedict gave Jessi the list of supplies that would be needed for the school year. "I have some papers for you, but I'm sure you're already accustomed to all this. What grade is it that you are teaching this year? You're at Edgerton, right?"

Jessi took the papers from her. "Yes, I'm teaching third at Edgerton. I've taught third grade for so long that I'm not sure if I'd remember anything else."

They discussed the school year and the schedule. Pretty much both school districts tried to follow the same break schedule for Christmas and Easter, although it wasn't called Easter break anymore. Aunt Merry would throw a fit about that one if she were to find out.

Olivia walked up to join them just as they were discussing transportation. "I just have one more form to discuss with you, and that is the bus schedule for Olivia to get to and from school."

Jessi looked alarmed. "Oh, she won't be taking the bus. I will drop her off on my way to school."

Olivia piped right in. "Mom, I want to take the bus. I've waited my whole life to take the bus. Why can't I?"

Jessi gave her daughter a "please not now" look. "Olivia, we'll discuss this at home."

Ms. Benedict hated to be the bearer of bad news, but she didn't see how it would work. "Our classes don't start until eight twenty. We have one of the latest start times in the county. You won't have enough time to drop her off at an acceptable time and still make it to your classroom in time for school to start. The bus would be picking her up early anyway, and then you would be free to leave for school yourself. If we had before-school care, it wouldn't be a problem, but we don't, so I don't see how it would work, unless, of course, you had someone else drop her off."

Jessi's mind immediately went to Mark. "No, I don't have anyone else. The bus is safe, isn't it? I mean how many accidents per year do you have?"

Ms. Benedict's smile was meant to reassure her. "We have not had an accident here in a long time. I'm sure Olivia would be quite safe in the care of our bus drivers. They are well trained and all have gone under immense scrutiny regarding background checks. I'm sure she would be fine."

Olivia begged her mother with her eyes. "Please, Mom, couldn't we just try it? I want to ride the bus so bad."

Jessi had to agree that her schedule would be really tight if she couldn't drop Olivia off at school until five minutes past eight. She had to let go of her fear at some point. "I guess we can try it."

Olivia started jumping up and down. "Thank you, Mommy!" She ran to the bird. "Did you hear? My mommy said I could ride the bus."

Ms. Benedict smiled and gave her the time schedule for the bus. "She'll be picked up at seven ten and then dropped off at three forty p.m. Will someone be there when she gets off the bus to pick her up?"

"My next-door neighbor will be watching her until I get home from school. I'll let her know that she won't have to pick her up at school now. She can just get her from the bus stop."

"Well, it was very nice to meet you, Olivia. I hear you and your mom are going out to lunch and then school shopping. You have fun. I'll see you right after Labor Day, okay?" Ms. Benedict turned her attention to Jessi. "I hope I didn't push you too hard about the bussing issue. Perhaps there is someone else you could talk to about dropping Olivia off for school in the mornings if you aren't comfortable with her riding the bus. Just let us know if you change your mind."

"I think we'll give it a try and see if it works out. I'm sure it's just me being an overprotective mom. Come on, Olivia, say good-bye to Ms. Benedict and the bird. It's time to go."

"Bye, Ms. Benedict. Bye, bird." Olivia followed her mother outside to the car. The rest of the day they spent eating and shopping and more shopping. Olivia fell asleep on the way home, reenergizing her for her evening with her dad.

• • •

At six o'clock sharp, Mark came walking up the driveway. Olivia spotted him first. "Daddy's here." She ran out the door and flew into his arms. He swung her around and then picked up the picnic basket he had set aside. They made their way to the field out back, and together they set up their picnic.

They spent the rest of their time together planning the birthday party for Jessi. She would never guess what they were up to. After cleaning up their picnic and watching Olivia yawn like there was no tomorrow, they headed back to the house.

Jessi got Olivia settled in with a movie and sat out on the front porch with Mark. She had become somewhat used to having him around. Part of her change of heart was the difference she saw in him. He wasn't the same man she had been married to. She was now sure the changes in him were for real. Not once had he let either her or Olivia down by failing to follow through with his promises. She was giving up a lot of her fears all at once, and she actually felt liberated. Freer. "You are good with her, Mark. I'm impressed."

Mark looked sheepish. He hadn't known what to expect, but it certainly wasn't a compliment. "Thanks. I love our time together." He wanted to say so much more but wasn't sure if their conversation would end up in an argument instead of settling on a visitation schedule. "I'd like to see her as much as possible. I don't know yet what I'll be doing for work, so I'm not sure what my schedule will be. I'm pretty sure, though, I won't be working on Sundays. I would like to take her to church with Julia and me. I know she would enjoy it. Then we could spend the afternoon together, and that would give you some free time. We could discuss a weekday afternoon visit time if my work schedule will allow for it. I'll know more once I get a job."

"I'm good with that. She's been bugging me about taking her to church. This way she gets to go and it's not me taking her. Works out perfectly for all of us."

Mark wasn't so sure about the "working out perfectly for all of us" comment but knew better than to disagree with her on this. God would work out her salvation in his own timing. He, along with Olivia and the others, would continue to pray until they saw the results that they all desperately wanted to see. "Well, then. I guess I will see you on Sunday morning. I'll call you with the time." Mark stood up to leave. Julia had pulled up a few minutes earlier and was waiting for him. He opened the car door. "Thanks, Jessi. I appreciate all you're doing."

Jessi just nodded and watched him go.

Sunday morning, Mark and Julia pulled into Jessi's driveway at nine o'clock. They were visiting a church in Janesville, and Sunday school started at nine thirty. They didn't want to be late. The church wasn't as big as the one they were used to in Oklahoma City, but maybe smaller wouldn't be so bad. It would be easier to get to know people at a smaller church. The pastor reminded Mark of his friend and mentor back in Oklahoma. He found Olivia's class, and she had no problem with giving her dad a kiss and joining in the fun. He decided to sit in on the pastor's class, and Julia joined a women's Sunday school class. There was hardly a seat to be had in the class he chose. The discussion was riveting, and he found himself totally intrigued when Pastor Jackson bowed his head to pray. He could hardly believe the class was over. After service he waited to shake hands and thank the pastor for the sermon. He'd have to see what Julia thought, but he liked what he'd seen so far. Hopefully she did too.

After church they went home and ate the pot roast that Julia had put in the oven before church. They finished planning Jessi's birthday party and then played board games until it was time for Olivia to go home. Everyone had a wonderful day. The next day Mark and Julia joined Jessi and Olivia for the Labor Day parade. Mark decided the fun in going was watching Olivia enjoying all the different parade participants. There were clowns and floats, marching bands, and lots of candy being thrown out to the crowd. She had a blast. After the parade they stopped for a burger and then headed home; everyone had a big day the next day. It was Jessi and Olivia's first day of school, and Mark had an appointment with his new parole officer. He wanted to apply for the ignition interlock device so he could drive himself to work and back. His parole officer also had some leads on some companies that might be hiring. Hopefully he would find something soon. He needed to start pulling his own weight and paying Julia for his living expenses and helping Jessi with the cost of raising Olivia. He desperately needed to make a difference.

27

Of all the things that were happening on Tuesday morning—Jessi's first day at school, Mark's meeting with his parole officer and job hunting, and Julia's shopping for furniture—none of it compared in excitement to Olivia's first day of kindergarten. Her new outfit was ready and waiting, and she was dressed and ready for school before Jessi climbed out of bed. Olivia stood over her mom, watching her sleep while deciding if she should wake her. She better wake her. Maybe the alarm didn't go off. What if she didn't turn it on. Then they'd be late for school. Olivia didn't want to be late for school.

She shook her mom. Jessi startled awake to find Olivia looking down at her. "What is it? What's the matter?"

Olivia looked at her mother. "We're late."

Jessi glanced at the clock. "What do you mean we're late. It's only five thirty in the morning. Why are you up? It's not time to get up yet." Jessi was awake enough now to see that Olivia was fully dressed, hair combed, shoes on, and ready to go with her new backpack in hand. "Were you too excited to sleep?"

Olivia nodded her head.

"All right, then, how about I get up and get showered and then I'll make us some breakfast before we have to leave. Do you want scrambled eggs and toast or pancakes?"

"Can we have chocolate chip pancakes?"

"I suppose so, just because it's a special day. You wait for me in the living room, and I'll be out as soon as I'm dressed. Do you want me to put in a movie for you?"

"No, that's okay. I will just look at my books."

Olivia headed out to the living room, while Jessi made her way to the shower. When she heard the shower going she picked up the phone and dialed her dad's house.

Mark was dreaming when he heard the phone ring. He felt like there was a war between sleeping and waking, and he was panicking because he couldn't wake up. Finally he opened his eyes and rolled over onto his side. He reached for the phone and at the same time looked at the clock. Five forty-five. Who would be calling this early? "Hello."

"Daddy, is that you?"

Mark jerked awake. "Olivia? Baby, is that you? What's wrong, honey? What's the matter?"

"Why does everyone think something is the matter? I have to go to school today, and I got up before Mommy and got dressed all by myself. The bus is going to pick me up at seven ten. That's what my teacher said. I have to be ready 'cause I don't want to miss the bus. Mommy is going to make me chocolate chip pancakes for breakfast as soon as she gets out of the shower. I am going to eat hot lunch at school today. The menu says we're going to have macaroni and cheese and pears. I like macaroni and cheese and pears." Olivia didn't let Mark get a word in. She was talking a mile a minute and was so excited about school that she didn't hear her mother come out of the bathroom.

"Olivia, who are you talking to?"

Olivia jumped and screamed at the same time. "You scared me, Mommy."

Jessi asked her again. "Olivia, I asked you who are you talking to?"

"I'm talking to Daddy. I wanted to tell him I was ready for school."

"Olivia, you need to ask permission before you make phone calls. Let me talk with your dad."

Jessi took the phone from Olivia. "Hi, Mark. I'm sorry about that. I didn't know she was going to call you. She was supposed to be looking at her books while I took a shower."

Now fully awake, he realized he enjoyed hearing Jessi's voice first thing in the morning. He couldn't remember appreciating that when they were married. "It's okay, Jessi. She's just excited, and I let her know it was okay to call me for anything. Even trivial things are important to me if they are important to her. It's not a bother or an inconvenience. I really don't mind."

Jessi really didn't know what to make of this new Mark. The old one would have been cursing and throwing a fit because his sleep had been disturbed, that is if he could have been awoken in the first place. Half the time he was still drunk at five in the morning. "Well, I just wanted to apologize. And thanks, Mark. For being so understanding, I mean. I appreciate it."

"You're welcome." Mark hung up the phone more hopeful than he'd been in a long time. Jessi had actually been decent and civil toward him, almost to the point of friendly. He looked upward and said, "We're getting somewhere, God. Thank you!"

Jessi drove to the end of the driveway and stood with Olivia until the bus picked her up. She couldn't help but snap a few pictures of her daughter as she was waiting and getting on the bus. Some of the teachers scrapbooked together and had invited her to join them. She'd always declined their invitation, but she decided it was time to put her memories of Ethan in a proper album for all of them to enjoy rather than hoard her mementos to sulk in them herself. While she was at it, she should also start Olivia's pictures as well.

Olivia was so excited when the bus pulled up. "Mommy, here it comes." Olivia looked so cute with her backpack and her new dress on. She was a beauty. It broke Jessi's heart to see her getting so big. It seemed like only yesterday when the doctors handed her, her life preserver, a new life to be responsible for, to give new meaning to her life. Now this little girl was growing up. Where was her life source going to come from when she was gone? She thought of all the people in the world who were constantly wishing away their lives. Jessi had learned long ago to live every moment to its fullest. Unfortunately, she was only starting to put it into practice.

Olivia waved as she got on the bus. "Bye, Mom. See you later."

Jessi waved back. "Bye, sweetheart. I love you. Have a good day."

After the bus pulled away from the driveway, Jessi drove to work, her thoughts returning to her conversation with Mark. Why did her thoughts often drift toward her ex-husband? What was she doing? She wasn't ready to completely forgive him for his actions. Why was she wondering about how his day was going and what he was doing? She knew he had a meeting with his new parole officer today, and she found herself actually hoping it would go well. This wasn't happening. She turned on the radio to drown out her thoughts.

Olivia loved her class. She loved her teacher. She loved the bird. And she especially loved her new best friend, Samantha, Sam for short. Sam sat next to her at the table they shared. Their cubbies were right next to each other too. Olivia was so glad to have a best friend. This was the best year of her life. She'd always wanted a dad, now she had one; and she always wanted a best friend, now she had that too. School was going to be wonderful.

When she got off the bus that afternoon, Mrs. Richards, the lady who owned the farm, was waiting for her. After talking with her mom on the phone she had a snack and helped Mrs. Richards with the horses. Her days were planned for the next nine months—school and then work with the horses. To her it was the perfect afternoon. She loved feeding the horses and brushing them down. She had no fear, and sensing that, the horses were not at all skittish around her. It proved to be the perfect job for her. She even earned a little pocket change from Mrs.

Richards, which she was going to save in secret to buy her mom and dad a Christmas gift all on her own.

The first week of school flew by, and before they knew it, it was time for Jessi's surprise birthday party. When Olivia and Jessi arrived on Saturday, Jessi thought she was just dropping Olivia off to spend the afternoon with her dad so Jessi could have some time to shop for scrapbook supplies. Mark met them in the driveway. Olivia got out of the car. Her eyes begged her father to do something. Mark gave Olivia a quick smile and a nod of the head. He bent down to the driver's side window. "Hey, Jessi, how are you?"

"Doing good. I'm just going to run to Janesville to get a few supplies. I shouldn't be more than a couple of hours."

"You haven't seen the house yet, have you? Julia wanted me to invite you in. She wants to show you around. It'll just take a minute, and then you can get on your way."

Jessi looked like she was about to decline.

"She'll be heartbroken if you don't come in. She doesn't know anyone here except you and me and Olivia, and, well, I'm not exactly the decorator type, if you get my meaning. She needs a friend at the moment, a woman friend, who can give her some suggestions and ideas on decorating. Please, if you just take a minute it would mean the world to her." He put on his best puppy dog eyes, hoping they would still work. "Please."

"Oh, all right. I suppose a minute won't hurt. Lead on."

When they entered the house, both Olivia and Julia had hats on and started to blow horns. "Surprise" they yelled between horn-blowing. "Happy Birthday, Mom." It didn't take Jessi but a moment to figure out what was going on and that she'd been duped.

The afternoon turned out to be very pleasant for everyone. Mark grilled the burgers while Julia got out the salads she had prepared. Jessi commented on the house while Julia was setting the table. "The house has turned out great, Julia. You have a knack for decorating, and I love the furniture. Have you decided if you are going to buy the house?"

"The inspector is coming next week. I want to have first dibs on the place since I'm already moved in and getting settled. I wouldn't want to have to move right away if it turns out to be a great buy and a good house to boot. I guess I'm just waiting to make sure there are no surprises in store for me, like termites or carpenter ants or something like that. If there are no major expenses involved, then I'll probably put in an offer. I really do like the place. It would be a little big for just me, but with Mark here too it seems to be just perfect. We each have our own space, so we're not tripping over each other. Things are working out all around."

"I'm happy for you. I think you'll like it here. I've enjoyed the change in the seasons so much since coming to Wisconsin, and I can't say I miss the red dirt back in Oklahoma. The ground is so fertile here for gardening. Aunt Merry will love it. She works so hard at maintaining her garden back home. She's always had to add to the dirt to make it suitable for growing. What plans do you have to keep you busy?"

"I've given that some thought as well. I don't have the friendships here like I did back in Oklahoma, so I'm going to have to find a way to keep busy and make some new friends. There's an opening at church for a secretarial position. I've been thinking about applying for it. It would give me a little extra spending money and keep me from getting bored. I'm not sure if they will consider me since I'm so new to the church, but it's worth giving it a try. I guess we'll see. I intend to ask for an application tomorrow when I run into Janesville. Here's hoping." She placed the last of the dishes on the table just as Mark and Olivia came in with the platter of burgers.

While they were eating Mark shared his news. "I got a job. I'll be working with a drywall construction crew that's based in Milton. The guy I will be working with even volunteered to pick me up until I'm able to drive. I start on Monday, and depending on the week I'll either work Monday through Friday or Saturday, which means I won't be missing church. I was so relieved when I got the phone. It seems there's a shortage of guys who do that kind of work around here. It'll be hard work, but it will be worth it." Everyone, including Jessi, seemed genuinely pleased for him. He had been making phone calls and filling out as many applications as possible to try to find work.

They all had birthday cake and ice cream for dessert, and Jessi was embarrassed when they insisted on singing "Happy Birthday" to her. Lastly, she opened her gifts. Julia had bought her some scrapbook supplies, knowing she had nothing for the new hobby she was taking up; Olivia picked out a pretty scarf for her mother when she'd stopped at the store after church the week before. The final gift she opened was from Mark. She wasn't sure what to expect. He'd never remembered her birthday when they were married. She carefully unwrapped the box. She pulled out the most beautiful music box she'd ever seen. It was in the shape of the two-story Victorian home she'd always dreamed of living in. Tears almost immediately filled her eyes. It was the most incredible gift she'd ever received. She wound up the box, and it played a song she remembered from her childhood, one that conjured up memories of home and family. She hummed along and sang the words as she remembered them.

If life were a song, I'd sing you a melody... hmm... If my heart were your home, I'd keep the fires burning... hmmm...

The song ended, and Jessi wiped the tears from her eyes. "Thank you, Mark. I will treasure this. It's beautiful." She wanted to ask him how he remembered, how he knew this song would touch her heart like it did, but it wasn't the right time or place. She would save that for later and let the tears tell him how much his gift was appreciated.

Olivia fell asleep on the short drive home, and Jessi hated to wake her, so she carried her into her room and changed her into her jammies, as Olivia liked to call them. She tucked her into bed and went to turn out the light. She was almost to the door when Olivia opened her eyes. "Mommy."

Jessi turned around and walked back to the bed. "I thought you were sleeping."

"I was. I just wanted to know if we surprised you for your birthday. Did we? Were you happy?"

It had been a long time since Jessi had truly felt loved by another person. Her daughter's devotion to her was so obvious she was barely able to contain her emotions. "I was very surprised. And you made me very happy. Was this all your idea?"

Olivia yawned. "I asked Aunt Julia and Daddy to help me surprise you. Even Aunt Merry helped us some on the telephone." Olivia curled up and closed her eyes. "I'm so happy we surprised you, Mommy. I love you so much."

Jessi tucked her in one more time. "I love you too, sweetheart. Good night."

This time she made it out the door without any interruptions. She checked her answering machine, and after listening to Aunt Merry's message, she returned her call. She told her aunt all about the party, even though she already knew the basics of it. When she mentioned her gifts she couldn't help but tell her about Mark's gift to her as well. She tried to play down the impact it had on her but didn't really succeed. After Aunt Merry wished Jessi her own birthday blessings and they hung up, Aunt Merry went to bed happier than she had been in a long time. She had just had her first sign from God that everything was going to work out. She fell asleep whispering her thanks.

28

Thanksgiving came in a hurry to Wisconsin, ushering in a blast of cold air. Everyone had been so busy with their lives, they barely saw it coming. Julia hosted and invited Jessi and Olivia, along with a few people she'd met from church. She'd made turkey and stuffing and all the trimmings. Jessi had pitched in with desserts, and Mark had provided all the drinks. It was a leisurely day of eating and watching football. Julia had started working at the church in the beginning of October and had met many super people. She'd met one man who had become of particular interest to her. He brought her a lovely bouquet of fall flowers as his contribution to the meal.

Jessi watched everyone as they enjoyed the day off from work and the regular routines in their lives. Olivia was keeping everyone entertained. She was going to be an angel in the Christmas play at church, and even Jessi had promised to be there to see her. Mark was lounging in the living room with a couple of guys, including the one who couldn't seem to keep his eyes off Julia, cheering on one of the football teams. Under normal circumstances, she would have been right there enjoying the game too, but she had things on her mind. It was only a month until Christmas, and there was so much to do before then. Aunt Merry was flying in the week before Christmas, and she still had to finish those journals before she came. It just seemed as though with the

Thanksgiving play at school and parent-teacher conferences, there was so little time for anything else. She'd been a little reluctant to continue reading them for fear of what she'd find. But she'd told Aunt Merry she would have them ready for her to take back when she returned home from her visit. She had no choice but to finish them.

Jessi went in the kitchen to help clean up and found Julia chatting with a couple ladies from their church.

Julia looked up from the dish she was drying. "Hey, Jessi, we pretty much have everything finished up here with the dishes. I stacked the salad plates on the kitchen table, so if you want to you can start setting out your pies. Laura brought a pecan pie as well, so I'm guessing with all you brought, we are going to have more than enough."

"Dessert time. The guys have been in there voicing their protest at having to wait until the dishes are done before they get pie. This is bound to make them happy."

She pulled out the two pumpkin pies, the apple, and the cherry pie she had made and set them on the table next to the pecan pie. They also had a double chocolate cake, banana pudding, and peanut butter cookies to munch on. The coffee was brewed and ready and the milk was on the table. All she needed was the whipped cream and ice cream. "I am so glad Thanksgiving only comes once a year. We have enough food to feed an army. If everyone is ready, I'll call the guys in."

The ladies started laughing but stepped out of the way regardless. Laura chimed in, "We wouldn't want to be trampled in here, now would we? I mean it's not like they are starving or anything, but how many times a year do you get pumpkin pie or pecan pie? They're like little kids."

Jessi opened the door to the living room. She called out, "Hey, guys, pie's ready." Then she stepped aside just in time to see four grown men dive toward the kitchen door to see who could be first in line, like there wouldn't be enough for all of them. It was a sight to behold.

29

Jessi sat by the fireplace with the last of Aunt Merry's journals. Olivia was tucked into bed, and Jessi had to pick Aunt Merry up from the airport tomorrow afternoon. It was now or never. She had a cup of hot tea and some of the Christmas cookies she had made earlier on a saucer for a snack, and she was all settled in for a good read. She turned to where her marker rested.

> Friday, May 28, 1964
>
> I went with Lester tonight, and he told me the most horrifying news. He's joined the army. I thought he was going to propose and tell me we'd move away to the city like he's always wanted to do. I can't stop crying. He told me he still loves me but we'd have to wait to be together. We only have two weeks together before he leaves, and he wants to spend every moment he can with me. It will be a long time before I will see him again, and when he does come home it will only be for a short while. He'll be away for so long. I will miss him with all my heart. I don't think I can bear this.

Jessi re-read the words and muttered to herself, "Probably the best thing that could have happened to her. Must have hurt at the time, but if he'd stayed, surely things would have turned out much worse for Aunt Merry." She continued to read.

> Tuesday, June 1, 1964
>
> I spent the day with Lester today. He wasn't able to spend any time with me this weekend because his family had lots of relatives come to say good-bye to him. He wasn't able to get away. But today we went walking in the country near his family's place and we spent time swimming at the lake. I know I made a promise to myself and to God, but how was I to tell him no when he is leaving so soon? Besides, we plan on marrying when he gets out of the army. He told me I'd always be his girl. It can't be all that bad if we plan on being a family anyway. God will understand that. It's like we're a family already. That's the way Lester said God sees it. He said in the Old Testament people didn't get married by a preacher. They just gave themselves to each other and then they were married. So I guess, according to Lester, we're married. Somehow I don't think Papa and Mama would see it like that if they knew what we were doing. Things will work out, though. I just have to believe that.

Jessi closed her eyes and wished she didn't have to keep reading. She didn't like where this was going. And for the life of her she couldn't understand why her aunt would want her to read this. This wasn't the kind of stuff you wanted your family to know. This was the stuff closets were made for.

> Thursday, June 14, 1964
>
> I waved good-bye to Lester today as he boarded the train. He's left us for the army. We hardly spent any time together, at least any quality time together. He managed to come and see me long enough to drive to the lookout, but we didn't do anything together that young lovers are supposed to do before they are

separated by lots of miles. I am already lost without him. He promised to write to me. I can always look forward to that. We can keep our relationship going strong through the mail. I can wait for as long as it takes. He will always be my only love.

. . .

Sunday, June 27, 1964

I haven't received one letter from Lester. I've written him three times already, and he hasn't responded to my letters at all. I even called his mother to ask if she has heard from him, and she told me he was doing well. He's been pretty busy in basic training, but she says he's doing fine. I was pretty upset that he has had time to write his mother and not me. I don't quite know how to take that news.

Jessi continued to read, already knowing things were going to turn out badly for her aunt. She felt like crying even before she read the dreadful news.

Wednesday July 20, 1964

I'm pregnant. I don't know what to do. I don't know who I can talk to. I wrote another letter to Lester, and I still haven't heard from him. I am hoping with this news he will feel compelled to write me back. This should seal our relationship and remind him of how important I was to him. I became the woman he wanted me to become for him. I feel sick to my stomach all the time and won't be able to hide my condition from my parents for very long if the sickness doesn't pass, not that it will give me much time in the long run anyway, as I'll be showing by the fourth month. I guessed I was pregnant when I didn't get my period in June, but I knew for sure when I still didn't get it in July. I'm sure everything will be all right when I get Lester's letter. He will come home and we'll be married, and then my parents will forgive me and help me with my baby. I have to believe still that everything will work out. I have to believe it.

There was only one more entry in the journal to read. Jessi pressed on.

> Thursday, August 5, 1964
>
> I received a letter from Lester today. I was so excited to hear from him that I tore it open as fast as I could. There was only a short note and some cash. I sobbed when I read the words that he wrote:
>
>> Meredith,
>>
>> Here is some cash and the name of a lady in the city who will take care of it. I've listed her name and address at the bottom of the page. Tell her I sent you, and she'll know what to do. I've used her before, and she'll take care of everything. I'm sure you're not so naïve to really believe that I would take leave and marry you. As I said, this has happened before, and everything works out fine. So don't worry; just go see Loretta, and no one will be the wiser.
>>
>> Lester
>>
>> P.S. I'm not sure it's a good idea for you to continue to write me. You are distracting me from my training, and I can't be letting that happen, now can I?
>
> I am not sure what to do. I don't know who I can talk to or even what the right thing is anymore. I am so confused and I feel horrible. I don't want this baby if Lester isn't going to love me. Why did he do this to me? Why is this happening to me? What should I do?

That was it; that's where the journals ended. No explanation of what happened or the decisions Aunt Merry had made so long ago were anywhere to be found. The journal was only half filled, and that was the last entry and the last book.

Jessi sobbed for her aunt. How alone she must have felt. The shame of her secret would have been too much for any teenage girl, especially one who was supposed to have been brought up in the church. Jessi cried well into the night, feeling the pain her aunt endured like it was her own. Finally she fell asleep in the chair by the fire, her tea cold and her cookies untouched.

The ladies took Merry to the airport in plenty of time to stop for lunch before dropping her off. All six of them in Mabel's Cadillac was a tight squeeze, but they managed it. Merry was a little nervous about flying for the first time, which was part of the reason she hadn't insisted on visiting Jessi in Wisconsin before now. "Girls, I'm getting too old for this. At my age the girl should be coming here, not me traipsing all around the country in something that doesn't stay on the ground."

Judy took her by the arm and led her into the restaurant. "Honey, if I can fly to California and back two to three times a year, I know you can do this. Why, you are so much braver than me, you'll have no trouble at all. Just remember that God is in control of everything, dear. Even airplanes have nothing on him." Feeling that her explanation was adequate enough to calm Merry's frayed nerves, she changed the subject completely and told Merry all about the new couple who had moved in next door to her. "They're just the cutest couple. Oh, and they have a little dog. I'm not sure what kind it is. They don't call them poodles anymore. It has some foreign name and I can't remember it."

Since Merry wasn't feeling too well due to her anxiousness of flying, she only ordered a cup of soup with crackers; which she barely touched. All the ladies seemed to be in good spirits and didn't notice that Merry was still nervous. She'd been given lots of good advice. "Make sure you use the bathroom before boarding the plane" and "Don't drink too much on the trip, or you'll have to climb over everybody's lap to get to the bathroom" were just a couple. They meant well, she knew, but all of them had flown before and had been doing so for years. She was the only one who had been stuck in her safe little world for so long without venturing out of it. It wasn't just the flying that was causing her stomach to be in knots. She could handle it if that were the only thing that was giving her cause to worry. What she was going to find once she got to Wisconsin was what was truly bothering her, or rather, how she would find Jessi's attitude toward her. Jessi had called her before bed last night and told her that she was going to finish the journals before heading to bed.

Lord, I know I was following your instructions when you led me to give the child my journals. I sure hope you know what you're doing. I'm scared I'm about to lose the only daughter I have ever known. Please give me strength to do your will.

Merry looked up as Mabel called her name. "We have to get going if we are going to get you there on time. Are you ready?" She looked at Merry's untouched cup of soup. She handed her a granola bar. "Here, put this in your purse. You'll probably need it for later." She took Merry's hand and led her to the car. Some of the ladies stopped off into the restroom, so Merry had a moment alone with Mabel.

"Mabel, you've been through a lot in your life, haven't you?"

Mabel thoughtfully looked at Merry. "Your anxiety is about a little more than flying, isn't it?"

Merry pursed her lips and nodded. She tried not to let the tears in her eyes spill over.

"Did you tell her about your past?"

"I let her read my journals. I'm scared, Mabel, that I'm going to lose my baby." Merry couldn't keep the tears from flowing now that she had voiced her fears out loud.

"Did God tell you to do this, Merry? Did he lead you in this direction?"

Through the tears, Merry nodded again.

"Then you have to believe he has it all under control. If it is his plan that you lose her, then you must face the fact that God knows best. We will pray that that is not in his plan. But, Merry, you know as well as anyone that God's plans are his own and no man understands his ways. We just have to trust him. It's hard to let him have control when you think he might change all you've ever known. Imagine what Abraham must have felt when God asked him to sacrifice his only son on an altar. At the last second, God stepped in by way of an angel and kept him from being obedient. Obedience is always better than sacrifice. You were obedient in doing what God has told you to do. You may also have to sacrifice, but we don't know that yet, do we? Trust God, sister. We'll all be praying for you."

Merry's full entourage followed her into the airport to say their good-byes. They were a comical sight, six elderly ladies making a ruckus and all dressed in various modes of dress—some loud and obnoxious and some very reserved—yet they needed and treasured each other as much as a child needed its mama. They all waved good-bye and then headed home with a little more room in the car to spread out.

Merry watched as everything she was used to grew smaller and smaller. The houses became little dots and then were completely gone underneath the clouds. She pulled her worn-out Bible from her purse and began to read, looking for comfort from the Creator of her soul. It wasn't long before the steward asked her if she'd like something to drink, and she chose a Sprite, as her throat was dry. They gave her a little bag of pretzels and an itty-bitty can of Sprite. She slowly munched the pretzels and drank her soda while she read. Before long the captain was describing the weather conditions in Chicago over the intercom system. The steward collected her garbage, and she put her Bible away as she was instructed to do.

She minded her business on the plane and didn't seek out conversation with anyone, not because she was a grumpy old lady, like some obviously thought, but because she was desperately trying to understand the Father's will in all of this. Once the plane landed and was at their terminal, everyone started getting their things from the overhead bins.

People were bumping each other, and all were in a hurry to be off the plane.

She waited until things calmed down, and even then the stewardess and the steward were holding on to their things, waiting for her to finish. When she finally stepped off the plane and walked down the tunnel into the airport, she was overwhelmed with its size. She followed signs that led her to the baggage claim area, and when she finally got there, she saw Jessi standing by her things, waiting for her.

Jessi had already spotted her and was watching from a distance, waiting for her aunt to notice her. When Merry noticed Jessi, she stopped for a moment and searched her face, looking for some sort of clue that would give her an indication of how things were going to go. After a moment Jessi smiled a big, welcoming smile that said "I still love you with all my heart," and Merry made quicker strides toward her and fell into her arms. "Oh, how I've missed you, child." Merry knew that this was really the easy part; she never explained or gave any indication in the journals of what her choices had been. She'd never finished the story of her life. It had always been too depressing to put it down on paper. Somehow, it had been easier to accept what she had done by not finalizing it or giving credence to it by written statement.

Together they walked to the car, Jessi leading the way with most of the luggage. "Do you think you brought enough?"

Merry considered her question. "Just enough, I think. Remember, I also had to bring Christmas presents, and I wasn't sure what I would need for warm clothes, so I pretty much brought all that I had. How long is the drive home?"

"At this time of day it will take us at least a couple of hours. Late afternoon in Chicago suburbs is like nothing you've ever seen before. If traffic keeps moving we'll do okay. If it doesn't, well, we'll be here for a while."

"Do you think we could stop and get a bite to eat when we've cleared the worst of it? I only had a couple bites of soup for lunch, and I'm quite famished. I'm buying."

"That should work out fine. Mark has Olivia, and I told him I didn't know what time I'd be home, so she is going to spend the night with him and Julia and then walk to school tomorrow from their house. She'll come home on the bus like usual, so I told my next-door neighbor that tomorrow she won't have to watch Olivia because you will be meeting her at the bus. Any ideas on what you'd like to eat?"

"Anything would be fine. I think I was a little too nervous to eat much before the flight. I'll leave it up to you since you know your way around here, and if we wait to get out of traffic before we stop, that's okay too. I'll survive. I have plenty stored up for occasions such as this one."

"We usually stop off in Rockford. It's about an hour or so up the highway. If you can wait that long we can get some seafood."

"I think that sounds just fine."

During the drive Merry rested her eyes and thanked the good Lord for his traveling mercies and the situation with Jessi going well so far. She prayed for his wisdom and guidance. She must have fallen asleep because before she knew it she was being roused and they were parked outside a seafood restaurant.

"You awake? We're here. You slept the whole way. I don't think we were out of O'Hare before you were snoring."

Merry was appalled at the idea. "I was not. I was just breathing loudly. I do that, you know."

Jessi laughed at her aunt as they made their way arm in arm into the restaurant. For the moment both women were not thinking about anything else but enjoying the little time that they had together. Later they would discuss what needed to be discussed.

30

Merry walked to the end of the driveway to wait for Olivia to come home from school. She'd had most of the day to herself to unpack and get ready for her visit. It felt good to get away, especially since she was at Jessi's. Julia had called and offered to pick her up and have her for lunch, but Merry declined, wanting to spend some time alone to rest and unpack. She was glad she did. She took inventory of Jessi's cupboards and freezer, and the contents left much to be desired. She'd not be able to cook too many meals with what Jessi had on hand. Maybe tomorrow morning Julia would take her to the grocery store so she could get some proper food in the house. She'd call her after their snack.

Merry watched the bus come to a stop and waited for Olivia to appear once the doors opened. Olivia bounded out of the bus at full speed. She squealed "Aunt Merry" and flew into her arms. She had found some packaged cookies for Olivia's snack then made a quick call to Julia, setting up the grocery store run for the next day, although it would be Mark taking her, as Julia had to work at the church the next morning. Since Mark had been approved to receive the ignition interlock device, he had recently purchased his own car with the money he'd been saving from work. Since work was a little slow this week due to Christmas, he was off work and was free to take Merry to the store. After that quick phone call, Merry sat back down with Olivia at the table.

"Tell me all about school, young lady. Do you like it?"

"I love it, Aunt Merry. My teacher is so nice. So is my best friend, Sam."

"Sam? Is your best friend a boy? I'm not sure that I like you having a best friend that is a boy."

Olivia giggled. "Sam's not a boy. Her name is Samantha, but she likes to be called Sam. Cool name, huh?"

Merry gave her a cocked grin. "Not as cool as Olivia, though. All right, then, tell me what you are learning about. Have you learned to read yet?"

Olivia looked around to make sure no one was listening, even though her mother wasn't even home from work yet. "Can you keep a secret?"

Merry nodded her head yes.

"I can already read; I just haven't told Mommy yet."

Merry looked perplexed. "Why wouldn't you tell your mommy you can read?"

Olivia spoke in hushed tones. "Because God told me not to."

Merry raised her eyebrows. "God told you not to? What do you mean God told you not to?"

Olivia wasn't sure she should have told her aunt about her reading. Now she had to explain her actions. "Well, if Mommy knew that I could read, she wouldn't read my Bible to me anymore. God wants Mommy to read Bible stories to me, even though she doesn't finish them most of the time. So when she leaves my room at night, I get my Bible back off the shelf and finish the story myself."

Merry couldn't believe her ears. This child was five years old, hardly old enough to listen to her mother, let alone God. Amazing. "How do you know it was God telling you to do this?"

"Well, I listened in my heart just like you and Daddy told me to. That's how I know."

until forever

"Well, I think it is very wise of you to listen to God. He is very smart, you know, and he wants what is best for your mommy."

They spent the rest of the afternoon talking, and Olivia helped Merry make spaghetti for supper. There was nothing but jarred sauce, so that would have to do. She'd survive this one time. After putting the salad together, she and Olivia talked about Christmas and the church play. There were so many things to discuss since they had last seen each other. The one thing Merry really wanted to know about was Jessi and Mark's relationship and how it was going. But she felt too guilty asking a five-year-old about it.

By the time Jessi came home, supper was on the table. It was a rare treat to not have to cook when she got home from work, even if it was spaghetti from a jar. She was pretty sure she would be hearing about the state of her kitchen from her aunt sometime soon. She'd meant to go grocery shopping before Aunt Merry came, but she'd run out of time. Now she would hear it. She'd have to leave some money for her to grocery shop with because odds would have it there would be a lot more to choose from when she got home from school tomorrow. Between bites she explained herself. "Aunt Merry, I'm sorry I haven't gone grocery shopping. I meant to, I really did. I just ran out of time. I'm figuring you've already noticed since you found something to make dinner with. I suppose you are going shopping tomorrow?"

"How do you think I would get there? I don't have a car."

Jessi doubtfully looked at her aunt. "You have your ways, Auntie. You can do anything you put your mind to. I know you pretty well, remember?"

"Well, it just so happens that I already have a ride set up for tomorrow morning after you and Olivia leave for school. But don't worry about it. There are things I need to get for Christmas. I'll just pick up a few things for around the house as well. Oh, and did you ask Mark and Julia to come for Christmas dinner like I asked you to?"

"I sure did, and they were happy to accept your invitation. I told them I would let them know the time once we figured it out. And I have some money for you for grocery shopping. It's my budgeted amount for groceries anyway, so don't say no. I just didn't get to them yet. If you want to just take the money and get something extra special for Christmas dinner."

After supper the three of them relaxed around the fireplace.

"It sure does get cold here. I was surprised there was no snow on the ground. I'm glad you have this fireplace. It sure does warm up the insides." She drank deeply from her mug. "That and this hot chocolate sure does the trick. Isn't tomorrow your last day of school before Christmas break?"

Jessi sighed. "It sure is, and I am more than ready for it. It's been a long fall. I need a break. We have ten straight days to do nothing we don't want to and everything we feel like doing. It is going to be pure joy to have you here, Aunt Merry. Usually it's just me and Olivia for Christmas. This year, with everyone here, it will seem more like an old-fashioned family Christmas. I've been looking forward to it for weeks." Jessi got up and collected the hot chocolate mugs. "I hate to be a party pooper, but it's bedtime for Olivia and me. One more day of school, and then you can stay up a little later." Jessi reached for her daughter's hand. "I'll run your bath while you get your jams."

Merry stayed by the fire for a while longer. She'd taken over Olivia's room and was glad that Jessi had gotten a double bed when she was shopping for her daughter. Last night, even though she was dead tired, she had slept poorly. Her mind was still on the discussion she would have to have with Jessi. She prayed that a good night's sleep was in the plans for tonight. She sat down at the table and made out a menu and grocery list before going to bed. She'd have to get up early since Mark would be here to pick her up at seven thirty. She wanted to get an early start so she could do some baking tomorrow afternoon with Olivia. She wanted to make cut-out cookies. This would be the first time that she got to make sugar cookies with her great-niece, and she was hoping Olivia would enjoy it as much as Jessi had when she was a child. She needed to get all the colored sugars and all the other candies that made decorating the cookies so much fun. She couldn't find any cookie cutters in Jessi's cupboards, so she was really glad she had brought hers. After completing her list, spending time reading her Bible, and praying, she went to sleep and slept the whole night without waking.

Mark picked Merry up precisely at seven thirty, just as they had planned. Merry wore her new heavy coat and warm boots. She was glad she had because it turned out to be a cold day. During the drive and while they were walking around the grocery store, Merry was able to talk with Mark about the things she was unable to talk with Jessi about, namely, how their relationship was progressing. "She doesn't tell me a thing, Mark. I'll ask her sometimes on the phone how things are going with you, and she is so vague. Oh, she'll talk about you and Olivia or you and Julia. She's even told me Julia is dating a guy from your church. But she has not said one thing about her feelings toward you. I don't know if she thinks I will disapprove or if she herself is unsure of her feelings enough to not want to discuss it." She continued pushing the grocery cart through the large grocery store, selecting an item here or there to add to her cart.

Mark looked a little sheepish. "I haven't pushed anything, Merry. I haven't even told her that I still love her. I was afraid I would scare her off. Yet sometimes I can see something in her expression, a tenderness maybe … oh I don't know, but nonetheless, I sense something is there. I was planning on asking her out to dinner while you are here so you could maybe watch Olivia for us. I was hoping then to be able to talk with her a little bit. Although I don't think I'll be sharing my continued love for her anytime soon."

"I will talk with her, Mark. There are things I need to share with her, and then I think—or maybe I hope—she'll be more open to the idea of considering a relationship with you. If I speak with her the day after Christmas, would that fit into your timing? And will you mind taking Olivia for some dad-daughter time? It will be easier to focus on what needs to be said if Olivia is not there to overhear or to distract."

The cart was overflowing, yet Merry insisted she would still push it when Mark offered to take over for her. "Think of it as a walking aid for an old woman."

"I'd be glad to keep Olivia the day after Christmas. You two take all the time you need. Jessi had already agreed to let Olivia stay overnight one night while she is on vacation, so why don't I keep her that night? I'm sure Jessi will agree."

After checking out and loading the car with all the groceries, Mark took Merry home and helped her carry everything in. Merry looked at him with an affection that she'd never before seen him with. "Mark, I want you to know how proud I am of you. You have made such tremendous changes in your life. Your walk with God is proving to me that you are a completely different man, completely new on the inside. God doesn't do anything halfhearted, does he? Nothing, other than Jessi finding her way with God, would please me more than if you and Jessi would find your way back together. You are a son to me, Mark. I love you very much."

Mark was unable to respond. In some ways it was still hard for him to accept love from others, especially from those whom he felt he didn't deserve to receive love from. He knew his actions in the past had caused Merry a great deal of pain, and for her to profess her love for him caused him a great deal of joy, but also a measure of guilt. God was teaching him the meaning of unconditional love. He murmured his thanks and quickly left, saying he would see her on Christmas.

By the time Olivia got home from school, Merry had several different batches of cookie dough made. Now she was just waiting for her favorite little girl in the world to help her make all these cookies. Jessi had already made peanut butter and butter cookies, much to Merry's surprise. Not that she couldn't bake, just that she rarely had time to bake. They spent the rest of the afternoon listening to Christmas music and baking their cookies. Neither Merry nor Olivia had realized how much time had passed until they heard the door open and Jessi enter the house. "Oh my, I haven't made a thing for supper."

One look around the kitchen told Jessi everything she needed to know. They would have enough cookies for an army, and she was going to run to Janesville to pick supper up. "How about I run and pick up some chicken and biscuits. That way you two won't have to give up all your baking just to make some supper, nor will you have to change to go out to eat. See, problem solved."

Merry looked at Olivia and Olivia looked at Merry and nodded their heads. They both looked at Jessi. "Sounds good to us," they both said in unison.

That night they baked seven different kinds of cookies and ate fried chicken by the fire because the table was too messy to eat on. After cleaning up, they all decided that tomorrow would be a good day to head into town to finish the little bit of Christmas shopping that had yet to be done. Merry was enjoying this visit with her family. She prayed that there would be many more like it.

31

The Christmas Eve service went off without a hitch. Olivia made a wonderful angel, unlike her partner in crime who tripped up the stairs and landed on his noggin. The parents were horrified, but everyone else laughed and enjoyed the moment. Somehow, it didn't seem like a play if somewhere on the stage a child wasn't messing up, at least a Christmas church play. It was like being given a moment to exhale and breathe in a new breath to carry you through the rest of the play.

After the play everyone said their good-byes and "see you tomorrows" and headed home. There was much to be done in the night hours before Christmas morning. After tucking in their little angel, Jessi began working on wrapping presents and placing them under the tree, while Aunt Merry started chopping celery and onion for the stuffing and getting various other things ready for tomorrow's dinner. Mark and Julia were coming in the morning so Mark could take part in Olivia's Christmas morning. There would be cinnamon rolls and hot coffee and chocolate to tide them over until the afternoon meal. Neither of the women got much rest. To Jessi, this was a normal part of having a child, but Merry hadn't had to think about such things in years. She was having the time of her life. To have family around for Christmas was the second best part of celebrating the holiday for her. Her Jesus and her family—there was nothing so important.

They both headed to bed around two a.m., and Merry figured she'd have to be back up by seven to get the cinnamon rolls in the oven, that was if Olivia didn't wake them up sooner. The rule was, though, that no presents could be opened until Mark and Julia arrived.

Merry's alarm went off way too early. She rubbed the sleep out of her eyes and headed to the coffee pot. *First things first*, she thought to herself. After getting the coffee on, she rolled out the cinnamon rolls, and while she waited for them to rise, she mixed the stuffing together and dressed the turkey. By the time Mark and Julia were knocking on the door, Jessi was up and dressed and a sleepy nightgown-clad Olivia had wandered into the living room to sit at the base of the Christmas tree, patiently waiting for the grownups to join her. It didn't take long to realize that a cinnamon roll before opening the gifts was not going to happen. Mark and Julia placed their gifts under the tree with all the others and waited for instructions as what to do next. Jessi looked to Merry to lead the group in prayer and a Bible story, as she had been taught as a child. It was not a custom that she normally followed, but because Aunt Merry was visiting this year, it was only respectful to do as she was taught.

Merry picked up her Bible and turned to Matthew, where she read the story of the first Christmas. As with the custom in her family, she pulled out four small gifts, each one beautifully decorated to use as examples of the gifts brought to Jesus, and handed them to the four people sitting in the room. She reminded each of them of the most wonderful gift that they could ever receive, and that was the gift that Jesus offered to all who would accept it, the gift of eternal life. His purpose in coming to earth as a baby boy, simply put, was to die. It was his mission.

Upon finishing the Christmas story, Merry asked Mark to lead them in prayer. He was honored. It was one of the things he was looking forward to when his family was restored to him. He bowed his head. "Father, I am so honored to be here today. It is a privilege to sit here with my family and honor and thank you for your love and for your sacrifice. You willingly gave your only Son, knowing he would be put through the most hideous death by way of the cross, yet without him, we would never be able to spend eternity in heaven with you. Please, Lord, help us always to remember what the true meaning of Christmas is. Let us never lose sight of all you have done for us. Please be with us now as we spend time together as a family. Thank you, Lord Jesus, for everything. In Jesus's name. Amen."

Mark looked to Aunt Merry for her approval, and when she smiled and shook her head, he knew he had done just fine. When he looked to Jessi, her eyes were fixed on something that she could not see. He truly hoped it was the Lord Jesus.

Olivia interrupted everyone's quiet moment when she addressed them all. "Can we open presents now?"

Jessi looked at Olivia, her only daughter. What a joy she brought to all of life, not just Christmas. "Yes, it is time to open presents. Do you want to help me hand them out?"

Olivia didn't hesitate in answering her. "Daddy will help you. I have a lot to open."

This brought some laughter from the adults, but it was also logical because she was right. If they waited on her, they wouldn't get to eat the turkey, let alone get to the cinnamon rolls, which were still filling the air with their sweet cinnamon scent. Mark got down on his knees next to the tree. He looked at Jessi. "How about we work on opposite sides of the tree?"

"Sounds like a good idea to me." She knelt down on the opposite side of Mark.

Mark pulled the first one out from under the tree. "Hmm, and who could this be for? Oh, it's for Olivia. Imagine that."

Olivia let out a squeal as she opened up the first of her gifts. They opened presents for a good hour. The adults received such gifts as new scarves and books, while Olivia received games and doll clothes for her American Girl doll, a sled from her dad, and a very pretty new dress from Aunt Merry. There were only two gifts left under the tree to hand out, and Jessi had both of them in her hand before Mark could reach them.

"I've got these two, Mark. I would like to hand both of them out."

Mark got to his feet and sat on the couch by Aunt Merry, waiting to see what Jessi was going to do with the last two gifts. He was surprised when after she handed Aunt Merry one of the packages, she handed him one too.

"I've been working on this nonstop. I hope you both like them."

Mark tentatively began to open his present. He really hadn't expected her to get him anything at all, so the fact that she'd thought to get him a gift nearly caused him to choke up. When he opened the gift and looked at what she had given him he couldn't speak. Tears filled his eyes as he looked to her for an explanation.

Aunt Merry was the first to speak. "Oh, Jessi, this is so beautiful. I will treasure it forever."

Jessi felt the need to explain herself. "I have decided to make a conscious effort to start remembering Ethan for all the wonderful memories he gave me instead of mourning him for the rest of my life. I made the decision to heal while I was in Oklahoma this past summer and have tried very hard to do that. I decided that making scrapbooks of him would aid the healing process, and I felt like I should share these memories of Ethan with the two of you. As I went through the pictures of him, I chose which ones would go in which album, depending on what he was doing. I hope that you both like them."

Mark was paging through the book. Each page was of Ethan at a different age or doing a different activity. She had managed to find a few pictures of Mark and Ethan together, and she put those in his book so he would have those memories to cherish. He openly wept at the thought and the heart that went into this gift. The only pictures he had of Ethan were the ones that Jessi would put in his wallet when she had them taken. Back then he'd barely taken the time to glance at them. Since going to prison, he'd treasured those pictures, trying to keep them as protected as possible. Now here he was with a complete album of him, starting with his newborn pictures. To think he'd ever been jealous of this sweet baby. "Oh, God, forgive me." He cried openly, not caring that anyone heard him. Aunt Merry wrapped him in her arms and wept with him.

Julia sat in the chair with tears in her eyes. What a beautiful gift he'd been given. He'd often commented to her that he wished he had more pictures of Ethan. When she suggested he ask Jessi for some, he'd shake his head no, saying he didn't deserve to have them. Jessi had just given the most treasured gift he would receive this Christmas.

32

The day after Christmas, Jessi dropped Olivia off at Mark and Julia's to spend the night, just as Mark and Merry had planned. When she returned, Merry had turkey sandwiches ready for their supper. After eating they decided to settle in by the fire. They both received reading material for Christmas, and the thoughts of a relaxing evening by the fire with a good book were just too good to pass up. At least these were Jessi's thoughts as she picked up the new book that Mark had given her as a gift.

Merry's mind, however, was far from the new book she was holding in her hand. Finally she worked up the courage to bring up the journals that she had given Jessi to read. She took a deep breath and started talking. "So did you finish the journals?"

Jessi instantly stopped rocking the rocking chair when she heard Aunt Merry's question. She resumed again, hoping Aunt Merry didn't notice her hesitation. "Mmhmm." She continued to read.

Merry watched her turn the page of the book. She wasn't going to let this go. She knew it was imperative that she speak with Jessi about the journals and the choices she had made. She decided to try a different tactic. She began by asking about Mark. "So, how are things going with you and Mark?"

This got Jessi's attention. "What do you mean?"

"Well, I guess what I really want to know is if you've forgiven him yet."

"He's here, isn't he? Olivia is spending the night with him." She made these statements with such a vengeance that Merry already had her answer. She just wanted Jessi to hear herself say the words out loud.

"I didn't ask if he was a good father to Olivia or even, for that matter, if you approve of him being here. I merely asked if you have forgiven him for being the cause of Ethan's death."

Jessi's face pleaded with her aunt to not go there. Merry returned her look with one just as demanding.

Finally Jessi began to speak. "You know what he did. How can you ask me that? I will never be able to fully forgive him. I'm nice to him, and yes, you're right, he is a good father to Olivia. For that I'm thankful. But where was he when Ethan was here. Why couldn't he have been the least little bit interested in his son? No, Aunt Merry, the answer is no. He doesn't deserve to be forgiven."

"I see," was the only response Jessi received. Now that she had her attention, she returned to the journals. "Jessi, I want to talk with you about those journals. I need to speak with you. You need to know what happened after that last entry." Merry walked over to Jessi and took the book from her. She took her by the hand and led her to the couch, where they could sit together. "After reading what you have, do you have any questions for me or anything you'd like to say?"

Jessi was quiet for a moment. She looked at her aunt with fear on her face. "Where is your child? That's all I could think of all this time is where is your child?"

Merry took a deep breath. This was going to be harder than she'd imagined, and that was saying something, because she'd already imagined this conversation to be the hardest one she'd ever have in her life. "Oh, honey, what I am about to tell you I am not proud of. As a matter of fact, I don't want to tell you this, but I'm doing it because you need to hear it. The day I received Lester's letter I was convinced that if I tried one more time, if I wrote to him and told him how much I loved him, he would change his mind and marry me and be happy that we were having a baby. Well, it wasn't to be. The only response I received from him was another note saying he didn't want it, to get rid of it, and he never wanted to hear from me again. I sobbed. I thought my life was over. Little by little I began to think about what I was going to do. I would take the money out of my drawer and look at it and wonder if what he was suggesting would be the best thing all around. I mean, what kind of life could I give a baby, right? I started to justify the act, and part of me was so numb, so hurt, that I really didn't think past the reaction of my parents and friends.

"I found myself in downtown Oklahoma City one Friday night when my parents thought I was at a movie, looking for this Loretta person. I wasn't sure I was going to go through with it. I walked into her place, and she asked me what I wanted. I looked around at the dirty room, and then I handed her the envelope with the money and the note in it. She read it and then led me into another room and told me to take my pants off and get up on the table. I did as she said, and she told me it would only take a few minutes. I felt the most horrible pain I'd ever felt, and then she said it was over. I was told I would bleed for a few days and then that would be it. Only, that was not it. I didn't stop bleeding. I continued to bleed, and when my parents took me to the hospital and they were told about what I had done, the horror and the shame that I felt was worse than anything I could have ever imagined. Telling them when I first found out that I was pregnant, or even when Lester suggested the abortion, would have been nothing to the shame I felt when they stood before me in the hospital looking at me as if they didn't know me. I had shamed them, I had shamed our faith, but most of all I had shamed myself. It wasn't until later, after the doctor at the hospital had stopped the bleeding, that I found out how much damage was done. Apparently Loretta did more than remove my baby; she also punctured some internal organs, which was causing the excessive bleeding. In order to stop the bleeding, the surgeon had to remove part of my insides." Merry stopped to take a drink of water.

She hadn't meant to ramble, but once she started she wanted to tell her everything. She wasn't going to leave out anything. Merry looked at Jessi with tears in her eyes and continued. "Jessi, I was seventeen years old when I was told that I would never again be able to bear children. I had dreamed my whole life of having a family. My sin, my decision to do something that I knew was morally wrong, resulted in consequences that I would have to live with my entire life."

Merry watched Jessi's face and saw the horror in her eyes. "After I was released from the hospital, I was completely withdrawn from everyone and everything. A couple of my friends tried to make contact with me, but I didn't want to see or hear from anyone. I ended up leaving school and moving to Oklahoma City to live with my aunt and uncle, where my parents thought I might have a chance at living a normal life without being judged by everyone who lived in our small town. I attended church with my aunt and uncle and eventually came to know Jesus as my Savior. It was the first time since the abortion that I had felt true peace. Eventually I met your uncle John, and he and I started dating. I was truthful with him from the start. Most men fall in love, marry, and want to have children. I had to tell him that he would never have a child with me. I was scared. I didn't know what he would do. I loved him and I was afraid of losing him, but I also knew that if I wasn't truthful with him from the beginning, I would definitely lose him in the end. This way, I would at least have a chance."

Jessi had remained silent up until this point. "What did he say?"

"He told he me wanted a day to think about what I'd told him. I understood, but it was the longest twenty-four hours of my life. The next evening when we got together he took my hands in his and told me that he had prayed about it and that I was meant to be his bride. Of this he was sure. He promised to love me and cherish me, no matter what mistakes I had made in the past. Right then and there, he got down on one knee and proposed to me, telling me it would be his honor if I would consider him for a husband. I started to weep. I doubted there would ever be a man who would love me after what I had done, and now here was this man of God who could look past all my sins and tell me he would be honored to have me, the person who killed her own baby, as his wife. I can't tell you how unworthy I felt. Part of me wanted to shout to him, 'Don't you realize what you are doing. Don't you know what I am? I am a murderer. I don't deserve to be loved,' while another part of me wanted him to put his arms around me and hold me and help me understand that true love was patient and kind and longsuffering, just like the Bible talked about.

"You see I didn't know what real love was, and here was a man who was willing to give up his dreams of a family because he loved me." Merry took a moment to wipe the tears from her eyes. Jessi was on her second tissue. "My story doesn't stop there, Jessi. There is still more to tell. I still had my dream of having children, but I knew that was never to be. What I didn't realize was just how big of a God I now served. He loved me too, and it hurt him when I was hurting. He looked down at me and saw my broken heart and decided that out of his mercy he would give me what I didn't deserve. That's when he gave me you. God loves you, Jessi. He's had a plan for your life since the day you were created."

Jessi couldn't stop crying. She embraced her aunt tightly and didn't let go for a long time. She pulled away and looked at her aunt. "I love you, Aunt Merry. I will always love you no matter what."

Merry gazed at the daughter of her heart. This was the part that was going to hurt Jessi the most, but she couldn't stop now. She had to go on. "I will always love you too."

Jessi started to get up to put on tea water, but Aunt Merry pulled her back down next to her. "Jessi, there is something else I have to talk to you about. I bet you are wondering why I let you read my journals, why I've told you all about my past mistakes."

Jessi had to admit she had wondered that very thing. "It has crossed my mind a few times."

"I'm sure it has. Do you realize that Mark and I aren't so different? That we are both guilty of the same crimes, except if you look closely enough, there would be evidence according to some that my sin would be worse? Not only did I ask someone to kill my child, but I paid them to do it. In Mark's case, he would have never willingly taken Ethan's life. Yes, he made an extremely poor decision, and the consequences of his actions happened to take someone we love very much away from us. In my case, my decision was to take the life of my child and the consequence was I was never to bear a child again. There is a big difference between the two, Jessi." Jessi was crying and shaking her head no. Merry still went further. "Yes, Jessi, I am no better than Mark. Are you able to forgive me now that you know what I have done? You said earlier that you would always love me, but I don't think you really thought it through. Your emotions were leading you and you were feeling the pain that I was going through. Because if you forgive me of my horrific sin, how can you not forgive the man you vowed to love you till death do you part? He has changed, Jessi. He is no longer the same Mark, but one who has found the love of God. He still struggles with his guilt just like I did, even after finding my faith. John saw fit to love me when I didn't think I was worthy. Do you know why John still loved me?"

Jessi shook her head no, the tears still flowing down her face.

"Because he knew that he was just as guilty as I was. God doesn't see our sin as being better or worse than anyone else's. He just sees sin. And it's all bad to him. You see, John knew that he wasn't any better than me. He also knew that if he trusted God, God would take care of everything. He would fill in the empty parts. So I ask you again, Jessi. How can you say you can forgive me if you are unable to forgive Mark? True, you didn't know my child; I didn't even know my child. Maybe that was what made it easy to justify. But that doesn't change the fact of what I did. I know that you have feelings for Mark. I've seen it in your eyes when you don't think anyone is watching. You have come to care for him again. Maybe in a way you didn't before. I don't know, but if you don't take the opportunity to find out you'll never know if you were truly meant to be. Jessi, follow your heart and don't keep holding on to not forgiving. It will keep you from the life you are meant to lead."

Merry left Jessi sitting on the couch with her thoughts and a box of tissues. In her room she got down on her knees and prayed like she'd never prayed before.

33

The snow started falling in earnest sometime after midnight, and when Merry looked out the window first thing in the morning, the entire landscape was shrouded in white. She had only seen such beauty in pictures. It had been a couple of days since she had confessed her past to Jessi, and, being true to herself, Jessi was taking a few days to think before she reacted. She'd always been this way.

Wondering if today was the day Olivia would hold her to the promise of making a snowman, Merry went about making the morning coffee. She liked having a few minutes to herself before anyone else got up in the morning. She'd spend some time in prayer and in her Bible while sipping on her coffee. It was a wonderful time of day. Being able to see God's creation as she sat at the breakfast table was also an addition to her morning devotionals. She was halfway through her Bible reading when the phone rang. It was Mark asking if he could come over and sled with Olivia on the back hill right after lunch. Assuring him that it would be fine, she set the phone back on its cradle and resumed her reading.

Shortly after she started pancakes and bacon, both Olivia and Jessi came wandering out of their bedrooms, wondering what smelled so good. Jessi poured herself a cup of coffee. "I think you should stick around here. The coffee is ready every morning and breakfast is in the making. I think you are a keeper." She set her coffee down and wrapped her arms around her aunt. "Have I told you lately that I love you?"

Merry smiled over her shoulder. "I think it's been at least a couple of days, so I am very glad to hear it again." Relieved that Jessi was in a better mood than she had been the past couple of days, she flipped the pancakes and turned the bacon with a song on her lips.

Jessi noticed her singing. "You seem awfully happy this morning."

"I get this way when someone I love has made me happy. Speaking of being happy, Mark called and asked if he could come over and try out that new sled he got Olivia for Christmas. What do you think, Olivia? Do you want to try out your new sled on the hill out back with your dad?"

Olivia ran to the window and looked outside. She let out a squeal. "It snowed last night. I get to go sledding. Maybe we can make a snowman too." She looked at her aunt. "Remember, you said you would make a snowman with me."

"I remember, child. I just hope I don't freeze out there. Should we gather up the stuff for decorating our snowman while we wait for your dad to come? He said he was coming right after lunch, so it won't be too long till he comes since you slept in so late. Maybe we can even get a head start on making the snowman while we wait. I think it is warmer out there now than it will be when you two are done sledding. After finishing breakfast, Merry and Olivia gathered up the carrot, hat, scarf, some licorice for the mouth, and two black buttons, which would have to do for the eyes, while Jessi cleaned up the kitchen. Jessi got out her new digital camera, a gift from her aunt, to take pictures of the two of them laughing and playing in the snow. Aunt Merry was like a child romping in snow for the first time in her life. They rolled and pushed and even tried to pull the biggest snowball they had ever made. They got Jessi in on it when they couldn't budge the thing from where it sat, which still didn't help. Therefore, Snowman Bob, as Olivia named him, sat right in middle of the uncovered walkway.

Aunt Merry volunteered a solution. "Guess we'll just shovel around it, or Mark might be able to help us move it later."

"We won't be moving it if we finish putting it together. I guess we can call him Greeter Bob. What do you think of that, Olivia?"

"I think it's great. What a cool place for a snowman. He'll say hi to everyone who comes over."

They had just finished putting the finishing touches on him when Mark pulled into the driveway. "What a great snowman." He kicked some snow up and found the sidewalk underneath and started laughing. "I'm assuming you do not want him shoveled off the walk." He grabbed the snow shovel that Jessi had brought from the garage and started clearing the walkway. It was a beautiful winter day. The sun was out and the temperature was just above freezing, a perfect day for making snowmen and sledding.

Jessi looked at the snowball in her hand one last time before letting it rip. He just made too good of a target to not give in to the temptation.

Mark ran for cover after the first snowball hit him right upside the head. He dove behind his car. "This is war!"

Merry ran for the house. She couldn't remember a time when she was happier. Jessi had just been hit by a fastball and was laughing so hard she was on the ground. Olivia was involved too, but not to the extent that Jessi and Mark were. They were having the time of their life. Merry gave thanks for this gift of snow. "This is exactly what they needed, Lord. Thank you."

The snowball fight went on for a good fifteen minutes until Jessi called a truce. While the three of them headed out to the hill behind the house for some sledding fun, Merry used up the last of the turkey to make some turkey noodle soup. It would be the perfect thing to warm them up and fill them up when they were ready to come in. When the three of them came in the door, making more noise than anyone should be capable of, she had the table set and a fire going. After they stripped off all their wet clothes and boots, they washed up and joined Aunt Merry at the table, all three of them talking at once, telling a different version of the same story. After finishing the light supper of soup and sandwiches, Olivia wanted to be read to. Merry quickly volunteered. "I'll read to her. I want to spend some quiet time with her. You guys go on and do whatever you want. I put the Yahtzee game on the counter. You could play that if you want."

Merry and Olivia went in the living room and curled up together by the fire. It was getting to be the hour where the light of day was giving way to darkness in preparation for a peaceful evening of rest. The way the darkness rested on the new fallen snow was a sight to behold, catching Mark's attention. He caught Jessi off guard. "Would you like to go for a walk? No snowballs, I promise. Scout's honor." He held up the scout sign with his hand.

"I didn't realize you were a scout." She looked at him slyly.

"I wasn't. But I promise I won't attack … that is, unless I'm provoked."

She looked at him for a moment, remembering the words her aunt spoke to her a few days before. "All right, it is beautiful out there. And warm, for winter at least."

They walked in silence for a while, seeing all there was to see, watching the landscape around them gradually become completely covered in darkness, until the only light left was the snow on the ground and the stars and the moon in the sky. It was a perfect night for a walk.

Mark spoke first. "It's beautiful, isn't it? The way everything is shadowed because of the snow. I've never been around snow like this before. I've only seen flurries, nothing that ever stuck around. It's been a wonderful day. I had fun. Thank you for letting me be a part of it."

Jessi remained quiet for a moment, deciding how she wanted to respond to what Mark was saying. "You're welcome. I enjoyed the day too." She looked at him pensively. "Actually, Mark, I've enjoyed all the times we've spent together lately. You've changed. You're not the same man I used to know. I like the new you."

Mark stopped Jessi and turned her so she was facing him. "I've always liked you, Jess, I just didn't know how to show it. I like you even more now that I can see you without anything to block my view. You are truly a wonderful woman. In all the different roles you play—mother, teacher, friend—you model the true meaning of beautiful. Can we begin again? I don't mean forget the past; I just mean start again." Mark pointed to himself. "This is the person I was meant to be. This is the person I want to be. I will continue changing for the better, Jessi. Would you like to go out to dinner with me tomorrow night?"

Jessi sighed. "Yes, Mark. I will go out to dinner with you. But I want us to go slow, and I can't make you any promises. I want to be your friend for now. Can you handle that? Then let's see where things go from there."

They walked for a little while longer, each quietly entertaining their own thoughts. They could see the Christmas tree lights lit in the window as they headed toward the house. The multicolored lights were Olivia's choice. If Jessi had had her way, they would have all been white and the tree would have been a combination of angels and family heirlooms, including all the beautiful handmade ornaments that her children had given her. Someday her house would be big enough to have two trees, a Victorian tree and a children's tree, as she liked to call it. For now, a children's tree was the priority.

Aunt Merry had warm spiced apple cider ready for them when they came home from their walk. Jessi poured them each a mug and included a cinnamon stick, and they joined Aunt Merry by the fire. She was knitting a pair of slippers by the light of the fire and the tree. Olivia was already fast asleep, worn out by her day of outdoor play. Christmas music was softly playing in the background, and peace was prevalent in the home. It had been a wonderful holiday, and Merry enjoyed being with Jessi and Olivia for Christmas, but she was beginning to miss home. She'd been here a week now and would be staying through the New Year. Jessi was taking her back to the airport the day before she and Olivia went back to school. She missed her friends. She missed being able to confide in them and trust them to pray for her needs and the lives of those she cared about. In short, she had her answer on whether to move here to be closer to Jessi and Olivia. The answer was no. She could always visit, and her home would always be open to them to visit, just as it always had been. Besides, where would they stay in the summer if she decided to move to Wisconsin? Jessi would still be going to Oklahoma each summer to visit Ethan's grave. No, as wonderful a place Wisconsin surely turned out to be, she would miss her home too much to leave it.

34

Jessi decided to dress casually for her date with Mark, hoping it would ease the possible tension she might feel. She wore jeans and a maroon turtleneck with a pair of warm-lined walking boots. She left her hair hanging straight down and pulled out her leather coat to finish off the effect.

Mark walked into the house at six to pick her up, and they took one look at each other and both started to laugh. He too decided to go casual, wearing a pair of jeans and a turtleneck, his being white.

Jessi looked down at herself. "I'll go change my shirt. It's a little closer for me." Not sure what to wear now, she looked into her closet and found a light blue sweater she hadn't worn yet this year. She put that on and changed her earrings to match. She kept the leather coat and they were ready to go. "So where are you taking me tonight?"

"I think that is better left as a surprise." He'd done his homework and wanted to take her somewhere that was nice and yet had a casual feel to it, a place they might make into a good memory. He headed south on I-90. It was a clear evening with the stars already glowing against the dark backdrop, perfect for a date with his favorite person. He would accept the fact that she called him friend, for now. It was more than he had hoped for in a long time. She wasn't calling him the enemy, and that was certainly an improvement. He had reservations for seven, so he took his time driving, not wanting to make her nervous driving with him for the first time since the accident. He stayed right at the sixty-five-mph speed limit. They chatted about Olivia and her school and Jessi and Mark's jobs. They talked about Julia and her beau and how serious things were looking for her. Mark also remembered to invite everyone over for New Year's Eve. Julia decided they would have a fun and games night. Jessi said it sounded like fun but would talk with Merry before committing to coming. They pulled into the Japanese restaurant at ten to seven, making their reservation in plenty of time and having the desired effect on Jessi that he'd hoped for.

She hurried out of the car. "I've always wanted to try this place, but it didn't seem like the type of place you'd go to by yourself, or with a six-year-old girl, for that matter."

Mark smiled, proud of himself. "I thought it sounded like fun. I hope it's as good as its recommenders say it is." Mark opened the door for her and followed her into the dimly lit restaurant. He gave the host his name and then waited with Jessi on a nearby couch to be seated. Finally they were led to a shared table with four other couples and watched a Japanese chef prepare their food on a grill right in front of them. They had such a wonderful time laughing and enjoying the company of complete strangers that neither one of them felt a bit nervous about being in the other's presence. The pressure to constantly carry on a conversation was also diminished because someone at the table was always saying something to cause everyone else at the table to double over with laughter. Mark and Jessi agreed it was a huge success for a first date. After leaving the restaurant, Mark surprised her and took her for her favorite ice cream. She had had a scoop when she was in Oklahoma this past summer but hadn't had any since, as the closest shop was in Rockford. "I'm not going to be able to button up my jeans." Her complaint was halfhearted, as she still ordered a double scoop of Rocky Road.

Mark watched her lick around the cone. "I can see you are really worried." He took his own cone from the girl wearing pink and grabbed some napkins. They were going to need them. "I would take Olivia some, but I'm afraid it would melt by the time we got home. We can bring her down another time."

Jessi savored her cone. "It could become a regular road trip if we're not too careful. Not that I would mind much."

Mark nodded in agreement, too content with his mint chocolate chip to speak. They sat in a comfortable silence while they ate their ice cream cones. Jessi drank some water while she waited for Mark to finish. "Still the slowest eater, I see," She chided.

Mark raised his eyebrows at her. "But if you'll think back to the lesson learned in all this, you'll remember that it is I who is still enjoying my ice cream." Mark smiled sweetly at her while he took a long, deliberate lick of his ice cream cone. They both started laughing when he felt the melting chocolate land in a big wet spot on his leg.

Jessi couldn't help but rub it in a bit. "I think the main lesson I'm going to learn is if one doesn't eat his ice cream fast enough, he'll end up with it all over his clothes."

He wiped up his mouth and clothes with a napkin, and they both ran to the car, already chilled from the cold dessert. He opened her door and then ran around to his side. When he dropped her off at her door nearly an hour later, he told her to call him about New Year's Eve and then he left. That was the end of the date. No expectations, no arguing, and no awkward silent moments that neither of them knew how to fill. They just had fun.

• • •

Merry, Jessi, and Olivia ended up going to Julia's New Year's Eve party. Merry was leaving the day after New Year's, and this would be a good time to be able to say good-bye to everyone, not to mention meet Julia's new friend. They played board games and TV guessing games, but the best part of the evening was playing charades. Everyone participated, and everyone laughed until they hurt. It was a wonderful evening for everyone, and while there was no kissing going on at the strike of midnight, there were a few looks that could have been interpreted as longing.

• • •

The next day, Merry and Jessi chatted and relaxed while Olivia played with her new Christmas gifts. Knowing tomorrow would be the last time they would see each other until Jessi returned to Oklahoma in June put a damper on their evening. They enjoyed being in one another's company, and Aunt Merry wanted to at least bring up her discussion with Jessi and see where she was at. They hadn't had time to finalize their feelings, and Merry didn't want to take any chances of leaving Jessi with hurt feelings. "Did you have a nice time with Mark the other night?"

"I was wondering if we were going to have this conversation tonight. And yes, I did have a nice time. He picked out the perfect place. We were around other people most of the time, and it really put us at ease. I was afraid we would be uncomfortable in each other's company, but it wasn't like that at all." Merry remained quiet because Jessi looked as though she wanted to say something else. "Aunt Merry, do you think I am failing Ethan in some way if I have a relationship with his father? Sometimes I think I'd like to get to know this new Mark. He still has the characteristics of the Mark I fell in love with and some new really great traits. I like him, Aunt Merry. I truly do. I just don't know what's right."

Merry chose her words wisely. "Jessi, did Ethan love his dad?"

Jessi looked confused. "Yes."

"Do you think that if Ethan had survived the accident and he was alive today that he would have forgiven his father and loved him anyway?"

"Ethan loved everybody, Aunt Merry; you know that."

"Yes, you're right, I do. The point I'm trying to make is I think Ethan would want his mom and his dad together. If he were here today, he'd want both a mom and a dad, and he definitely would want his little sister to have both parents. I think right now he is looking on saying, 'Look, God, your plan is working. My dad and sister know Jesus now. I'm just waiting for my mom so she can spend eternity with us too.' Jessi, do you remember what I taught you when you were a little girl? That nothing happens on this earth without God's approval?"

Jessi remembered the talks she and her aunt had when she was younger, before she had an attitude with the church. "I think so."

"Then you'll remember how I told you about God being all powerful and all wise. His power gives him the ability to do anything he wants. That includes making people do what he wants. But in his wisdom, he knows that a person needs to be able to make their own decisions. He tries to warn us of the consequences. Sometimes we choose not to hear, and other times we heed the warning and listen to his voice. In the end, if we choose to love him, he will make something good happen out of the bad. I believe that is what you and Mark are going to see: good things coming from a very bad situation. First, though, you need to find your way back to God. He's the only way that all of this is going to make any sense. If you open your heart to him, he will not hurt you; that I can promise. He loves you, Jessi, and he wants you to be filled with his love and his joy. I need to ask you something, and I wouldn't do it unless I thought you were ready. I haven't pushed you or nagged you about your faith, and I don't intend to now. I do ask that you start attending church with your daughter. She needs to see you as an example, someone she can look up to. Will you do that for me? Whatever else happens—whether you and Mark end up together or apart, or maybe you meet someone new you want to spend the rest of your life with—you need to get right with God. It's the most important thing you could ever do. So, will you start going to church with Olivia?"

"I've thought about it for a while now. I never told you that I was going to start going to church right before Ethan died. I was going to tell him that. Then the accident happened and I blamed God instead of finding solace in him." Jessi became thoughtful and then spoke again. "I'm not saying I'm all ready to serve him or anything, but I will start going to church. You are right; Olivia doesn't need my grudges or bad feelings to be passed on to her as she gets older. I have to at least try. I'm also going to start seeing Mark on a regular basis. We are going to take it slow and see where we end up, but at least it's a start."

They finished the evening out with some small talk, plans for Easter, and when Jessi was planning to come for summer this year. After tucking Olivia in, they called it a night and got plenty of the rest for the next day's travel.

Checking in for a flight out of Chicago was much more hectic than at the little airport in Oklahoma City. It was amazing how large O'Hare was. There were trains and tunnels, moving sidewalks, and musicians playing for money. It was almost like a carnival. After checking her luggage and saying good-bye to Jessi, she had two hours to sit and wait to board her plane. She wasn't nearly as nervous about flying this time as she was the first. Hopefully it would get easier each time.

At the gate she took out her Bible and began to read. At times she would take a break and watch and pray for a certain person as the Lord directed her to. Mostly, though, she just read and waited.

Time passed quickly, and before she knew it she was buckling into her seat on the plane. This time she was a bit friendlier and talked with the person sitting next to her, and that helped the flight pass quickly. When she stepped off the plane in Oklahoma City and started in the direction of the luggage pickup, she heard them before she was able to see them. Mabel had something to say, and the rest of the group was carrying on like there was no tomorrow. When she came into sight, they all started talking at once and even louder than they were before they saw her. She smiled to herself as much as to them. She was home. She had missed it as much as she missed them. They were almost as much a part of her family as Jessi and Olivia were, the best friends a woman could have. After hugs all around, they led her to the baggage claim and helped her carry everything to Mabel's Cadillac. This time when they stopped for lunch, she had no problem eating her meal. Mabel caught her eye halfway through the meal and winked at her. Merry replied with a great big bite of the best homemade mushroom soup and a satisfied grin.

35

It felt wonderful to be home, and not just because the weather was warmer, although she wasn't going to complain, that was for sure. Merry walked into her living room and sat down in her favorite chair. She closed her eyes and thanked God for a safe trip and allowing Jessi to be open and willing to listen to what she had to tell her. It was here in this home that she had raised Jessi and loved and cherished her husband, John, until death did them part. After sitting for a few minutes, she got up and walked around her living room looking at the pictures scattered around her room. Her parents' wedding picture, her in-laws' picture, along with her and John's picture, hung together above the piano. She studied her own parents for a moment. "Lord, I know the worry I put them through. I'm going through just that now with my own Jessi. The hours of prayer and petition on my behalf must have been overwhelming at times. It's comforting to know that I will see them soon and spend eternity with them praising you. I pray that I will have the same level of dedication when it comes to praying for Jessi. I still stand on the promise, Lord, that she will come to you before she leaves this world."

The pictures on the piano were of Jessi at various stages in her growing-up years, from birth through her college graduation. She had never understood purchasing art for her walls when she could have pictures of her loved ones hanging throughout her house. If she wanted to see beauty, all she had to do was step outside her door. The other open spaces were occupied by pictures of Ethan and Olivia. She carried the scrapbook Jessi gave her for Christmas and added it to the table that held various frames and knickknack types of gifts she'd been given over the years.

Merry went into the kitchen and rinsed her teapot out before putting water on to boil. The house was nice and toasty because Mabel had stopped by and turned the heat up before she'd picked up the others to head to the airport. The wind still had a bite to it, and it gave Merry a case of the chills. It should be getting warmer on a permanent basis here soon, she thought to herself as she made her tea. The house was quiet, something she was going to have to get used to again. She spoke out loud, just to hear the sound of her own voice. "It's just you and me again, Lord."

Merry picked up her Bible and read from the book of Psalms, 28.

36

Mark put away the containers of Chinese while Jessi tucked Olivia into bed. Their lives had become pretty predictable in the past two months since Merry had gone home. They had gone out to dinner, to see plays, to watch a movie, they hit the museums in Chicago and Milwaukee, you name it, and if Olivia could join them for the activity, they probably did it. Every weekend was busy. Privately, both Jessi and Mark felt as if they were playing catch up, trying to see and do everything they possibly could because they had done absolutely nothing as a couple with Ethan when he was alive. Of the activities and outings that they had gone on, according to Mark, there was none as important as the fact that every Sunday since Aunt Merry left, Jessi had been going to church with them. Mark didn't know what happened to prompt the change, but he was happy she was going. She didn't participate much, but she did listen to the message each week and respectfully thank their pastor each week when she shook his hand. The Word didn't return void. He would stand on that promise from God's Word. Everything she was hearing was a seed being planted and taking root. Eventually those seeds would grow into plants, giving fruit. He finished cleaning up and waited for her to come out of Olivia's room. She returned just as he was stoking the fire. "Ah, and is our girl off to dreamland?"

"Yes, she was so tired from everything we did today that she dropped off before we even finished her Bible story. That's become the norm lately, especially on weekends when we have been going so much." Jessi watched Mark, trying to read the look in his eyes. They had become good friends, and she enjoyed spending time with him. They almost felt like a family. To the outside world, they sure looked like they belonged together, especially with Olivia calling them by "mom and dad." She'd heard people murmur about how nice a couple they made. She wondered if they ever noticed that she and Mark weren't wearing wedding bands. She looked down at his hand where a ring should be and noticed that he was wearing his old wedding band. How long had that been there? Jessi walked over to Mark and lifted his left hand and questioned him with her eyes.

Mark looked from the ring to Jessi. He had been wondering when she would notice. He'd been wearing if for the past two weeks. "Yes, it's my wedding ring. I never got rid of it and I, well, I felt like I should be wearing it. In my heart of hearts, Jessi, I know we are meant to be. Through everything—or in spite of everything, I am not sure—but together regardless of it all. I will never love another woman. You are the only one for me." He lifted her chin until her eyes met his and gently kissed her on the lips. It was a light sweet kiss. Nothing overly passionate, just tender, a kiss that said "I honor and cherish you." Mark let go of her and walked out the front door to his car.

Jessi watched him pull out of the driveway, her fingers still lingering on her lips. Her emotions were betraying her. Her initial reaction was stunned. After he left she worked up the courage to be angry. but that dissipated almost as quickly as it came. What she ended up with was a longing for the man she had fallen in love with, the one who held her heart in his hand, the one who knew her like no one else ever would. She still loved him, even with their history. She wasn't sure how or when it happened, but she'd fallen in love with her husband all over again. Jessi went to bed dreaming of a man she'd spent the last six years trying to hate.

Mark drove around a little while before heading home. He hoped he hadn't overstepped his bounds by kissing her. He wasn't able to help himself any longer. He'd wanted to do that for so long that when she looked at him with those beautiful eyes questioning him about his ring, he wasn't able to stop himself. He would begin to win her hand in earnest now.

Monday morning before work, Mark called and ordered thirteen red roses to be delivered to her classroom that afternoon.

The note read: *A single rose for Olivia, the daughter I love with all my heart.*

A dozen roses for Jessi, the woman who owns my heart.

I love you both. Mark

He spent the rest of the day painting and wondering if she'd received his gift yet.

Jessi had just finished her lunch when the deliveryman came with the flowers. She knew who they were from. Who else would send her roses, especially to work? Her eyes glossed over as she read the card. The rest of the day everyone she worked with noticed she was considerably happier. At home she put Olivia's single rose in a small vase and her own in a larger one. Then she called Mark to thank him. The phone rang a couple of times before he answered the phone. "Hello." He and Julia didn't have caller ID.

"Hi, Mark, it's Jessi. I wanted to call and thank you for the flowers. They are beautiful."

"You are welcome. I was hoping you would like them."

"Yes, I do like them. They were the envy of every woman at work today. I was wondering if you would like to come to dinner on Friday night? I know we talked about the three of us going out to dinner, but I thought I would make something here instead. Would that be okay with you?"

"Well, sure, but will Olivia be disappointed? I told her she got to pick where we eat this time, and I'm fairly sure we were going to that pizza and game restaurant."

"No, I don't think she will be upset. She's spending the night with a friend on Friday night, so it will just be us. I think it's time we talk. Things seem to be changing between us so fast, and I want us both to be on the same page regarding our relationship. I've done nothing but think since Sunday night. I need to share some things with you."

"What time do you want me to come?"

"Say six?"

"I'll be there."

"See ya Friday."

"See ya Friday."

Mark hung up the phone wondering where this was going to lead. "Lord, I hope I didn't mess things up with that kiss."

Each day seemed to crawl for Mark. He might not be so antsy about having dinner with her alone if she hadn't told him she wanted to talk with him. Now he spent each day wondering and worrying about what she wanted to say. On Friday he stopped on the way to her house and bought a pie. He couldn't think of anything else, and he didn't want to show up empty-handed.

Jessi watched Mark get out of the car with something in his hands. He looked horrible, like he hadn't slept all week, the cause of which was probably her fault. She should have told him that what she wanted to say wasn't bad. As a matter of fact, she guessed he would think it was very good news. Jessi held the door open for him as he climbed the front porch to the door.

"I brought pie." He handed her the box that held the peach pie and walked in the front door and kicked off his wet shoes. After hanging up his coat, he followed Jessi into the kitchen, where she had the table set and some wonderful smells coming from the oven. "What are you making? It smells delicious in here."

"We're having stuffed pork chops with twice baked potatoes and honey-glazed carrots. I was just going to cut up a loaf of French bread to eat with our salad when you rang the doorbell. Grab whatever you would like to drink out of the fridge. I've got a glass of water already."

Mark grabbed a Pepsi from the fridge and set it on the table in the place where he normally sat and waited on Jessi to finish slicing the bread. Jessi placed the salad on the table, and Mark prayed over their meal. He didn't walk on eggshells around Jessi regarding his faith. She knew what he believed, and he wasn't going to diminish how much it meant to him for anyone's benefit. He didn't push it on her, so it surprised him when she brought up the subject as they started eating their salad.

"Mark, I've been thinking about us and how God fits into the equation. I mean, if we were to get back together, would you expect more out of me in the faith department than what I'm willing to give?"

Leave it to Jessi to just blurt out whatever she was thinking. Mark put down his fork and took a deep breath to give him some time to think. What was she saying "if we get back together"? Mark walked around the table to the open chair closest to Jessi. He took her fork from her and set it on the table; then he took both her hands in his. "Jess, what are you saying to me? I mean the 'us' part."

Jessi looked from the table to Mark. Then she lifted up her left hand so he could see the ring she had put back on her own finger. She never knew why she had kept it. For some reason she couldn't bring herself to throw it away, and after seeing Mark wearing his old ring, she found hers in the bottom of her jewelry box. It was a plain band. They didn't have the money for a diamond engagement ring when they'd first gotten married. She knew it would send the message she didn't trust herself to deliver by voice—that she too wanted her family back.

"Do you really mean it, Jess?"

She couldn't trust herself to speak, so she just nodded her head yes.

He had to answer her questions before going any further. "Jessi, I am going to trust God in bringing you to him. If you are willing to keep doing as you are doing, I believe we will still be honoring God in being together. It's how we started. I won't expect any more of you until you are ready to give it. Does that answer your questions about faith?"

"I can accept that. I don't know that I'll feel differently, but I will still go to church each Sunday with you and Olivia. I just don't know how much more I have to give right now. I'm trying to see God in everything. It's just hard for me to accept him being so powerful yet unwilling to intervene."

Mark got down on his knee before her. "Jessi, I have to do things right this time." He pulled a box from his pocket, one that he'd been carrying around for the past six months, hoping and praying that the right time would come to use it. "Jessi, would you do me the honor of becoming my wife? I promise that I will love you and honor you for the rest of my days." He opened the box, and Jessi gasped. Inside was the most beautiful ring she'd ever seen.

Tears sprang to Jessi's eyes when she looked at the ring and thought of all that it meant. "Yes, Mark! I've been happier these past months than I've ever been, even more than when Ethan was here, and I'm not sure I like the sound of that, but I can't help it. I'm happy, Mark, and I want to be happy forever. I like being happy. You and Aunt Merry and Olivia have been right all along. Forgiveness brings a freedom that I'd never expected. I forgive you, Mark, and I love you. I think I forgave you some time ago. I just felt if I let go of those hard feelings, I'd be letting Ethan down somehow. I didn't realize until I talked with Aunt Merry that Ethan would want me to forgive you. It's what he would do if he were here today."

Mark took the ring out of the box and slipped it on her finger. They would have to take it in and have it resized. Her fingers were smaller than the original bearer of the ring, so the ring was a little loose. "This ring belonged to my grandmother, Jessi. I was very close to her up until she died, and I wasn't made aware that she'd left this ring for me until we moved here. When Julia was going through her things, unpacking, she came across it and the letter from our mother. I believe it's God's perfect timing in her finding the ring now. I want to grow old with you, Jessi. I want to hear children's laughter in our home for as long as we live."

Jessi noticed the smoke first. It was rolling out of the oven door. She jumped up and threw the oven door open. When she pulled the pan out of the oven, they both knew this would be a story to pass down for generations to come. The pork chops were completely black and rolling with smoke. She turned off the oven and looked at the mess sitting on top of her stove. Jessi looked at Mark and couldn't help but laugh. "So much for a nice homemade supper."

Mark couldn't agree more. "Put your coat on. I'm taking you out to celebrate. We'll stop by the mall and have the jewelry store resize the ring for us."

The rest of the weekend flew by in a blur. Plans were made for an early June wedding and a family honeymoon to Oklahoma City. Aunt Merry and Julia cried when they heard the news, and Olivia jumped up and down screaming. Finally, she was going to have a real family.

37

On Wednesday the unpredictable March weather brought in a snowstorm. Jessi had spent most of the winter worrying about Olivia going to and from school on the bus, especially when the weather turned nasty, but nothing had ever happened, so she rarely thought of the road conditions anymore. She'd pretty much gotten used to the weather and the roads, like most native Wisconsinites.

Stan tried to keep his eyes on the road ahead. Looking around and thinking about the poor conditions were not going to do him any good. He had to keep his concentration on climbing the hill in front of him. The hill he was climbing was the steepest hill in the county, and it was part of his normal route. Usually it wasn't a problem, but with today's surprise snowstorm, the road had become a problem. The snow had blown over onto the road, and while he could gauge where the road was, he wasn't able to see if there was ice on the pavement. He still had fourteen kids on the bus who were heading home. Why did they send him out in this? He yelled back to the kids. "Everyone sit down and be real quiet, okay?" He was starting to lose momentum. The bus was slowing down. If the bus came to a stop on this road, he would never get it going forward again, and being halfway up the hill, he was sure to slip backward. He was scared to death. He tried to accelerate, making the tires spin. The bus started rolling backward, picking up speed as it went.

He tried to use the brake, hoping he would hit a dry patch in the road and at least keep the bus from falling off the side of the road. The road must be a solid sheet of ice. The bus started to slide sideways. He could feel it. Braking wasn't doing anything.

Stan looked at the direction they were heading. "Oh, Lord, help us!" He cried for the kids to brace themselves, not that they knew what that meant. The bus slid to the side of the road where there was a decline in the terrain. Stan felt the bus begin to tip over. The bus did a half roll and ended up on its top, wheels still rolling in the air. Stan never knew what hit him. When the bus rolled a young tree trunk pierced his driver side window, killing him instantly. The small children were thrown about in the bus. Some were still conscious but didn't know what to do, while others were knocked unconscious.

A driver heading down the hill was the first person on the scene. He dialed 911 as soon as he saw the bus. He ran to the bus, still talking to emergency, trying to get a grasp on how much help was needed. "Oh no! We need ambulances now. Children are laying everywhere. The bus driver is hanging upside down, bleeding." Whimpering was coming from the back of the bus. He kicked the door as hard as he could and tried to get to the children who were crying. "Some of the children are crying in the back. I'm trying to get to them. Hurry!"

He shut his phone off so he could use both hands. Another car pulled up behind his, and the driver got out to help. Together they were able to get the door to give. Not wanting to move the kids, in case they would injure them more than they already were, they tried to calm them down by talking in quiet tones to them, all the while praying that help would get here quickly. The sirens coming from a distance were welcome sounds. It took eight ambulances to get everyone to the hospital.

Mrs. Richards was the first person to call for Jessi. "Hi, Jessi, I'm sorry to bother you at work, but I've been waiting for the bus to drop off Olivia and it hasn't come yet. I'm beginning to get a little bit worried."

Jessi looked at her watch. The bus should have dropped her off almost a half hour ago. "I'll check into it and call you back. If you hear something first, will you call me and let me know?"

"Of course I will."

Jessi hung up the phone and dialed Olivia's school's number. The secretary answered the phone. "Hi, this Jessi Jensen, Olivia Jensen's mother. Olivia hasn't arrived at home yet, and I'm just wondering if anything has happened?"

"The bus driver did call and say that the roads were pretty bad and they were running late. I'm sure it's just the snow keeping them from being on time."

Jessi was persistent. "I would feel better if you tried to radio your bus driver to make sure that things are okay."

"I'll have to call the bus company and have them contact him. If you don't hear from me, assume they are just running late from the snow."

The secretary hung up before Jessi could say anything else. She walked down to the office of her own school. Susan, the assistant principal, was walking out of the office as Jessi was nearing the door. "Jessi, the bus Olivia takes home from school was involved in an accident. She's been taken to Mercy Hospital in Janesville with the other children."

Jessi began to shake. Susan, not knowing what Jessi had been through with Ethan, tried to calm her down. "Jessi, sometimes these things happen. Most of the time the children are just taken to the hospital as a precaution and they are released as soon as their parents arrive. I'm sure they slid into a ditch or something and they are all fine. I will go down and take over your class so you can get to the hospital. I'm sure Olivia is scared and needs her mom." She smiled at Jessi and patted her shoulder as she left her standing in the hallway.

Jessi ran back to her room and gathered her coat and her purse. She left her classroom to the assistant principal and her aide. When Jessi saw the conditions of the roads, she became dizzy and had to hold on to the side of the building. She called Mark from her cell phone to let him know what was going on and where they would be. "Mark, I'm so scared. I can't do this again. I just can't."

After hearing what little she knew, Mark tried to comfort her while making his way to his own car. He'd have to hurry if he was going to arrive at the hospital anywhere close to when she did. Thank God he was working fairly close to the hospital. "Listen, sweetheart. The principal is probably right. Those buses are so big, the odds of the kids getting hurt in an accident are very low. Let's wait till we get there to see what we're dealing with. We'll probably give her a big hug and be able to take her home right away."

Jessi pulled into the hospital parking lot and saw one of Olivia's classmates leaving the building with his mother. He was still obviously upset and crying but seemed to be more scared than anything. His mother smiled at Jessi as she ran past them toward the hospital emergency entrance.

Mark saw Jessi running and yelled to her, "Jessi, wait up!"

She heard him and watched him run to catch up with her. They both hurried into the emergency room. There were parents and grandparents everywhere. One woman was sobbing, while others looked like they were waiting to see what their fate was. Mark approached the check-in desk. "Hi, we received a phone call that our daughter was in a bus accident. Our daughter's name is Olivia Jensen." He pointed to Jessi. "This is Jessi Jensen, her mother, and I am Mark Jensen, her father. Can we see her please?"

The receptionist wrote down their names. "Do you happen to have a picture of your daughter, Mr. Jensen?"

Mark pulled Olivia's picture out of his wallet and handed it over.

She glanced at the picture and left to show it to a doctor who was just coming out of a room. After looking at the picture, the doctor followed the woman to where Mark and Jessi were standing. He extended his hand in greeting. "Mr. and Mrs. Jensen, I'm Doctor Carlson. We have been waiting for you to arrive. I will take you to see Olivia. She has been asking for you, but first I need to talk with you about the injuries she has sustained. Olivia has a damaged spinal cord. The CAT scan shows she has fractured the fifth, sixth, and seventh vertebrae in the thoracic section of her spinal cord. We will have to see what her limitations are. While she seems to breathing just fine on her own, we are still watching her in ICU to make sure there are no respiratory problems. It is important that you are both positive. Her attitude in rehabilitation is going to be key in how much progress you see in her ability to overcome her injuries. She will feed off your attitudes. If she sees you being negative and worrying, she will be negative and worry. If you are positive and see her getting well in your attitude, then she will think that getting better is the only option. Come on. She's been asking for you."

Mark took Jessi's hand and led her behind the doctor through an open room with only curtains separating the patients. Dr. Carlson looked back at them. "Don't be surprised when she doesn't reach for you. Presently she has no ability to move her arms and hands. She is scared. Try to be calm." He continued walking and pulled back the curtain where a nurse was sitting with Olivia.

The nurse looked at Jessi and smiled. "This must be your mom and dad now. I told you they were on their way. I'll just leave so they can fit in here. It's kind of small in here, isn't it?"

Olivia looked from the nurse to her mother. Tears filled her eyes and the corners of her mouth made a downward turn. Jessi rushed to her side, desperately trying to keep herself from crying. "Hi, sweetheart. I heard you had a bad accident. Your daddy and I got here as quick as we could. I hope you weren't waiting too long on us."

Olivia looked at her mother. "Momma, can I have a hug?"

Jessi reached down and held her daughter close, resting her cheek on her daughter's.

Mark and Jessi spent as much time as they could keeping Olivia company, reading to her, telling her stories, and doing their best to bring laughter to her lips. The reminder of days in intensive care with Ethan were always close at hand, and for Mark, the guilt at not having been there to support Jessi during the stress of those days was sometimes overwhelming. He just thanked God that he was here now.

They both took breaks to call and inform everyone of Olivia's injuries. Jessi called Aunt Merry. The answering machine that Jessi insisted Merry buy when she was there activated instead. "Aunt Merry, this is Jessi. Olivia's been involved in a bus accident. I really need you to pray, and get everyone else praying too. They say her spinal cord is damaged and she may never walk again. Call me on my cell phone when you get a chance. Love you."

Mark called the church where he and Olivia attended. It wasn't long before people all over were praying for Olivia.

When Jessi and Mark sat down in the waiting room while Olivia was being taken to have an MRI, Jessi about lost it. "I am not going to make it through this, Mark, if something happens to her. I won't make it. I just know I won't. I can't do this again."

"Jessi, nothing is going to happen to Olivia. I have a peace about all this. I trust that God knows what he is doing, even though we don't understand why this could happen, not again, not after everything that happened with Ethan. God is God. I know you haven't come to accept that yet. But you are going to have to make some decisions, Jessi. You say you cannot handle this, and you are right. But you won't lean on the One who will help you get through it and trust in him no matter what the outcome is."

Jessi's eyes betrayed a deep-seated fear as she spoke. Her words already sounded defeated and without the strength he was used to hearing in her voice. "What if she doesn't make it, Mark? What if she never walks again? Am I supposed to just accept that is God's will and be happy about it?"

"If ultimately it is God's will, then we will have to accept it. But I don't believe for one minute that this is God's will. I have a peace, Jessi, that our little girl is going to walk again, and soon. I believe she is going to astound the doctors and nurses and all the naysayers. But until that happens, we have to let God be our strength."

Jessi looked like she had retreated into a place where Mark couldn't reach her. Her facial expression alarmed him, and he began to take hold of her. She almost whispered. "I shouldn't have let her ride the bus. It's all my fault. I knew better. I didn't listen to the voice in my head. How could you even think of loving me, Mark? I am such a horrible mother. I don't deserve to be a mother."

"Jessi, you have to stop taking the weight of the world upon your shoulders." Mark grabbed her by the upper arms and shook her slightly. "Jessi, look at me. Someone with much bigger shoulders has already done that." Jessi still looked away with that look that proclaimed her failure at trying to be perfect once again. Mark shook her once again. He practically shouted to get her attention. "Jessi, look at me!" Jessi turned her face toward him, he who had begun to mean something in her life once again. What was he saying to her?

"Listen to me, Jessi. You have to let go of blaming God and blaming yourself. You have transferred the blame from me to yourself and God a long time ago. He isn't the taker of life, Jessi. He's the giver of life. He's the one who gave you Ethan to love and take care of. Yes, he ultimately is in control, and yes, technically he could have put his hand forth and stopped everything that happened. But think about it, Jessi, that would be no life for us. We'd never know pain and sorrow and choose—and yes, I mean choose—to love our God, because we need a Savior who has chosen to love us first, through it all. He loves you Jessi, and he wants to carry all your pain on his shoulders. It's time for you to give it up. Give it to him, Jessi."

Jessi felt the sobs erupt from deep within her soul. She couldn't do this again. She couldn't square her shoulders and make it through another tragedy. She needed God to give her the strength she so desperately yearned for . She cried out to him. "Oh God, help me. Be my strength, oh Lord."

Everything she ever knew about him came pouring over her. His love, his strength, his patience, his loving-kindness, and especially his forgiveness filled a void in her that started in her toes and washed up through her to the top of her head. A refreshing river of life completely filled her being. Jessi wept in Mark's arms. Together they prayed for their daughter and all the other children who were in the bus accident. Together they prayed for a miracle for their little girl.

Olivia was transferred to the rehabilitation center after the results from the MRI were confirmed. There were no blood clots or anything else forming that would have to be surgically dealt with. Now was the time to watch and see just how much damage was done. Sometimes Mark and Jessi spent time with Olivia together, and sometimes they took turns, one going to read to her and one going to the chapel to pray. Already Jessi could tell what a difference God made in the waiting process. Even though there was sadness, she wasn't without peace. It made all the difference.

When Merry got home she saw the light on the new machine blinking on and off. She had tried to tell Jessi she didn't need the thing. If something was that important, the person doing the calling would call back. But Jessi insisted, saying that every person should have one. So she had relented and let her pick one out and help her hook it up. Now the thing was blinking. She walked over to it and pressed the play button. After listening to Jessi's message, she sat down in the chair, not trusting herself to stand up right without falling. "Olivia? In an accident? Oh, Lord, please help her now. Touch your daughter, Lord, and please give Jessi peace of mind, Lord. Lord, I don't understand this, but I trust you and I believe your will, will be done." Merry picked up the phone and dialed Jessi's number. Mark answered the phone.

"Hello."

"Hi, Mark. It's Merry. I just got Jessi's message. What is happening there?"

"At the moment we're just waiting. Apparently, when the bus rolled, the kids were thrown about pretty good, and one of them landed on top of Olivia. Of course, there is no way to tell exactly what happened, but the position she was in, along with the position of the child on top of her, indicates that the child was thrown with some force into Olivia's back. Maybe an elbow or something strong hit first; that's our best guess. Things could be much worse, Aunt Merry. A couple of children were Med flown out of here to the university hospital in Madison, and two of the children, along with the driver, died in the accident. We are very blessed. Things could be much worse."

"I doubt Jessi is seeing it that way, though."

"Actually, Jessi is holding better than you'd expect. She accepted Christ through all this. As a matter of fact, while we've been waiting, she has been offering to pray and talk with other parents who are in the same place as we are."

Merry instinctively understood that God, in all his wisdom, knew that Jessi would have to hit bottom before she would be able to look up. "My Jessi finally has a place in heaven. Oh thank you, Jesus." Merry was quiet a moment before she remembered Mark was still on the line. "Mark, I'm calling the airline now and booking a flight as soon as I can. I will call you back with all the details."

Merry hung up the phone and called the airline. The next flight was for seven the next morning. She booked the flight and called Mabel and the others for two reasons—first, to see if Mabel could take her to the airport again, and second to see if she and the ladies could gather together tonight for an impromptu praise meeting. Her Jessi had given her heart to Jesus. If ever there was a time to celebrate, it was now. Jessi might not have understood how they could bring themselves to be happy at a time like this, but give her time and growth in their Lord, and she would eventually understand. She called Mabel first and then the others. Everyone was coming over at seven o'clock. She had just enough time to throw a casserole in the oven.

Jessi went from person to person in the waiting room. She didn't know all the parents yet wanted to encourage them as much as possible. There were as many different types of injuries for as many different children as there were in the accident. The initial assessment of the bus driver was penetration of a tree branch directly to his heart. They found him still strapped into his chair upside down with a piece of the tree protruding from his chest. He died quickly from rapid blood loss. One of the children who died was Olivia's best friend, Sam. She and Olivia had been sharing a seat when the bus rolled over. Jessi was trying to console her mother, Kristy. She had arrived shortly after Jessi and Mark and was just told about her daughter. Her husband was on his way, and Jessi was sitting with her until Tad arrived.

Jessi took Kristy's hand in hers and held on to it. From experience, Jessi knew there wasn't much you could say to a grieving mother that would do any good. It was best to let them cry and not offer any excuses or explanations. In time there would be closure and the healing would begin; for some sooner than others. It wasn't too long before a man walked in and called out Kristy's name. Jessi wrongfully assumed he was her husband. She'd only met the man once and couldn't remember what he looked like. Kristy stood up and hugged him. "Oh, Pastor Dave, what am I going to do?"

"God will strengthen you, just like he strengthened Linda and me when Jeremy was taken from us in that car accident. You will be with her sooner than you can imagine, and then you will have eternity to spend together." He pulled away from her and addressed her lovingly. "I'm not saying it's going to be easy. It will be anything but easy. God will not let go of you. He will be walking along side of you the whole way. Where is Tad?"

"He's on his way. He should be here any moment."

Pastor Dave looked from Kristy to Jessi. "And who is this?"

Jessi extended her hand to shake his and introduced herself. "I'm Jessi Jensen; my daughter, Olivia, was involved in the accident as well."

Pastor Dave covered her hand with his. "How is Olivia doing?"

"She's going to have a tough road ahead of her. Her spinal cord was damaged and the doctors are not sure if she'll ever walk again."

Kristy's reaction to Olivia's condition surprised Jessi. "Oh, Jessi. I'm so sorry. If there's anything I can do, please let me know. We will be praying for you and Olivia."

Tad walked in at that moment, and Kristy turned to him, explaining what had happened to Sam. Pastor Dave listened in, but Jessi wanted to give them her privacy, so she walked around the room, watching the reactions of the parents around her. Kristy amazed her. If that had been her and her daughter had just died, she never would have even thought about anyone else's problems and here Kristy was offering her kindness and compassion. She looked around the room and saw Mark watching her. She started to walk toward him. She had so much to learn. He stood and wrapped his arms around her.

"Have I told you how much I love you lately?"

"Yep, but I could stand to hear it again. Mark, Olivia is going to be just fine. Even if she never walks again, she'll be fine."

"Hey, while you were talking to Sam's mom, the nurse let me know that Olivia is all tucked into her new room. She's ready and waiting for us to get there. And Aunt Merry called. She'll be on a plane first thing in the morning, and everyone at church is praying, along with all her friends. There is nothing greater than the prayers of the saints, Jess. And we've got a whole lot of them praying right now. I wouldn't be surprised if she were up walking when we get to her room."

"Knowing Olivia, she'll be walking soon enough. I don't think there is anything that will keep that girl down."

Mark and Jessi walked hand in hand to room 223 in the rehabilitation center of the hospital to remind a certain little girl of the strength that was in her, an all-powerful force that nothing could keep down: the God of the universe, her very own wonderful and loving God.

38

Merry had just hung up the phone with Jessi when the doorbell rang. The ladies started coming in twos and threes until everyone was there, talking at once. It was a happy group because there was so much to celebrate. Jessi, after much prayer, had finally given her heart to Jesus. Tonight was going to be a praise and worship night. Merry had the piano and the sheet music ready to go, and after eating the bounty of the Lord, they would praise him for his wonderful faithfulness. Tonight's celebration was what she had been looking forward to for a long time. True to tradition, Merry had to tell the whole story while everyone else ate. She snuck in a bite here and there while telling everyone about Olivia's bus accident, resulting in Jessi needing to rely on God for her strength. "I just talked with the girl myself, and I'm telling you this is not the same Jessi that I just spent Christmas with. She's a changed woman. She has a peace she says about Olivia and her walking; that means whatever happens, she's trusting God for his will to be done." Merry looked toward heaven. "I don't know what you did with the old Jessi, Lord, but thank you for this new one. I sure appreciate it." Everyone started laughing. Things were a little more solemn when she spoke of Olivia, and she asked them to all consider her in their prayers when praying at home.

Everyone looked as if they were finished with their meal, so Merry started in to the living room and sat at the piano. She took out the prayer journal and attached Jessi's picture and the day's date. She placed the journal on the piano and then started to play songs of praise and continued on to energetic songs of high praise. The ladies were dancing around the living room giving thanks and praise to their God for yet another answer to prayer. It looked as if Merry Duvall was having the party of a lifetime in her living room. In her haste to get to praise, she forgot to close the living room window curtains.

Jeff and Debbie had just moved into the neighborhood and enjoyed walking in the evening with their lab, Smooches. They didn't have children yet, and with both of them working, this was their time to unwind and spend a little quiet time together. They had been enjoying the same walking route now for the past two weeks. It was a nice neighborhood with nice people. They were only a few houses down from their own when they couldn't help but stop and stare at the events happening inside their new neighbor Merry's house. Jeff spoke first. "What in the world?"

Debbie just shook her head and then cocked it to one side. There were a bunch of old, gray-haired women dancing around the living room like wild banshees waving their arms all around.

Jeff looked at his wife. "Did she remind you of someone who might do drugs when she brought that cake over the other day to welcome us to the neighborhood?"

Debbie still couldn't believe her eyes. She shook her head no.

What Jeff and Debbie didn't realize was the celebration had started much earlier in the day. As a matter of fact, it started right after God and Jesus watched and heard Jessi call out the name of Jesus and confess him as her Lord. When Jesus took up the pen and wrote her name in the Lamb's Book of Life, a host of angels started the party. If for some reason God opened their eyes and they could see at that very moment into heaven, they would witness angels dancing and singing and blowing on horns, praising and celebrating right along with the older ladies in the house, and Jeff and Debbie would be the only ones standing out in the whole scene playing out before them.

As it were, they continued on their walk, wondering what that was all about. Within the next six months they would know. Merry had just lost her last loved one's soul to pray over and she would need a new one to take its place. Any guesses as to whom she chose?

39

Merry's flight arrived right on time, and Julia was there to pick her up. O'Hare wasn't nearly as frightening the second time around. Julia filled her in on Olivia as they drove toward Wisconsin. Mark and Jessi had taken turns sitting with her during the night so if she woke up she wouldn't be scared. They took turns sleeping, each in a room reserved just for parent use, for two hours at a time. Merry was going to insist both of them go home and get some rest when she arrived at the hospital. She would stay and keep Olivia company. She brought Olivia a new book and a new doll, another of the American Dolls, with matching sets of pajamas. She was sure to love them. Olivia mentioned the fact that she would like to have them someday. Maybe the doll would be an inspiration to her to start trying to move her hands and feet.

Julia pulled into one of the overhead rest stops on the highway, and they both got some lunch to go. When they entered Olivia's room, they found Mark and Jessi both looking terrible, sitting in chairs half falling asleep. Merry looked to Julia. "Would you look at this?"

Jessi was the first to look up at her aunt. She got up and hugged her tightly. "Thank you for coming."

"You couldn't have kept me away if you had tried."

Mark followed suit and gave Merry a hug. He smiled a thankful smile and offered her his chair.

"Actually, Mark, Jessi. I want to spend some time with my niece. She and I have some things to discuss. I want you both to go home and get some sleep." She looked at Mark. "And maybe a shave. Then come back this evening after you've gotten some rest. That will give Olivia and me some time to talk about what's going on here." She picked up their jackets and helped them put them on. "Julia, would you drop these two off at home and make sure they get some rest." Jessi started to object, and Merry interjected before she could barely start. "No, you don't need your car. You will fall asleep driving, and then I'll have another accident victim on my hands to be praying for. I mean, I know you accepted Jesus, but I don't want you to be going home to him quite so soon. Julia will come back for you later on. Get going, both of you."

Merry turned her back on the three of them and gave her entire attention to Olivia. "Well, my dear. Here we are. So how are you today?"

Olivia looked at her aunt. "I'm not doing so good, Aunt Merry. Did you hear I was in a bus accident?"

"I heard about that. I am sorry to hear that you were hurt. Your mom and dad are pretty worried about you, do you know that?"

"I'm sorry I'm making them so sad. I try to be happy, but I can't make my mouth smile. I'm just too sad inside."

"I can understand being sad inside. Maybe you need something else to think about that will make you happy inside."

"I could try that. Do you have something for me to think about?"

"I think I do. That is, if you think you could handle it. It is going to be some hard work, but I think together we could make you think of something else besides yourself. What do you say? Do you want to give it a try?"

"What is it?"

"Do you want to do something to make your mom and dad really happy and very proud of you?"

"Yes."

"Then let's you and me try to help you move your fingers."

Tears filled Olivia's eyes. "I already tried. I really did, and I can't."

Merry was moved with compassion for the child but couldn't give up the goal. "I know you tried your hardest. You always try your hardest. But do you remember who is stronger than you are? Jesus, right?"

Olivia nodded.

"Did you pray to Jesus to help you move your fingers? Did you ask anyone else to pray so that you could move your fingers?"

"No, I just tried by myself."

"Well, how about this time we pray first and we ask some other people to pray too, and let's see if Jesus will help you move your fingers, okay?"

"Can we pray right now?"

"We can, and let's call some friends and have them pray too."

Merry used her new cell phone to call the ladies in Oklahoma and get them praying. Then she and Olivia closed their eyes and asked God to begin to heal Olivia. They prayed for few minutes—as much as a five-year-old would stand for—and then they began to work on Olivia's hands. Merry began to massage each hand, one at a time. She used herbal lotion and worked it into the muscles, praying as she went.

Jessi fell into her bed, exhausted. She didn't remember ever being this bone weary. If it weren't for Aunt Merry coming to the hospital and taking over, she would still be there, trying to do something when there just wasn't much of anything she could do. She prayed for Olivia's healing and her acceptance of God's will no matter what that came to before she completely passed out.

Mark looked at the clock one more time to make sure he had set the alarm. If he didn't set it he was afraid he wouldn't wake for at least a good ten to twelve hours, maybe more, and Julia would be back to pick him up at seven. He read his Bible before he laid his head down and prayed one more time, not just for Olivia, but for all the injured children and their parents. He slept peacefully and without remembering any dreams. When his alarm went off at six thirty he felt as if he'd been hit by a Mack truck, totally out of it and not ready to get up. Julia had offered to spend the night at the hospital tonight so he and Jessi could get a good night's rest. At first he didn't want to accept, but realizing the shape he was in, and knowing Jessi was the same, made him give in to her offer.

He took a quick shower, put on some clean clothes, and had just finished brushing his teeth when Julia pulled in the driveway.

"Hey, you're up. I thought I would have to throw a cold bucket of water on you to get you out of bed."

"If it wasn't for Olivia, not even cold ice would have done the trick. I'm so tired. The nap helped, but you're right, we need to get some real sleep. We'll need to be clearheaded to keep up with everything that's going on and make good, solid decisions. I think I'm going to talk to Jessi about your offer. Then, once we get caught up on some sleep, we can start taking turns sleeping with Olivia in her room."

"I can sleep in that recliner in her room, no problem. You guys can relieve me in the morning so I can go and get cleaned up. It will work just fine."

Julia and Mark pulled into Jessi's driveway at seven fifteen. She was dressed and ready to get in the car. "I talked to Aunt Merry a little while ago, and she said she and Olivia have a surprise for us. I hope she found a way to put a smile on that little girl's face. If she is going to improve at all, it has to start with her attitude. She was so depressed earlier, and I don't know what to do to bring her out of it."

Mark agreed. "Yeah, it's not like we can get her new toys; she'll just be reminded daily of why she can't play with them."

"When I just think of the words *quadriplegic* or *paraplegic*, my stomach turns. I am praying so hard for a miracle here, Mark. You have a closer relationship with God than I do. What do you think he is saying?"

Mark looked at Jessi, knowing what she wanted to hear yet afraid to speak anything but the complete truth with her. "I do have a peace about the whole situation, but that doesn't mean God's will is my will. I've had to learn that simply means trusting God to know what is best and believing that he has my best interest in mind when making his decisions. I'm sorry it's not exactly what you want to hear, Jess, but it's the best I can do. We have to trust him."

Jessi spoke out loud something that both of them had been thinking about since the accident happened. "Mark, I don't think we should have the wedding until Olivia is well enough to be there. The doctors say she could be in therapy for some time, that is if she gets any movement back at all."

"I agree, Jess. But I don't want us to wait forever. Even if she doesn't regain mobility, it will take the two of us to properly care for her without wearing one of us completely out. It is going to be all right. Somehow I know that much."

Julia pulled into the hospital parking lot, and the three of them walked together to Olivia's room. The first sounds they heard were giggling. Jessi was so happy she almost had tears. Not wanting to ruin the moment, whatever it was, they stayed outside the door to listen for a minute. They had not heard Olivia laugh since before the accident, and the sound was beautiful to their ears.

After eavesdropping, they walked into the room bearing gifts. Mark brought in a big bouquet of daisies that had a silly balloon tied to it, something that he was sure Olivia would like. Jessi brought the DVD player and a new movie that Olivia had been wanting to see, hoping that would keep the boredom to a minimum. The smile they saw on Olivia's face stopped them all in their tracks. She was glowing, absolutely glowing. Jessi put her bags on the table and went to her daughter. She held her face in her hands. "Your smile is the most beautiful thing God has ever created."

Olivia pulled away from her mother's embrace. "Mommy, I think your smile is the most beautiful." Then she lifted her hand ever so slowly and traced her mother's lips. Everyone in the room started crying at once, including Aunt Merry, who was already aware of what God had accomplished that afternoon. The doctor who had stepped into the room wiped his eyes when he witnessed the scene. The girl had worked awfully hard this afternoon and had surprised everyone when she began to move her fingers. Now she was not only moving her fingers and hands, but lifting her arms as well. It really was nothing short of a miracle.

Jessi stayed with Olivia while Mark took Julia and Aunt Merry to get some dinner. He promised to bring them back something really good to eat. Jessi hoped so because she felt like she could eat a horse. After they left, Jessi pulled out Olivia's Bible to begin reading to her. Olivia took the Bible from her mother. "Mama, can I read to you?"

She helped Olivia hold onto the Bible. Olivia began to read in an almost perfect manner. Jessi was astounded. "Olivia, when did you learn how to read?"

"I didn't want to tell you before because then you wouldn't read my Bible to me."

How did this child get to be so smart? "So you figured I would make you read the stories all by yourself?"

"Sometimes you did that already. You didn't finish some stories, so I would read them after you left my room."

Jessi didn't realize Olivia knew the difference. She never gave the child the credit she deserved. She was a smart one, this child of hers. "Yes, I did do that, didn't I? I'm sorry that I hurt your feelings. Sometimes Mommy wasn't ready to hear about Jesus and the things he did. I knew that if I chose to let Jesus love me I would have to love him, and if I loved him, then I would have to change some things that I wasn't ready to change. I'm sure that doesn't make a whole lot of sense, but it's how I felt then."

"Aunt Merry told me you love Jesus now. Do you?"

"Your Aunt Merry is correct. I do love Jesus very much, and I am very thankful that he loves me too."

"Now we can be a family, right? And live together in the same house like mommies and daddies do?"

"Pretty soon, sweetie, we will do just that. First, we have to get you better. That is the most important thing to your daddy and me. Then we'll think about having the wedding."

"Mommy, I want us to still have the wedding when we said, when school is out, so we can go visit Ethan together on our honeymoon. Why do they call it a moon?"

Jessi laughed. "I really don't know why they call it a moon. I've never thought of that, Olivia. I suppose it's called honey because you go with the person you love and sometimes you call that person honey. I have no idea why it's called a moon, though. Maybe your aunts or your daddy will know the answer to that. We'll ask them when we get back. Would you like to finish your story now? I really like you reading to me."

Olivia finished reading, and they were halfway through a game of Sorry, with Jessi being sorely beaten, when the two aunts and Mark got back from dinner. He had a box with cheese pizza in it, and Olivia was glad to be able to eat the pizza all by herself.

Now that everyone knew what she was capable of, along with the fact that Jessi had not flat out refused her request to keep the wedding in June, Olivia had the desire to succeed, the attitude to make great strides in her therapy, the support of her family, and God, the most powerful ally she could have.

40

Mark and Jessi, with the help of Aunt Merry and Julia, fell into a good working routine with Olivia. On the way home one afternoon, Jessi brought up the discussion she had had with Olivia about the wedding. "She still wants us to marry when we originally planned; that's why she has been working so hard. If we don't, it's going to break her heart." Jessi looked at Mark for his opinion.

"Well, let's tell her nothing's changed, then. If need be we'll wheel her up the aisle in a wheelchair. Wedding's on, just as we planned."

"Should we tell her tomorrow when we go in? I think the news will give her even more determination to get better."

"It looks like we're getting married in June. Should we start making plans when we go in each day? You know, talk about the cake and food and colors and all that? It might keep her mind busy during the tough times."

"I think that is a good idea. Maybe tomorrow we can stop and pick up some invitation samples on our way." Jessi reached over and squeezed Mark's hand.

Mark pulled into Jessi's driveway. Julia was spending the night tonight with Olivia, and today was Aunt Merry's day to stay home. They both went in and found a pot of beef stew on the stove and some fresh bread, hot and ready for supper.

Mark gave Aunt Merry a kiss on the cheek. "Thank you. This smells so good." He washed his hands and sat down at the table, waiting for the ladies to sit with him. "Julia was in her pajamas and all ready for bed when we left. It was really nice of them to let us put a rollaway bed in her room. I didn't relish the idea of Olivia waking up in the night scared and not sure or awake enough to get the help she needs."

Mark ladled out stew into everyone's bowl while Merry sliced the warm bread.

Jessi buttered her bread and dipped it into the stew. "I think our schedule is working out pretty good." She took a bite and sighed. Jessi spent Friday night, Sunday night, and Wednesday night at the hospital, Mark was there Monday night and Thursday night, Julia spent Tuesday night and Saturday night, and Aunt Merry spent five days a week at the hospital praying and working with Olivia, reminding her why she was working so hard at becoming well. The miracles were not instantaneous, but they were miracles all the same. Each day brought new victories.

Aunt Merry agreed, although she had been more than willing to sleep at the hospital, seeing as everyone but her had to go to work the next day. "I have to admit, things have been going well. The hospital has been so understanding about us being there with Olivia."

Mark was not saying too much; his mouth was full most of the time. "This is really good. I was so hungry. We were too far out of town working for me to make a fast food run for lunch, and I didn't grab anything when I stopped by the hospital 'cause I knew you'd have something awesome for supper." He took another bite. "And I was right." He filled up his bowl again.

Jessi watched how much he was eating. "Where do you put it all?" She shook her head, unbelieving. "Aunt Merry, Mark and I have some news." Jessi looked to Mark and continued on. "We have decided to continue with our wedding plans as they are. We debated putting it off until Olivia was better, but Olivia wants us to keep the plans, and we think it will give her reason to keep working hard at getting better."

"I couldn't agree more. I think you will see that child fly through therapy. If she can manage to manipulate her hands and arms in one day, imagine what she can do in two months if she puts her mind to it, with the Lord's help, of course." Merry rose from the table and took a pie out of the oven.

Mark looked from his half eaten bowl to the pie. "You could have told me we had pie."

Jessi started laughing. "I don't think you are going to have a problem finding a place to put it, Mark."

They finished eating, and Mark helped clear the table and wash the dishes before he left for home.

On Sunday after church, everyone met at the hospital to eat lunch with Olivia. Mark, Julia, and Aunt Merry went to church together in Julia's car since Jessi would stay the night with Olivia. Jessi announced the wedding news to Julia and Olivia. "We've decided to go with your suggestion, Olivia, and keep our wedding date the same. You have been doing so well, we don't think it will be a problem for you. So we stopped and picked out some invitation samples. We'll have to send them out really soon."

Everyone helped in getting ready for the wedding, and it wasn't long before things were falling into place quite nicely. After six weeks of therapy, Olivia was able to sit up on her own, feed herself, and manipulate all the fingers and thumbs on both her hands. She had some feeling in her toes and was beginning to wiggle them. She was doing amazingly well.

The plans for the wedding were also progressing. The invitations were sent out, and Jessi and Julia were trying to find spare time to pick out dresses. Julia decided to take her laptop to the hospital and look at ordering dresses online, that way Olivia could be part of the decision-making process. Jessi picked out a tea-length ecru dress, and Julia and Olivia fell in love with mint-green summer dresses with matching hats. She placed their order. "Well, that was easy enough. We're having the wedding and the reception at the church, and Mark and I already picked out the menu. We're having true picnic fare. A local catering company is providing all the food, and when we went to counseling with the pastor this week, we talked about the actual service. It looks like everything is working out." Jessi let out a deep breath. "I wasn't sure if we were going to make it. It's been a long six weeks."

Julia leaned back on the chair, listening to Jessi and watching Olivia brush her own hair. Just watching her do the simple things most took for granted gave her pleasure. Julia hadn't told anyone her own news yet. She and Bert were going to get married. They had so much in common and they both shared the same dreams. It was hard living day to day without him. He owned his own business in town and was able to get away during the day to bring lunch. They spent many afternoons talking about their past and where they saw themselves in the coming years. There was so much going on that she really didn't want to add anymore to the list, but she didn't think she'd be able to keep it in any longer, let alone keep the ring off her finger when she was around family. She decided to tell Jessi and Olivia. "Hey, you guys. I have some news of my own. I wasn't going to say anything with everything else going on and all, but I feel like if I don't tell someone I'm going to burst. Bert asked me to marry him and I said yes." She held out her hand to show Jessi and Olivia the ring. "We are waiting until August, when you guys will be back from Oklahoma, and I thought I would ask Mark to give me away."

Jessi gave her a big hug. "I am so happy for you Julia. He seems like such a nice guy in the little bit of time that I've gotten to know him. Look at you. You're practically bursting as it is. How didn't I notice before?" Jessi blew out a big breath. "I'm sorry, Julia. I should have noticed how happy you are and guessed."

"Oh, don't be silly. I've done a pretty good job of hiding it until things settled down, at least somewhat."

Julia gathered her things to leave. Jessi was spending the night with Olivia, and visiting hours ended at eight; it was ten to.

...

The weeks continued to pass quickly, and before everyone knew it, it was only a week until the wedding. The dresses had been fitted; the seamstress even came to the hospital to fit Olivia. Everyone was impressed with her services. The cake had been ordered, and the only thing left to be seen was if Olivia would be able to go on a trip. She had not been allowed to go home yet. In the three months that Olivia had been in therapy, she had learned to do almost everything, everything, that is, but walk. Her latest victory was using a walking crutch to make it across the room. This was the plan for walking down the aisle.

Jessi and Mark purchased a small house that was set up for handicapped access. Hoping that Olivia would be able to come home after the wedding, they had everything ready for her.

Aunt Merry would be flying home a couple of days later. Although she volunteered to drive to Oklahoma with them to help with Olivia, they said it would be better if she flew and prepared her own place to make it easier on all of them. Olivia wouldn't be climbing stairs this time, so she would need a place to sleep on the main level. So that was the plan. There were things she could change, things that she had used for her husband's care when he was still alive, things she could put to good use now with Olivia.

Olivia was permitted to spend the night at home on the eve of the wedding to see how she would fare. Jessi and Merry spent the night with her at the new house, making use of the equipment that was purchased to ease Olivia's transition to home. They stayed up too late talking about the wedding, and it was after midnight by the time Olivia was sleeping soundly. After Aunt Merry went to bed, Jessi called Mark, knowing he would probably be asleep but wanting to hear his voice. "Hi, were you sleeping?"

A sleepy voice answered, "Uh, no... I mean, maybe I just dozed off."

"I'm sorry I woke you. Olivia just went to sleep and I wanted to hear your voice. And I wanted to tell you I love you. That was all."

"I love you too. We haven't had much time to spend together, just the two of us lately. I miss those times."

"I know; I was missing our time together too. I guess that's why I called. I'll see you in the morning."

"It's going to be here soon; you should try to get some sleep. It won't be long before we'll have more time together. Know that, okay?"

"I guess I better get to bed. It's going to be a long day tomorrow. Good night."

"Good night."

Jessi hung up the phone, wondering how she had come full circle. There was no doubt she loved this man, more than she ever had. God's grace was more than she'd ever hoped for. She drifted off to a wonderful place in her dreams.

41

The morning of the wedding was clear and sunny. It was going to be a beautiful day for a wedding. Jessi stretched and looked outside her window. Having a house in town was going to take some getting used to. She put on her robe and peeked in Olivia's room. She was still asleep. Jessi took a hot shower and dressed in a pair of sweats until it was time to get ready for the wedding. Aunt Merry had coffee on and a light breakfast of fruit and muffins on the table when Jessi emerged. Julia would be here around eleven to help her get ready. The ladies at the church were taking care of the decorating, and the caterers would be arriving around noon. The wedding was taking place at one o'clock, and lunch would be directly afterward.

Julia arrived with bags and baskets, makeup and hairstyle products. It took a good hour and a half to get everyone ready. Aunt Merry didn't want to be fussed over but still admired herself in the mirror when she looked at the job Julia had done on her hair.

Julia drove the four of them to the church, and Jessi and Olivia hid away in the women's bathroom until it was time to walk up the aisle. Jessi's parents were unable to come for the wedding, which didn't come as a big surprise, seeing as they hadn't made it the first time she and Mark wed, so going against tradition, Aunt Merry was walking her down the aisle.

Jessi looked in the mirror at herself, trying to see what Mark might see when he looked at her from the front of the church. Her hair was piled up on her head with curls cascading down here and there. Her makeup was perfect, and the dress was a bride's dream, so why was she so nervous? Maybe because this was her wedding day? Because she was marrying the same man she had been married to before? What if this was a mistake? What if she had allowed her emotions to control her and not her head? She couldn't believe after all they had been through together lately that she was still questioning him and his character, but a small voice kept creeping up, whispering in her ear. Aunt Merry chose that moment to enter the room Jessi was waiting in. "Are you ready?"

Jessi still stood in front of the mirror looking at her image. "I guess I'm as ready as I will ever be."

Merry took her hand and pulled her away to the sitting area. "It's only natural that you are asking yourself some hard questions right now. You are marrying a man who brings some painful memories of the past into your relationship." Merry looked from Olivia, who was napping on the couch, back to Jessi. "Do you love who Mark is today? Do you want to spend the rest of your life with him? Can you see yourself living without him? I know I'm asking some very pointed questions, but they are questions you will have to answer before you can say 'I do.'"

Jessi already knew the answer to all the questions. "Yes, I do love Mark, and no, I can't even begin to imagine living without him. We are meant to be. I guess I just have a case of the nerves. There have been so many changes in the last few weeks, and now I'm getting married." What she said was just beginning to sink in. "Aunt Merry, I'm getting married. I've been so focused on Olivia and her therapy and planning the wedding that I've hardly given any thought at all to getting married. Maybe that's why I'm so nervous. I haven't prepared myself for the actual marriage to Mark."

Merry looked at her watch. "I think you better wake Sleeping Beauty; the wedding is supposed to start in a few minutes."

Instead of being scared, Jessi was now excited. She gently nudged Olivia and woke her from her light sleep. "Hey, it's almost time. Are you sure you feel okay enough to do this? We can still get your chair up here."

"No, Mom. I can use my crutches. It's not that far to walk." They both heard the music start to play. Olivia smiled and with Jessi's help, stood up. With a crutch under each arm, she made her way to the door. "I'll be right outside if you need me, Mom."

Aunt Merry held the door open and joined her. "We'll be waiting for you. Come out when you are ready."

They both left the room, and Jessi felt the excitement begin to build. She was going to have a husband again. Someone she could share her dreams and goals with, someone to laugh with, someone to love and to be loved by, and someone to fight with; of course, making up always used to be fun. Yes, this was what she wanted. She walked out the door ready to get married.

Julia walked down the aisle first, and then Olivia followed. Halfway up the aisle, she handed her crutches to Bert and took a basket of rose petals from him. She looked to the back of the church to her mother and smiled a great big smile and continued forward, without crutches, sprinkling rose petals as she went. Jessi really didn't want to cry, but after seeing Olivia walk, even for the short distance that she had, she couldn't help but shed a few tears. It truly was a miracle watching her daughter overcome her obstacles. She focused on what she now had to do. They had written their own vows, and though she had hers memorized, she was afraid she would forget them. The wedding march began.

Mark watched the most beautiful woman in the world walk toward him. She was the epitome of grace and beauty. Every day since she said yes he'd thanked God for his wonderful mercy. He didn't deserve to be here. There were many places that he did deserve to be, but this was not one of them. He smiled at Olivia, who was standing across from him. After today, they would all be together as family, both in God's sight and in the natural. It was a day he had been looking forward to for a long time.

Jessi reached the front of the church. Mark smiled and took her hand, hoping to put her at ease. He knew she was nervous doing anything in front of crowds. There were only a hundred or so guests that came—some friends from school, some of Mark's friends from work, and the church family—but Jessi would still see a multitude of faces. As long as she only looked at him and their pastor, she would be all right.

Pastor Tim started the ceremony. When it came time for the vows, Mark began. "Jessi, my dearest Jessi. I promise that I will cherish you, honor you, lift you up when you are weak, and love you as Christ loved the church and gave his life for it. You will always be the center of my life. I would forsake everything to be by your side. Your needs will always come before my own, and I promise to provide for us to the best of my ability. I will stay near when you become ill and wipe your tears when you cry. I will rejoice with you when you rejoice, and I will mourn with you when you mourn. I promise to love you all of my days." When it came time for her to say her vows, Jessi felt her voice wobble slightly, but she remained strong. "Mark, I promise to love you, to honor you, to encourage you, and uplift you. I will stand by you every day for the rest of our lives, no matter what circumstances come upon us. You will always be the one I look to for leadership, love, and friendship. I will remain loyal to you and be your companion all of my days. All of my love will be yours till death do us part."

Mark placed the ring on Jessi's finger, and then Jessi placed the ring on Mark's finger. They kissed and were pronounced man and wife.

Before sending the couple down the aisle to wait in the receiving line, the pastor made an announcement. "Everyone is requested to make their way out to the back of the church by the pond where chairs are set up for your convenience. After the outside portion of the service is concluded, the bride and groom will have a traditional receiving line."

Mark and Jessi left the platform of the church by way of the side stage doors. They changed into summer clothes, and when they found

Olivia changed and ready, they headed out to the pond. Everyone was already seated and wondering what was happening. Pastor Tim let them know. "Mark and Jessi have requested something very special as their first act together as a married couple. They would like the whole family to be baptized together. I am going to baptize Mark, Pastor Gregg will be baptizing Jessi, and our children's pastor, Pastor Mike, will be baptizing Olivia. While Mark and Jessi are going to be baptized by immersion, the manner our church normally baptizes, we will be doing things a little bit different with Olivia. Because of her recent accident, we don't want to shock her system, and the water is still pretty cold from the long winter, so Pastor Mike is going to baptize her in the manner of our Christian brothers and sisters who choose to baptize by sprinkling. Our biblical view of baptism indicates that by being baptized we are telling the world we are Christ's. I believe that God will see Olivia's heart and know that she wants the world to know that she is truly his. First Corinthians tells us that baptism symbolizes that when we are going under the water, we are burying our old self, and when we are lifted up out of the water we are being resurrected with Christ. Therefore, by dying with Christ, we choose to live with him."

The pastors led Mark and Jessi into the water. Pastor Mike lifted Olivia into his arms and joined them. Pastor Tim led the baptismal service, and all three were baptized at the same time. It was a glorious day for a wedding and a glorious day to be baptized.

Merry watched as Jessi's head went under. She was so proud of her daughter. She had overcome so much in the past year. It was one year ago that she found out Mark had been released from prison and had given thought to hiding from him. One year later, and she was married to the man. God had a sense of humor.

After the baptism service, Mark, Jessi, and Olivia changed and they formed the promised receiving line. Jessi had to laugh when so many people commented on her hairdo. The lovely up-do that Julia had spent so much time on was gone. Now it hung limply to her shoulders, still damp from only being towel dried.

The afternoon was filled with fun and more food than they could possibly eat. There was fried chicken, sliced ham, potato salad, sliced fruit, and much more, with plenty of sweet tea to go around. The church had set up volleyball nets, and horseshoes were being played. The little ones played on the playground. Mark and Jessi's celebration turned out to be a lot of fun for a lot of people. They were both glad at the end of the day that they had chosen something that everyone could enjoy.

Olivia returned to Julia's house with Merry, while Jessi and Mark went to their new home. Olivia really wanted to go with her mom and dad now that they were a family, but Aunt Merry put her foot down. "Tomorrow you will go home. Tonight you get to spend the night with me and Aunt Julia."

She was so tired after the full day that she fell asleep in the car on the way home, and Julia had to carry her in the house and tuck her in after she managed to get her changed.

Jessi was nervous when she and Mark returned to their new home alone. "Mark, do you want something to eat?" She opened the refrigerator, pretending to look for something to eat.

"No, I am just starting to feel human again after eating so much at the church." Mark smiled at his wife and pulled his shirt off.

"Well, do you need some Rolaids? Are you not feeling well?"

"I'm feeling perfectly fine, Jessi. I don't need anything but you." He pulled her close, and she forgot all about Rolaids, food, and anything else that might have crossed her mind.

Epilogue

Mark watched Jessi as she approached Ethan's grave. From this very spot he had watched her two years ago and realized how much he still loved her. She was an amazing woman, his wife. He still gave her a moment alone at their son's grave before he joined her. It was their custom to then come together and tell Ethan about the previous year. He began to walk, anticipating her need to have him by her side. He was almost there when she turned to motion him to her, and she gave a small laugh when she saw where he was. It was little things like this that had drawn them together so close.

He put his arm around her. "How was your visit with your son?"

"I hope you don't mind that I already told him about his little brother."

"And to think we were going to do that together." He drew his very pregnant wife into his arms. "Something tells me that Ethan already knew about his little brother. I wonder if he had any say in picking him out for us." He grinned down at her. "God does have a sense of humor, you know."

"Oh, I think God had him picked out a long, long time ago. Before the foundation of the world is how I believe it goes."

Mark kissed her nose. "Yes, I believe you are right."

They both heard her before they saw her and turned toward the very rambunctious Olivia running toward them. She had fully recovered to the point that you would never have known the doctors thought she may never walk again. "Mom, Dad, I don't know why I couldn't come with you guys. Aunt Merry took so long in getting here. She had to stop by the store for something. Did you already tell him everything?"

She waited for their response. Mark answered her. "Your mother already told him about the baby, if that's what you mean."

"Ugh! I thought we were going to tell him together." Olivia plopped down on the ground and waited for Aunt Merry so she could complain some more.

Jessi reached up and rubbed noses with her husband. "Have I told you lately that I love you?"

Mark scratched his head and pondered the question. "Nope, I don't believe you have."

"Well, my dear husband, I will love you until forever."